WINGBOUND

WINGBOUND SERIES: BOOK ONE

HEATHER TRIM

This is a work of fiction. All characters, places, and events portrayed in this novel are either products of the author's imagination or are used fictitiously.

WINGBOUND

www.heatheraine.com

Published by TrimVentures
www.trimventures.com

ISBN 13: 978-0-9987415-5-0

ALSO BY HEATHER TRIM

THE WINGBOUND SERIES:
Wingbound
Wingless
Wingspan

Supernatural Superheroes

Join the email list for new releases and more. Go to
www.heatheraine.com

"Unexpected, funny, serious, wonderful,
and above all; magical."
-Fantasic Books & Why to Read Them

"Spellbound by Wingbound... I was swept away
by visions of the castle in the sky."
-Author A.C. Gaither

"Sprawling castles and desolate oceans
in a soft, simplistic fairy-tale writing style."
-Bookish Creature

"A new world, new cultures, adventure, danger, triumph,
true-to-life characters, humor, romance, and dragons."
-Author Melissa Keaster

DEDICATION

To my fam,
You make me fly.

THEY DESCEND 1

I need to see for myself. I am told they are vicious and wild. Their wings are sharp as spears. It is harvest. They always come during harvest. I look to the skies. The clouds lie in long heaps of yellow and blue, soaking in the setting sun below and the sky above. Conflicting colors that shouldn't exist together, but they do.

"Ledger, I bet you five heads of corn, they will be here within the next three nights," challenges Angus. He strokes his unruly red hair.

Looking up at him, I shake my head. "Angus, no one cares about your stupid corn."

Tolliver, my older brother, and my cousin, Angus, recline together atop the last haystack they raked. I am the only one still working.

"What about you, Tolliver?" Angus offers, picking his teeth with a piece of hay. "Got any man in ya?"

Tolliver holds out his hand. "Three nights?"

They shake.

The wind picks up around us, throwing dust and hay in

our faces. My dark curly hair swirls in the wind. We all stop and look to the skies, suspicious of every gust.

When the Sky People come, they require a portion of our harvest. They always take, since before I was born, before my mother and father were born. But no one can stop them. They come on the wind and soar down with swords and wings. They kill. They take.

They come from the southwest, beyond the fields and briars, a tangled mess of thorny vines and shrubs. It protects us from threats on the ground but doesn't fortify us against the Sky People of Ellery. I squint at the horizon hoping to catch my first glimpse.

Tolliver joined the ranks in early spring. He trained throughout the summer for the Clash. I overheard Mother pleading with Father to keep him off the frontlines. Father and Tolliver overruled her.

This will be Angus's second year. Maybe that is why he let his beard take over his face. He is a man. He will fight with Tolliver by his side. Tolliver, with hair like corn silk, is as powerful as Angus, but bales smarter. Sadly, I am left to tend to the women and children another whole year while they get to see the Sky People face to face.

As I watch them wrestle and tease each other over five heads of corn, the cry comes from beyond the thick briars. The Protection had been scouting the skies for weeks. As soon as the first cold spell hits, they are on duty. Our warriors watch and wait, carrying shofars made from hollowed out ram's horns.

The horn's tone starts low and grows higher the longer it is blown. It stops and blares again. Low, high. My heart skips. I hold my breath, peeking at the briars. I consider burying myself in the haystack and watching them approach. I need to see them.

Angus laughs and demands his corn, but Tolliver is all business now. He leaps down from the hay and I race to keep up all the way back to Balfour. Tolliver and Angus scatter in different directions—Angus to the armory and Tolliver to prepare the horses. My legs are not as long as theirs. I make it to the edge of the village in time to see them dash between the first set of cottages. Out of the corner of my eye, I catch a flash of yellow. An evergreen branch swings out and smacks me clean across the face. I stumble backwards with stinging eyes to the sound of a girly giggle from the underbrush.

"Hollis!" I snap. She emerges, blonde hair flailing about as she convulses with laughter. I can't help but crack a smile after spitting out the bits of pine needles at my friend. "I don't have time for this," I say with a stifled laugh, trying to be serious as the horns blow in the distance.

"You should really watch out for those pine trees. They're unpredictable," Hollis says with a grin. She wipes her sappy hands on her dress and abruptly runs off in the direction of her cottage.

I hurry home. The village is filled with action. Families are running about closing the shutters and doors of their log cottages. Everyone knew this day would come. We are prepared. The cellars are cleanly dug and stocked for nights of hiding away.

Still stinging from the branch that grazed my face, I enter my father's workshop. Gathering the tools from beside the furnace, I put them away over the workbench. I lean close to a sword hanging on the drying rack and peer at my reflection, relieved there is no blood or welts on my face. I shake my head. Typical Hollis.

My father, Fergus the Blacksmith, is standing at the forge using the hearth rake to spread out the red coals to cool off. He has a sculpted jaw and a bulbous nose crowned with a heavy brow. His caterpillar-like eyebrows pinch together in concentration as the coals turn black and gray. I have his dark curly hair and brown eyes. Sometimes, I am proud that I look the most like him of his children, even more than fair-haired Tolliver. Maybe when I am a man, I will have Father's bulky chest and muscular arms. I peer down at my spindly limbs and sigh. Maybe.

Father silently places a heavy hand on my shoulder. His solemn dark eyes remind me of all the responsibilities he's already laid out for the Shield of our home: keep it locked up tight, ensure there is no fire till morning, and never let the children outside. Tolliver will not be the Shield this year. I am the eldest now, commissioned to keep our home safe.

Father slips metal armor over his leather tunic. His helmet covers the bridge of his nose. He steps out into the evening. Slamming his right hand over his heart, he nods at me. The sound of metal still echoes in my ears as he mounts the horse beside my brother. They ride toward the falling sun, the end of day and the beginning of war.

The alarm sounds again with three fast tones on all sides of our village. It means, "They descend." My heart quickens. If only I could climb to the roof to catch one small glimpse. But I can't. I know my responsibilities. I run from the workshop to our cottage behind. Crashing through the heavy wooden door, I find Mother holding the cellar hatch open for Mila and Killian who are climbing down the stairs beneath the hardwood floorboards. The baby is asleep, strapped to Mother's chest. I sweep the room with my eyes acknowledging the closed shutters, dead coals in the fireplace, and blankets missing from my parents' bed in the back room.

"Ledger, come," my mother calls from the cellar. Her words do not hasten my steps.

I want to see them come. I have seen neither their wings nor their beasts. Every year I have been alive, nothing has ever happened inside the village. The Protection takes the fight beyond the briars. I've only heard stories of their enormous feathery wings. I obey, pulling the cellar door shut and tiptoeing down the stairs to our hiding place.

***

As the Shield, I am the first to step out from the cellar in the morning, checking to make sure it is safe. I am the only one allowed outside to fetch food from the garden or necessities from the workshop, which means I can sneak my first peek at Ellery.

On the second night, I hurry through the dark workshop, grabbing a spyglass, and scrambling up the ladder on the far wall. Scaling it in seconds, I push the door out of the way and heft myself onto the roof. To the southwest, the orange and red sunset streaks the sky with warning. I put the spyglass to my eye. Ellery is an upside-down mountain, wider and deeper than our North Mountain. Two of our villages could fit atop. At the center is a large castle of tan stone, wrapped in wispy clouds.

On the third night, I see the winged people flying down from their floating island as it skirts by our village. They come in small groups, one after the other like swarms of bees raging from their hive. I cannot see the Protection on the ground, but they are there, fighting and defending our land.

On the fourth night, the island is almost over the eastern lake. The Clash must be ending soon because no Sky People appear. I soak in the sight of the mysterious island and just when I decide to head home, movement catches my attention. It shoots from the surface, away from the battle. I lose it momentarily in the ginger-pink clouds. Putting down the spyglass, I wait for it to emerge from the clouds. The sun glints off brilliant wings again as the figure darts to another cloud. Watching it like a firefly dancing toward me, I squint to keep my eyes on it.

Doesn't anyone else see it? I wonder, scanning the village below for anyone in view. The Protection has sentries posted on the outskirts of the village. I search for each man through the spyglass. The two I can see are not looking in the direction of the intruder.

The spy maneuvers surreptitiously through the sky toward the woodlands to the northwest. Someone has to do something, and I am the only one who sees him. I scramble to the ladder, slide downward and race from the workshop. After checking that the house is shut tight, I grab my father's bow and quiver. It is full and ready for his next hunt. It slaps against my back with every step. I catch movement from the corner of my eye as I round the backside of my house.

Hearing the sound of footfalls, I catch a glimpse of Bernhard making his rounds. I consider calling him to help me hunt down the intruder, but he would send me back to the cottage with the children. I need to see the Ellerian for myself. My heart pounds as I take the only chance I have and run, grass slashing at my legs. I aim for the Hundred Harvest Tree, where the winged trespasser must have landed.

Maybe they are trying a new tactic this year. Scouting our numbers? Spying on our crops? Sending an assassin to take out women and children? I imagine.

Low hanging branches of yellow and orange welcome me as I rush along the path into the woods. The treetops high above my head have stolen the light from the evening, plunging me into momentary darkness. As my eyes adjust to its depth, I trip on branches and vines along my route, but keep going. The leather on my feet barely protects me from the stones and brambles on the path.

I scurry through a mess of fallen yellow leaves as I come within view of our sacred Tree. I stop. Wait. Listen. The dust and leaves settle around my throbbing feet. The sounds of the forest awaken. The treetops sway together. The evening song of the twillerbird drowns out my heartbeat. Then I hear it. The snap of a twig, and a whispered, "Ow."

I tiptoe toward the sound. I consider going back to alert a sentry, but I can't. I want to see for myself. Then I'll go for help and back to my post as Shield. Circling the Hundred Harvest Tree is a wide grassy area where our ceremonies are held each year. Streaks of golden light touch only the far edge of the clearing. The mist has already begun to pour from the North Mountain and seep into the woods. Out of habit from regularly hunting with my father, I pull an arrow from the quiver, place it on my bow, and draw the string back. I muster all the strength I can find, even though my gut is telling me to run away. Peeking around a tree, I locate the spy. My chest seizes. I can't breathe as I fumble the poised arrow.

It is a winged girl.

SKYBOUND 2

She is sitting in a mess of vines entangling her feathery white wings. Dark disheveled hair hangs in her face. Her olive skin is dark against her brilliant wings. She bends a branch and pries it from around her slender body. Her small hands pull at the last vine, but thorns bite at her palms. "Ow." Her cry draws me to her. She wipes her soiled hands on her pale green dress and jolts to attention.

Turning her heart-shaped face toward me, she meets my eyes, and I am instantly entangled in her gaze. Seeing me approach from halfway across the grassy space, bow drawn, arrow ready, she whimpers and shrinks back from the light.

Following my first instinct, swinging the arrow toward the ground and disarming. I don't know if it is the right thing to do, but I don't want to scare her away. She is unarmed, after all.

"Don't be afraid." My voice emerges as a croak. I place the bow on the ground and shrug the quiver from my arm. "I can help."

Pulling at the vines again, crimson drips from her grip.

The sun filters through the trees like long arms pointing at her, making it difficult not to stare. She is so different from anyone I have ever seen.

I slide a knife from my belt and tiptoe closer, crossing through the evening rays.

Her brown eyes are wide and terrified. I kneel slowly and gently pull the vine from her feathery limb, avoiding the thorns. She lets out a panicked gasp as I slice the vine, freeing her.

Wings burst from her sides and she takes flight in an instant. They are easily twice the width of her outstretched arms.

"Please don't go," I blurt. My hands tremble, knife outstretched.

Already at the treetops, she turns midair and scrutinizes me. Her dark eyes search my body, my face, my hands. I toss the knife to the side and step forward, hands extended. The light reveals I have nothing else to hide, not even my curiosity.

Suspended in the air above me, her giant wings thrash, keeping her aloft. Wings beating once more, she slowly descends before me. Her leather-shod feet touch the ground before I can figure out what to say. Watching me closely, she folds her wings against her back, unable to hide their enormity behind her petite frame. They extend at least another head above hers.

"I… I… Welcome to Balfour." Gently touching my fist to my chest in a proper Balfourian greeting, I nod. Four steps it would take to touch her, but I remain motionless, worried I might ruin this moment.

"I'm not supposed to be here," she whispers and steps back.

"It's okay." I desperately wish for her to stay a little longer. "I'm Ledger."

She touches her flushed cheeks in worry and looks to the sky. "Alouette."

"Is that your name?" I breathe deeper.

She nods, and I take a small step closer. She shivers, cradling her wounded hand close to her chest, but doesn't move away. As daylight fades, I ache to have a few more moments of light to memorize her face, her eyes, her wings.

"Yes," she sighs. Her enormous feathery limbs twitch as if ready for flight at any moment.

I toe closer. "You are one of the Sky People?" It isn't really a question, but she answers anyway.

"Yes." She brushes her hands down the sides of her dress. "I wanted to see for myself."

Raising my eyebrows, I am surprised at her response. I hoped for the same thing every year. And now she is here—one of them. I dismiss the worry clawing at the back of my mind, telling me I shouldn't trust her or any Ellerian. I swallow back years of Father's warnings. "Now you see. What do you think?"

"You're smaller than I imagined. They make you sound like land-walking giants."

I laugh. She covers her mouth, hiding a smile that makes me unsteady.

"No giants here. Although, I am a little short for my age." I am blushing, but I don't care.

"You are not full grown?"

I shake my head and take a step closer within arm's reach. "I am twelve. Another harvest and I will be a man. Then I will join…" About to admit I will join in a war against her people, shame washes over me. I can't believe I am standing with one of them, the Sky People, enemy of Balfour, and I don't feel threatened. She is so small, gentle, and beautiful. Every belief I've ever held about them rewrites inside me.

"I am already thirteen and almost fully grown." She tilts her head to the side and peeks behind me. I expect another person, but we are alone. "No wings," she notes. "How do you stand it?"

"What?" I turn around so she can see my back.

"Walking everywhere."

We giggle together, but then the sound of the shofar wails in the distance. She jerks, and wings unfurl behind her. I fall back a step to see their full extent.

"What is that?" Her eyes search the forest for an answer.

"They are calling in reinforcements."

"Oh," she says, shoulders drooping. Her downturned eyes give away her feelings of worry. She squeezes her wounded hand close to her chest.

I reach my hands in my pockets, one holds a trinket I created today, and the other has a handkerchief. It isn't clean, but I offer to help her. "Can I bandage that for you?"

She hesitates, debating whether it is safe. Startled by a squirrel scampering from tree to tree, she looks around warily. Definitely not a spy. Just a curious girl. I approach her slowly. She is taller than me by a few inches. I pull the trinket out of my other pocket and offer it to her. Finally, her brow eases, and she takes the toy. I win her.

"I am a blacksmith, well, my father is the blacksmith. I'm technically still apprenticing."

Taking her delicate hand, my chest flutters at the touch of her soft skin. I wipe the blood away. She winces a couple of times but allows me to wrap the handkerchief around it.

"There." I smile, and she returns the expression. Her shoulders relax as she sighs. "I make tools and weapons. I invent things too." I point at the trinket I made from metal pieces leftover from my father's nails. "It's a windmill," I explain and twirl the sails. "You can have it if you like."

She looks at me and we are frozen still. My head buzzes with excitement. I don't move, though my heart pounds out of control. Her eyes slide from my gaze to my mouth. My breath catches in my throat. Her wings slowly expand behind her and all the senses in my body stand to attention.

"Thank you." She looks at the mechanism in her hands and smiles with one side of her mouth.

"Um, you're welcome."

Her wings fan out once lifting her off the ground in a graceful leap. She is quite unlike Hollis, who often squeals and flails clumsily as if her legs are uneven.

Hoping to keep her here a little longer, I point at the giant tree in the middle of the clearing, "This is our sacred ground under the Hundred Harvest Tree. We gather here twice each year, where our first-fathers settled. We have a feast every harvest after the Clash—" I put my hand over my mouth, worried that I've offended her.

"It's okay. I am not offended at you saying our people are at war."

My confidence is boosted. "We have a feast after the

Clash and if there are any ready for marriage, we hold a ceremony."

"What's that like?"

"The hunters bring a wild boar and the women cook—"

"No, what is the ceremony like?" Alouette's wings fold behind her as though they are praying. Her fingers mimic the same motion and her brown eyes widen in anticipation.

"The fall leaves of the Hundred Harvest Tree are gathered into a long path from our village to that area over there." I point to the mark in the ground where the grass is scarce from the many ceremonies held there. "The sun hits that spot during sunset and the Tree looks like it is on fire."

"I would love to see that!"

I reach out and touch the hem of her soft green dress. It's like a mixture of feather and linen. "What is this made of?"

"Oh, it's just dove-down-silk. Tell me about your family." She kneels beside me.

I look around, making sure we are still alone and join her on the ground. I marvel at the way she easily sits without damaging her wings. It's like they have a mind of their own.

"Tolliver is my older brother. Mila is eight. She is really annoying." I keep talking and watching her warm brown eyes soak in my every word. "Killian is nearly two and has only just started talking. My baby sister was born during the summer."

Alouette rips out the grass in bunches and piles it in her lap as she listens. Her small hands remind me of Hollis. "My friend, Hollis is a gatherer. Her family picks from the berry bushes and herbs throughout the woods."

Alouette smiles and rips out another fist full of tender

grass, piling it on her feathery dress. "What's it like having such a big family?" she asks with a sigh.

"It's okay," I say, though I've never thought about it before. "Tolliver is only one harvest older than I. Next harvest, when I turn thirteen, I will be a man and become a blacksmith, same as my father. He is on the council of our village and has many duties outside of our workshop. But it's okay; I can do everything now anyway. I'm hoping I can build a few of my ideas to help our farmers do better during planting and harvest."

"I wish I could see how you get the plants to grow all in a row in the fields like that." She picks another blade and drops it in the breeze. It floats to me and lands on my leg.

"I would love to see what that looks like from the sky." I lean toward her. "Can you fly carrying another person?"

She leaps up and the grass wafts into the air. I bounce to my feet and her wings stir the ground beneath us. "I carry my little neighbor around all the time," she says.

I wonder how I will hold onto her small frame. She steps behind me, wraps her arms around my waist and squeezes my stomach. I gasp as the ground shoots from beneath me. We are above the trees in a flash. Her wings swoosh around us. It's as if I am a part of a spectacular flying contraption. My village isn't visible from here, but her sky island is in plain sight. She darts toward the mountains away from my people and hers. We fly along the treetops, dodging the spiky tips of the fir and pine trees.

Following the rise in landscape, we sail up the side of the mountain. Turning southward overlooking Balfour, I see the lined pattern of our fields in the distance. Our crops are in semi-straight lines and each field is like a square on my grandmother's quilt.

From this skyward view, the evergreen trees look like wispy green feathers stuck in the soil. The rest of the forest looks like a swirl of red, yellow and orange that surrounds my village. The cottages of Balfour are laid out in three concentric circles.

Alouette's arms tighten around me as we drop to the rocky ground on the side of the mountain. It is cold up this high and I shiver as my feet touch down. She releases me, and I shout, "That was amazing! I can't believe you get to fly whenever you want."

She smiles and nods. "This is what our ground is like on Ellery." She kneels and scoops a handful of rocks and dust. I notice the absence of grass or trees around us.

"Is that why your people take our crops?" I am nervous about being so forthright.

Her eyebrows push together. "Yes. There are civilizations on our path that willingly provide us with food." She drops the rocks to the ground. "Yours is the only one who fights against us. The Guardians train for this interception every rotation and it's all they talk about." Her eyes close in thought. "They have a strategy to refrain from killing as many of your people as possible so that there will be enough of your men to tend the fields. I heard a story from ages ago that our people triumphed over the Balfourians and had killed so many men, the next year they couldn't provide enough food for Balfour and Ellery."

Remembering the stories of the Great Loss, I don't know what to say. In the distance, the floating land has no trees, only rock from top to bottom.

Wordlessly, she wraps her arms around me again and heaves me from the mountainside soaring head first toward my village. My whole body enjoys the mixture of exhilaration and terror. I laugh at the wonderful feeling of flying. The wind shear dries my wide eyes and gaping smile. My stomach doesn't catch up with my body even after we level off and glide across the treetops.

As we soar, I spot several sentries sprinting into the woods toward us. Panic rises in my throat. I swallow it back as we drop into the clearing around the Hundred Harvest Tree. She lets go of me, and I stumble forward.

"They're coming! I have to go," she cries. Her wings swish around us and dust billows in the twilight. With her hand still in mine, she hovers just above my head.

I shield my face from the whirling dirt. "Will I ever see you again?"

"We will be out of range by tomorrow. I will not be able see you until next harvest. Be safe, my friend." Alouette places a hand to her lips and blows a kiss. My heart wrenches at her sudden exodus as I watch her dart into the sky.

"Farewell, Alouette," I whisper as I think about the fact that I was flying. It is the most magnificent thing I have ever felt.

GROUNDED 3

Several men from the Protection tromp hastily into the clearing. They help me to my feet and search the sky with swords ready. But it is too late. She is gone. They ask me if I am okay, but her absence left a deep hole in my heart where only moments ago delight had been. I fear it will not be filled again for a long time. An entire harvest season long.

Father believes I was kidnapped and refuses to listen to my story. Mother always says, "Honesty first, in all things." Around the evening fire while Father and Tolliver are still on duty for the last night of the Protection, I sit beside Mother telling her about my rendezvous with Alouette—whether she believes me or not. She mends Father's tunic and Killian's britches. The children are in front of the hearth playing quietly, fortunately ignoring us. I tell Mother about Alouette's beautiful wings and our flight up the mountain together.

I stop when a sudden thought hits me. Next year, I will join the Protection, train for the Clash, and fight against her people. Becoming a ground warrior is what I have hoped for since I was Killian's size. Tolliver and I used to practice with wooden swords. He taught me to be quick because I am not strong. But the thought of slaughtering one of Alouette's people makes my head reel. Dread fills my periphery and the room spins around me.

I realize I cannot fight her people, her family.

I grit my teeth and admit it aloud. "Mother, I cannot join the Protection," I say holding a spool of thread in my hands. She stops and looks at me for the first time since I began talking. Her brows raise and her chin quivers. I can't figure out what she is thinking.

"Your Father will not allow you to sit around doing nothing." Mother continues stitching and says, "It would be wise to request a role behind the lines."

Everything I've imagined about who and what I wanted to be unravels inside me. I will never be a warrior. I didn't think there would be anything that could stop me from joining the ranks when I turn thirteen.

"What role won't have to fight?" I ask barely above a whisper. Mother doesn't answer as I consider delivering meals to the men. My lip curls in disgust. Maybe a village sentry? They rarely see combat. At least they carry a weapon. But that would pull me away from the blacksmith shop during the year.

Maybe I can be a weapons supplier. My heart sinks at each disappointing job that isn't a famed warrior. My shoulders slump realizing I'll never do anything important enough to be included in the retelling of Balfourian history.

I catch a partial smile peeking at Mother's cheek. Of course she is pleased that at least one of her sons will not lose his life to our annual war. A memory wraps around my mind of the harvest before when I overheard Father and Mother arguing about what role Tolliver should fill. Mother pleaded to keep him behind the lines stating, "He's different and you know it." Father wouldn't stand for it. Tolliver demanded to be front and center—such is his nature—and Father agreed.

I am not my brother. Maybe Father will understand. I look down at my hands and realize I've wrapped my fingers up in the spool of thread. One of my fingers is turning purple. I unwind the twists anxiety has threaded around me.

***

Each year, winter passes slowly. Spring is full of hard labor in the fields and smithing work. Summer is hot and restless. After Alouette visits in the fall, I recount each adventure to my mother.

When I am thirteen, I show Mother the small, smooth sandstone carving of a blue lark Alouette brought me. It fits in the palm of my hand. She is so thoughtful, and I like that she thinks about me throughout the year.

***

When I am fourteen, I describe the feel of the wind on my face and the thrill of soaring through the clouds. I don't show her Alouette's gift. It is a regular rock on the outside with purple crystals on the inside. She calls it a geode. Mother listens and I sometimes wonder if she thinks I am making up a tale. Maybe I should show her the rock.

***

When I am fifteen, I tell Mother about Alouette's family, her responsibilities as she becomes a woman of Ellery, and some of the people they encounter around the world on their floating island. I wrap the jingly bracelet Alouette gave me around my mother's wrist. It is from a country who welcomes them with a musical ceremony.

Each time I finish, Mother touches my face. The only thing she says is, "Thank you for your honesty." I walk away worrying that I am doing the wrong thing by telling her everything. I'm afraid she will suddenly decide to forbid me to see Alouette ever again. But she doesn't. With each passing year and every confession my insides churn with apprehension.

***

Now I am sixteen and awaiting the one person that makes me feel alive. I hope she recognizes me. I've grown several hands taller since last season and my voice has lowered. I hope she will be impressed with my changes, even though I'm more tall and lanky than muscular. Tolliver's voice lowered by the time he turned fourteen and it took me two years longer to really sound like a man. He still pokes fun at me when my voice cracks.

Alouette's dainty silhouette soars around the backside of the mountain and descends to our favorite meeting place. I notice a few things about her maturing form, the curve of her waist, the fullness of her breasts and length of her legs.

She lands in front of me, igniting my heart. I am dizzy and excited to see her. Even she has changed over the past year. She is an exotic woman with wide cheekbones, small chin, and smooth tan skin. Alouette rushes to me and gives me a brief hug.

"Alouette," I say into her hair. She hears the depth of my voice and looks up at me.

"Ledger," she says raising her sculpted brows. "You have a man's voice!" Giggling and dancing out of my arms, her dark hair swishes around her heart-shaped face. "I'm so glad to see you." Her slender form lifts from the ground, and she curtsies in her emerald green dress in the air. "Shall we fly?"

"Do you think we can visit your land?" My eyes are wide with hope.

"Ledger, there is no way for us to get on the island without the entire Guard seeing us," she says, letting me down gently.

"Then how do you manage to avoid detection?" I ask, not intending to argue.

She grinds her teeth. "I pay the Guardian." She sighs as if telling me the truth is unbearable. "I was found returning on our first visit. He saw me board through an underground cavern."

"Why didn't you tell me?"

"I didn't want you to think that it is too dangerous and tell me not to come." Alouette crosses her arms.

I feel a little guilty for making her defensive, but her defiance amuses me.

"I wouldn't have told you not to come," I admit. "I look forward to your visits. But please, always tell me the truth."

She looks up at me through her long dark lashes. "I will."

In one blink she whirls behind me, pushes her satchel aside, and grabs me around the waist. She jolts upwards, but my big feet stay planted. She pulls harder on my stomach and I nearly lose my midday meal. Her hands slip from around me and she lurches upward.

"Ledger," she says, mussing her hair to the side. "You have a man-sized body!"

I smile awkwardly, flaring my nostrils and shrugging, unsure of what to do.

"It's okay, we can walk." Alouette says sliding her hand in mine. We walk the path down the backside of the mountain between the tall pines. I am embarrassed and disappointed in myself.

She asks about my family and about the weddings this season. There haven't been any, but I still give her the full narrative of our dull life here on the ground. She tells me of some news on Ellery, but she is out of breath walking through the fallen pine needles. Her legs and feet are wrapped in a short-haired white animal skin with a crisscross pattern of twine.

"You don't have to walk," I say, prodding her into the air by lifting her delicate hand over my head.

Alouette flutters her wings and is floating in an instant. She isn't accustomed to the amount of walking I am. I tromp along the path with a flitting bird on my hand until we are out of view of Balfour and Ellery.

"I feel like I should be able to lift you. We can try again with the strap from my satchel," she says. Landing gently beside me, she removes her satchel. We strap ourselves facing each other. Her hair smells like lavender and rain. As we wrap our long arms around each other, my insides stir at how closely we are bound together. Maybe with the help of the strap and both our arms, we can fly again.

"You might have to cut off your legs," she laughs. Our bellies jiggle in unison with the rumble of our laughter. Her wings give several heaves as she attempts to lift me off the ground. She groans, and we squeeze each other tightly as the weight of our bodies is lifted from the dirt. The dust flies faster into the air than we do. I imagine we are above the trees, but I peek below and realize I can extend my toe and touch the soft path.

"Alouette. It's okay," I whisper in her ear. I feel like I'm squeezing the life out of her.

She sets me down with a huff and drops her arms in defeat. Breathing heavily, her words are barely audible. "I'm sorry, Ledger. You are bigger than I am now." Her body goes limp. "I'm sorry," she whispers. Still tethered to her, I hold her up for a change. Cradling her in my arms, I carry her to a nearby patch of drying grass. We are both sad about the end of our skyward adventures.

"No need to apologize." I console. "It is not a lack of commitment, but our bodies that fail us."

I set her in a circle of wilting daisies and pull the leather strap over our heads and up over her drooping wings. Her sad eyes search mine and I smile hoping to comfort her.

Our inability to put distance between us and the ground hangs like a dark cloud over our joyous yearly rendezvous. There must be another way to join her in the sky.

We spend the rest of our time together picking dead

flowers, tossing them down the cliff side and talking about our separate lives that only overlap for four days. When the sun touches the western horizon and the forest looks like slouching silhouettes, I hear footsteps coming around the mountain pass.

I leap to my feet in an instant and Alouette is in the air at the next. I push her toward the bushes on the upside of the path.

"Hide," I whisper and pull her to the ground. "If you go now, you might be seen."

I gaze up the path as a voice calls, "Ledger!"

In a panic, I tuck Alouette's wings beneath the branches and attempt to crawl in beside her. I am too big, again. I cannot be completely concealed.

"Ledger!" Tolliver says.

Realizing there is no hiding my giant gangly body, I scramble toward him. "Here I am." He comes around the edge of the trees and jogs the rest of the way to me. I stop him from coming into view of the hidden winged girl.

"Where have you been? What are you doing out here?" Tolliver asks, slowing his pace. His tunic is dirtied on the front. He must not have worn the leather apron in the shop today. His face is red from hiking and his sandy hair hangs limp with sweat.

"I'm not doing anything."

"Father sent me for you and Mother said you were out here." He looks around, one eyebrow up and pauses when he hears rustling in the bushes behind me. I grab his arm, pulling him away. "Wait. There's something—"

"It's nothing," I say, trying to lead him away until a

muffled sneeze comes from the leafy mass.

Tolliver knocks me to the side with his broad shoulders and crouches down, looking beneath the branches. "Hello," he greets.

"Hello," answers Alouette's small voice.

"Who are you?"

She sneezes again and attempts to stand, but the branches are wrapped through her wings. "I am Alouette."

"Who is this?" Tolliver turns to me like her name isn't enough. "I've never seen her before."

"She is a visitor." I am impressed by my quick answer. I hope he simply accepts it and walks back to the village. Without me.

Instead he says, "From where?" He politely offers her his hand. She accepts it and he pulls her free of the bushes. Her enormous wings snap out of the shrubs and into the air behind her. Tolliver gasps and pulls his hand away like Alouette is suddenly contaminated.

"Tolliver, I can explain," I say.

"She is Ellerian!" His eyes are blazing, and a vein protrudes from his neck as anger spreads through his body like wildfire.

"I know. It's okay though. She's not a threat."

"Not a threat? She is one of them!"

Alouette leaps into the air above us, distancing herself from the yelling.

"Wait, don't go," I call with one hand reaching out to her. "I know she is one of them, but…" I stretch the other hand out to Tolliver.

"Does Father know?"

I shake my head and wish for words to explain. I need time to think, time to figure out what to say and how to say it so he will understand. My delayed mind and words fail me.

Tolliver stomps off. I look to the sky as Alouette drifts farther and farther away. "Please, don't go!"

Tolliver says, "This is unacceptable."

I call to her again, "Please stay."

I hear the distance in her voice, surrendering to the lost moment. "Goodbye, Ledger." She darts to the cloud layer. She is concealed instantly in a blanket of navy and gray.

Tolliver's face is contorted and looks like he's ready to fight.

"Please calm down," I beg.

"How can you do this? Betraying your own people!"

"It's not betrayal. She's my friend."

"That's exactly what betrayal is." Tolliver's fists clench over and over.

"She was just a little girl when we met. She was curious about us." I explain. "Mother knows, but no one else can."

His jaw tightens, and he says nothing for several moments. I'm not sure what he is thinking, but all he does is growl and walk away.

"Please, Tolliver. No one can know," I say. He leaves me alone on the hillside in a circle of dead daisies. I drag my feet toward the village to answer my father's summons.

4
SKY AND DIRT

I heat and bend the rods of metal until it is all connected. Hiding my contraption from my father has been difficult and risky. Not that he doesn't allow me to create strange objects, but I would be in undeniable trouble if he found out what this one can do. I have been able to fold it up and prop it under my leather apron in the workshop, but now that it is all together, I'll have to move it. Attaching the last piece, I sigh. The smithing task is complete. It has taken weeks of hiding, sneaking parts, and working late.

I pull the contraption in two directions on the workbench, joints moving outward in a wing-like form. I am overjoyed at its finished shape and do a silly dance flapping my elbows and kicking my feet in the air. I gather myself and prepare to cover it in fabric so that it will hold the air and I can fly with Alouette.

Several days ago, I had traded a tool and a sack of nails for a spool of thread and two pieces of thick cloth big enough to cover the wingspan. The brown fabric has a small weave and I expect it will be strong enough. The better question is: Will my sewing skills be strong enough? I carefully lay the first piece of fabric across the length of the wing. It will definitely fit. Relief spirals through my gut. I pick up the spool of thread and unravel a long strand, snipping it with my teeth. I pull out the needle and bring it close to my face. I've seen my mother do this many times. I lick the thread the way she does and poke it at the top of the needle. The end of the thread bends awkwardly, and it doesn't go through. I step closer to the window to use the afternoon light, making a second attempt to thread it.

His voice booms down the path before I see him pass the window and I accidentally poke myself with the needle. Stabbing it into the windowsill for safekeeping, I dart for the wings spread out on the table. I swipe the fabric onto the floor and collapse the wings. There is only enough time to drop them to the floor, kick the cloth over top and stumble to the furnace as Tolliver saunters through the door.

I forget to put on the thick leather gloves and nearly grab a piece of hot iron out of the fire.

"Whoa! Little brother, are you trying to singe off all the skin on your hands!" he says, stopping me from excruciating pain.

I snatch my hand back suddenly and shake it in the air as if I had burned it. My heart pounds and my face burns with embarrassment. "Thanks, Tolliver. I guess I wasn't paying attention."

"Truth be told you haven't been paying attention a lot lately." He approaches and hovers over me the way a tall pine looks down on a sapling. It irritates me when he does that, and I resist the urge to stand on my tiptoes. I sense a confrontation coming. He's going to say something about Alouette now that we are alone. I've been avoiding him for weeks and now the conversation is inevitable. I hold my breath as he speaks.

"Father needs Kitching's new sword. Show me which one it is so that I may deliver it."

I exhale loudly and say, "Oh, yes. Okay." I awkwardly point toward the cooling rack knocking a chisel off the anvil, feeling like a fool. Tolliver watches it fall but doesn't say anything.

Swallowing hard, I lay the sword on the green cloth. Tolliver wraps it gently and inserts it into the long leather bag already hanging from his hip.

He makes his way back to the door. "Get your head out of the sky, Ledger."

The wood door slams behind him and I consider how true his statement is and how unlikely it would be. My heart hammers out of control. I rest my hands on my knees as though I just finished a long-distance run. I take a deep breath and reach for the wretched needle on the windowsill.

Three bleeding pinpricks and one angry howl later, the needle is threaded. I stretch out the metal wings with the fabric atop and sew them together. Wrapping, sewing, wrapping, sewing as neatly and quickly as possible.

The second wing doesn't take nearly as long now that I am in a good rhythm. My imagination flits wildly with the idea of sailing through the sky with Alouette. She with her white feathery wings and I with my brown metal wings. What adventures we will have.

Finishing the last stitch, I tie it off. The wings open and

close freely. It's not quite done. I need to figure a way to secure it to my body. Then a thought hits me. I collapse the wings, whip off my heavy leather apron and lay it on the worktable. The shears slice roughly into the leather as I cut a two-inch strip off the bottom. Cutting it in half, I tie one to each wing below the major elbow joint. I am giddy with anticipation, chuckling aloud as I work.

Now I need something to tie it to my back. I look around the dirty workshop, at the forge, at the tools on the eastern wall, the workbench and the cooling rack on the western wall. I see our cottage through the backdoor window and have a brilliant idea. I race out of the workshop, through the cottage door and to the clothing cupboard near my parent's bed. I open the top doors. Nothing but clothes. I pull open the drawer below, hitting myself in the knee. Pain shoots through me as I find what I am looking for: Father's old belt. Mother is saving it for when he slims down. It's been years since he used it. I rub my sore knee and kick the drawer shut. Dashing back to the workshop, I remember I left the wings out on the workbench. My heart drops into my gut and I swing through the workshop door. Jarvix is standing in front of the cooling rack.

He is a pudgy old man whose belly hangs all the way over his belt.

"What are you doing in here?" I blurt. He looks at me with eyes wide and before he can say a word I correct myself, "I mean, what can I help you with?"

"Yes, I was dropping in to see if my sword is ready. Kitching just received his and I am looking forward to seeing mine." He rubs his mustache and looks at me expectantly.

Eying the worktable, my wings are fully visible. I walk along the cooling rack on the other side of him so that he is not looking toward my secret project.

"Oh, yes. Let me find it for you." I try to breathe normally, but my body is starved for oxygen and I'm nearly panting. Luckily, his sword is finished and hanging in the corner. I reach for it.

"Thank you for stopping in. Enjoy," I say and push him ever so slightly out the door.

Seeing Father pass Jarvix, coming this way, I careen through the door and slap the wings shut with a clunk. I wrap my leather apron around them and heave the whole thing behind the chair beyond the workbench in the corner. I kick the scraps of fabric under the bench and sit.

Father stomps through the door and I pretend to be bored. I pick my nose and wipe it on the seat. He smiles at me and commands, "Stop digging for potatoes and help me with this."

He heaves a large bag from his shoulder.

"I have finished all of my projects, Father."

"Well," he says. "I am impressed."

"Jarvix even picked up his sword today."

"I saw that. You are a dedicated worker. Why don't you take the rest of today and enjoy yourself?"

My eyebrows shoot upward along with my heart. I imagine soaring from the backside of the mountain in the warmth of the day.

"Thank you, Father!" I smile and nearly hug him.

He raises a single burly eyebrow at me and says, "You're welcome. Now get out of here before I change my mind."

I scramble for the door looking back for a moment toward the chair and my hidden secret. How do I get my wings out of there without him seeing?

Then I have an idea that might work so I wait for the man to leave. I am dizzy with fear as if I'm about to have a nosebleed as I enter and lie to my Father, "Mother asked to see you."

"Yes, yes," he says absently. "In a moment." He is fully engrossed with inspecting something in his hands. I wait outside and around the corner for him to leave. Good thing I'm not counting the seconds because it takes him over ten minutes to respond to my mother's fake summons.

As soon as his bulky body is out of sight, I have only moments to grab my things. I race in and pull the contraption from the corner with a loud scrape on the stone floor. The leather handle accidentally snags on the workbench. I growl while unlatching it and dart out the workshop door. I run straight for the woods just in time to hear my father yell my name and something unintelligible. Relieved to be out of his sights, I slow to a walk.

Reaching the North Mountain, I follow our path around the backside and head for the cliff. It is only a ten-foot drop and there is more dirt than gravel at the bottom. The wind sweeps up the side tossing my hair in my eyes. I smile because this amount of wind will give me good lift.

Spreading the wings out on the ground, my haphazard stitches show all the way around. I wring my hands; nervous they may not hold. I string the belt around the middle of the metal bones and lay my body down on it looking up at the sky. I imagine racing Alouette from cloud to cloud. I have a lot of practicing to do to catch up with her skilled flight. Pulling the belt tightly around me, the metal digs into my back. I grab the loops attached to the upper joints, and stand up with the wings fully mounted to my back. I flex the wings in and out. My triumphant laugh echoes down the mountain.

Stepping to the edge of the cliff, my heart thrums, the wind picks up and the wings flap outward. It lifts me slightly and hope inflates my chest. Don't think. Just fly.

I back up four steps and take a flying leap off the overhang. The wind hits me coolly in the face and fills the wings. I keep them level the way Alouette pushes us away from the ground. But the weight of my body is more than my arms can bear and the wings cut through the thin mountain air. I flap and flap, losing more altitude than I gain. Then I hold my arms out hoping to glide, but my arms are nearly ripped from their sockets as my body plummets to the rapidly approaching ground.

Suddenly, dirt, gravel, metal, and pain consume me. I roll head over feet several times. The metal bends and clangs, tearing at my flesh. All I can see are flashes of sky and dirt blurring into one. I land in a tangled agonizing mess.

5
HUNDRED HARVEST TREE

Balfour is abuzz like squirrels scampering about the forest floor this morning. All families have their tasks. We are the village blacksmiths, so we bring the sky lanterns. This year, there are three deaths to honor.

While finishing my chores, I consider my next flying idea. I cringe at the thought of my first failed attempt to fly and the resulting weeks of walking around pretending I'm fine but needing to limp. My knees and elbows took the brunt of the damage. Wearing long sleeves in warm weather concealing the missing skin on my joints is almost unbearable. The sweat makes the clothing stick to my scabs. This is one story I will not tell my mother.

Hanging the tools on hooks around the furnace, I imagine welding all the wing's joints outstretched and unmoving. I was almost gliding. But I wouldn't be able to gain height. I need lift. Running a dirty hand through my hair, I notice a figure beside me and leap like a startled mouse.

"What are you doing?" Hollis bounces on the balls of her feet, unaware she's scared the life out of me.

"Nothing." I scowl, as blood courses through my veins.

"Good. I need your help." She is in her usual blue dress that makes her eyes look like a clear summer sky. Her blonde hair is mussed and falls haphazardly around her face. There is a smudge of dirt on her cheek. She is only two years younger than me but it's taking her longer to grow up.

"With what?" I ask.

A mischievous grin blossoms on her face. "Come on," she says, yanking my arm. I flinch, anticipating pain from my nearly healed wounds, though there is none. I let her pull me out the door, wary of what she is dragging me into this time.

Hollis and her family are preparing for a wedding. Her brother, Cullen, is marrying the miller's daughter. Following her through the square and beyond the last row of cottages on the east side of the village, we stop at a patch of holly bushes. She holds up a single branch and points. She is gathering holly branches, representing her family. Except holly leaves have little spikes at the tips.

I laugh.

Hollis swats at me with the branch. I turn just in time for it to hit me on the side, barely missing my exposed skin.

"You have any mittens?" I ask.

She pouts at me with puckered lips and rumpled eyebrows.

I shake my head at her unfortunate task, knowing she'd much rather run down a musk ox than pull branches from holly bushes. At least she could have a wild time riding an ox. I jab my hand into the bush and quickly yank out a branch. It pricks me in each knuckle and I loudly screech,

"Aah!"

Hollis joins my howls, "Aah!" She laughs and reaches for another spiny branch. "Aah!"

We scream and laugh and pull at the greenery until the basket is full.

"Thank you, Ledger." Hollis smiles and gives me a quick punch in the arm. "Let's run to the river and wash our hands. Someone will think we murdered someone with all this blood."

"Don't exaggerate. It only looks like your ugly old cat attacked us." She punches me again with her boney little fist, sending a shooting pain up my arm.

We walk up the lane toward the miller's house. The wash maids launder upstream from the cows and horse pasture, but no one is working today. We follow the well-worn path down to the bank. The river is wide and slow moving at this point, knee deep all the way across. The water glistens in the sun and we bend to rinse our hands.

The water cools the punctures on my palms. They are mere scratches compared to the wounds from my crash. I watch as red fades from my hands when I'm suddenly heaved to the side.

Splash!

As I emerge from the water, soaking wet, I hear Hollis laughing. Her voice echoes down the riverbank.

"Hollis! Look what you did," I howl, pointing at my wet clothes. I slip on a slimy rock beneath my feet. Another splash.

Her laughter grows louder as she dives at me and wrestles me until my face is back in the water. She knows how much

I hate swimming so I am trying not to get upset. She giggles and gurgles the water in her mouth. A chuckle bubbles up from my belly and I can't help but join her hysteria. Finally, she loses her footing and we come to rest on the river bottom with only our heads sticking out of the cool flowing stream. My mother will not be happy that my only clean tunic is drenched. I look in Hollis's clear blue eyes, unsure if it's water sprinkled over her cheeks or if happy tears stream down her face.

"Oh lands, you should have seen your face as you fell in the water!" She opens her eyes, mouth wide, mimicking my expression. She giggles and splashes water in my eyes.

"Hollis! Stop it!" I spurt and choke on the water. "Let me breathe, you wild twillerbird! Has your father taught you no manners?" Frustration bubbles in my chest, reminding me of the time she challenged me with who could climb higher and faster up the Hundred Harvest Tree. I lost, nearly falling to my death only because she cut in front of me and stepped on my fingers.

"Who needs manners with you?" Hollis sucks water into her mouth and squirts it at me.

I gasp as it hits me in the ear. I leap at her and push her pretty little face in the water and run for the dry bank. I slip once or twice but finally reach the grass. She slips and trips her way toward me and accidentally falls on top of me. I catch her tiny frame. As I am about to push her away, I look in her bright eyes. Out of breath, we pause with a confusing moment between us. Our faces are close, our breath blending and our hearts beating hard. I know the rules, no intimate contact until a contract is made. A thought flashes through my mind. I imagine her being my bride. Pretty, spitfire, playful Hollis. But it's her. Annoying, persistent, feral Hollis.

I set her down beside the flowing river. I shake the strange thoughts from my head. Wringing her soaking hair and humming, she isn't fazed by the awkward moment. I accidentally revisit the thought and look away, ashamed that I allow it to flood through me. She is my friend.

A bell tolls in the distance and we look at each other. We clamor to our feet and run back to Balfour with her basket of holly branches. Music is playing as we enter the village.

Hollis tugs the basket from my hands and I bid her farewell with a smile. She winks and dances away. I watch her hips sway and that strange feeling fills my gut again.

Tolliver jolts me from the confusing thoughts. "You are going to hear it from Mother," He laughs at me. I'm seventeen now and I'm supposed to represent the men of Balfour. Dread floods over me.

***

Standing near the fire pit, my clothes eventually dried out, but Mother made me attend the wedding around the Hundred Harvest Tree in my sopping wet clothes. The men of Balfour stack wood in the pit preparing for the ceremonial retelling of Balfour's history. I've heard it so many times; I almost have it memorized. Each year, new details are added to the story from the previous harvest and I always wish to hear my name in the particulars of our lives. But I'm only a blacksmith's son. I dream of contributing in some way, but when I opted out of direct combat, it killed any chance of that. Now I am just a measly weapons supplier.

As I gaze at the first star of the night, someone sneaks up and grabs me. Pulling my head under his arm, I smell sweat and iron. My teeth grind as I struggle and punch him in the stomach until he releases me.

Facing Angus, he pats my cheek and says, “What’s with you not wanting to be a warrior? I know you are smart and could outwit every one of them.”

I scoff at his proposition because he has no idea what he is asking me to do—who he is telling me to fight.

“My only concern is your skinny little arms.” He holds up my limb for Tolliver to inspect.

I see a glimmer of something in Tolliver’s eyes. I want to ask him what he is thinking because he knows about Alouette. We have never spoken of her and I ache for him to say something. Anything.

Angus leans in and bites my upper arm. “Aaaaaangus!” I scream. I don’t want to rip my arm from his teeth for fear he might take a chunk out of it. So I pound on his curly red head, bruising my knuckles.

Tolliver slaps Angus on the back, and he releases instantly like an obedient dog.

Angus dusts me off and says, “I just think we can use all the help we can get against those rabid flying beasts.”

His insult hits me in the chest and my breath is taken for a moment. My brow furrows, and my mouth drops open ready to blurt something. But I can’t argue. They are our enemy.

Looking at Tolliver, I see the warning in his eyes as he shakes his head once. Then he grabs me by the neck, wrestles me to the ground and pins me with little effort. Angus laughs and cheers for Tolliver. Pain shoots through my shoulders and stomach. Tolliver releases me when Kava, the only daughter of the village healer, approaches.

"Would you be a darling and fetch me a cushion?" she asks with a manipulative pout. I want to throw something at her, but Tolliver smiles and heads off to find one.

Kava straightens her dark gray dress as she waits. Her right arm is adorned with the red ribbon worn by the healers and their apprentices. They care for the wounded men in the Protection. There are two apprentices, Rylan the son of Elder Jubal, and Kava.

As I come around the stack of wood, I notice Hollis in a little yellow dress standing with Angus. I sigh. She won't go away, but maybe these feelings eventually will.

As Tolliver returns with a pillow under his arm, the shofars blare all around us. Our five leaders with torches blazing, my father included, enter the clearing. The crowd parts for them making a direct path to the woodpile. Standing beside the stack of firewood are three families. The head of each family holds a papyrus lantern representing the death of one of their family members. One by one the elders light the lanterns. They release them as we stand in silence honoring the dead as the lanterns drift skyward. Watching them float, I imagine flying with Alouette again. My mind wanders back to the glider. It isn't going to work, but there has to be some way for me to join her in the sky.

The five leaders toss their torches on the pyre. Our people cheer as it swells with heat and light.

"It's about time. I thought I was going to freeze to death,"

Hollis says as she dances over, rubbing her shoulders. My first instinct is to wrap my arm around her and share my warmth. But I stop myself. That's what yesterday's Ledger would have done. He would have done it without thinking anything of it. But today, it would mean something, and I have no idea how to feel about it. So I let her stand there and shiver as if I didn't hear.

I step closer to the fire's warmth. My cheeks burn with true heat as an arm slides around my waist. I brace myself for Tolliver or Angus to slam me down in some way, but the arm stays gently wrapped around me. It is Hollis. She smiles and gazes into the fire. My body buzzes with more of that nauseous excitement and I start sweating. When I move my arm to return her embrace, Angus bursts between us and falls to the ground catching a pinecone at the same time. Tolliver gets ready for the next toss. I take it as a chance to walk away and escape all that Hollis makes me feel. I want to choose whom I love, and this body will not fool me into choosing whoever is closest. I look to the sky where I desire to find my destiny. But there is only starlight and moonbeams.

I walk toward the North Mountain, into the woods where I walked with Alouette five harvests in a row. I remember her smile and miss her gentle flittering wings. Could I ever marry a winged girl? Is that even possible—according to nature? I know it isn't possible according to family and heritage. But I don't really care about that.

Noticing the lanterns drifting through the sky toward the mountain, I imagine being small enough to ride one, gently meandering through the air. I stop in my tracks and wonder if I could build a larger lantern. I walk back to the celebration with a new revelation and hope rising in my chest.

DOVE-DOWN SILK 6

Full of anticipation and excitement, I weave my way through the people of Balfour in search of my Father. He is standing on the far side of the bonfire, face lit with gold and yellow. He is talking loudly and laughing with several other men. Hollis's father is among them. He is a fair-haired witty man, who seems younger than the men standing around him. I slow my pace and breathe deeply, calming my racing heart. I put my thoughts in order, so I can ask efficient questions. It annoys Father when I fumble and mumble through our conversations.

I approach and Father bellows, "There he is!" His big arms raise and grab me by the shoulders. I am confused for a moment at his unrestrained attention. He winks noticeably to the other men. They walk away, and I realize something is awry. Hollis's father straightens his collar and follows the other men. Maybe I messed up a sword or tool in the workshop. Am I in trouble? My stomach churns and I choke back my fear of the oncoming conflict.

Father's tone lowers, "I'd like to talk to you about

something, son."

"Yes, Father."

"You'll be of marrying age next winter. You and Hollis get along well. Have you considered her as your match?" He looks at me with serious eyes, scrutinizing my reaction. I flinch and blink, confused that I'm not in trouble. "I know you spend a lot of time with her."

My throat aches as it suddenly dries out. I attempt to swallow. No words come to mind. I am floundering to say something. Shouldn't he be talking marriage with Tolliver? Not me. I clench my sweating fists, frustrated at my inability to think quickly.

"What say you, son?" He smiles big, with eyebrows raised, as if doing so will force an answer.

"I will have to think about it," I say finally.

"What is there to think about? She is your best friend. It is perfect."

"I would just like some time—" I stop, contemplating a better excuse.

"Fine, fine, I know you have your own way of doing things," he agrees, much to my surprise.

"Thank you, Father." I breathe deeply and puff up my chest, feeling more like a man now that he is respecting the way I am.

As he walks away, I scurry to catch up. "I have a curious question, Father."

"What is it?"

"I was wondering if you could explain to me how the floating lanterns work."

"Oh boy, that is an explanation for another night."

“I’m just curious,” I state as if it didn’t matter.

“Not now, Ledger,” he says. Father laughs loudly and shakes his head. “My curious boy.” I descend to feeling ten years old again as he pats me on the head and walks away.

Villagers are all gathered around the bonfire and I hear my grandmother’s voice, “Balfour searched high and low for the perfect place to settle and came upon a tree. Full of life and light, this tree sat in the center of a clearing that called to him. He brought the twelve families from the west to settle around the Harvest Tree. That first night many slept beneath its boughs and all across the clearing under the stars.” The old woman waves a bony hand at the night sky of black and white.

This season’s storyteller is Grandmother Huyana. Her name means falling rain. Grandfather said she fell into his life like the rain and soaked his soul with her compassion. I can’t help rolling my eyes at his sentimental words. Grandmother is the best storyteller among them. She makes the best parts more exciting and even sings the voice of Laurel who saved Balfour’s sister from drowning and eventually married him. My stomach tightens again as I listen to the tale of Laurel and Balfour’s wedding beneath the Tree.

I listen to Grandmother’s version of the story and marvel at the sparkle in her brown eyes. The bonfire’s flame lights her face, but her heart lights her eyes. “That first harvest brought plenty from the flat fields beside the river but with it brought a shocking sight. An island in the skies with winged people. Did they bring life or death? Balfour and two elders journeyed south beyond the briar to meet them. Their wings carried them down with ease, they accepted the presence of one another and we welcomed the Sky People of Ellery.

"While feasting around the Harvest Tree, they bestowed gifts upon each other. Rayven, the King of Ellery, gave garments of white and new instruments made from ram's horn. Balfour gave Rayven a portion of our crops to take to their people atop the floating mountain. For it was all we had to share.

"They found their rhythm as Ellery came and went each harvest season circling our world with the moving winds and seasons. The shofars would announce the return of their friends and the anticipation of a feast, until one harvest season when the winds changed."

Grandmother clears her throat and sips from her cup. My mind drifts back to the floating lantern. Can I possibly make a man-sized lantern? It would have to be enormous. I look around for an idea of where to start or what to build it from.

Looking directly at me, Grandmother continues the next few lines of the story holding my gaze. "During the last feast of peace between Ellery and Balfour, Rayven's youngest granddaughter was lost in the woods around the village. No one had seen her for a full day and Rayven went mad—" Grandmother coughs and looks away from the fire. Grandfather reaches for her hand. I watch a look that flashes between them. A look of sadness.

Were they sad that Rayven went mad and started a war with our people? Is Grandmother too tired to continue telling the story? She catches her breath and continues. I notice a small glimmer of a tear at the edge of her eye.

"Rayven, bent with rage, declared war on our village." Grandmother coughs again and again. I rise from my seat in concern. She leans into Grandfather and coughs into his tunic over and over. When she sits up there is an obvious spot of blood where she had been. Mother gasps along with many others around the clearing. I rush to her aid.

Grandfather gives her his handkerchief and motions for me to help. I guide her to her feet and she wavers. I catch her and scoop her into my arms. I am surprised I can lift her by myself. She seems lighter than seven-year-old Killian. I look at Grandfather, his white brows pinched with worry. "Take her to the cottage, Ledger." I scan for my parents. They are gathering the children. Mother nods, telling me to go. I follow the path of petals as the moon guides our way back to the village.

I walk north around the outer circle of cottages as Grandmother has another bout of coughing. Inside, I set her frail body on the bed. Grandfather neatly tucks her in and strokes her wrinkly cheek, as Kava and Healer Clovis rush in with a medicine bag.

He gets to work sifting through his bag pulling out several bottles and a small mixing bowl. He is a little man with a round balding head. His tunic is too big for him and hangs loosely over his elderly frame. He hunches over the bowl grinding something and Kava adds a drop from each of the bottles. Her dark eyes are focused. She has been helping him all her life. Her mother died in childbirth and Clovis raised her alone. They work together seamlessly as though she can read her father's mind.

Clovis shuffles to Grandmother with the completed tonic. His small hands hold the bowl to her lips and she swallows it down. Grandmother's barking cough startles me. It twists my stomach in knots at the thought of her pain. Grandfather and Clovis discuss her condition. It is possibly a lung infection, something old people die from regularly. I clench my teeth and watch her trying to get comfortable in the bed. Grandfather assists her, adjusting her pillows.

"I'll be right back, my dove," Grandfather coos. "I must speak with Clovis."

She half smiles and half winces.

He follows Clovis and Kava out the door. I wonder if they are talking outside because she is worse than he is letting on.

A single candle on the windowsill next to her bed flickers in the darkness. I walk to Grandmother's bedside and touch her hand. Speaking over her body, I tell it to heal. Her eyes open, reading my face.

"Don't be sad, little Edgy."

I give a smile at the endearing nickname. I kneel beside her bed and hold her small hand for many silent moments until she speaks in a hushed tone. "Your mother has been telling me of your harvest time adventures."

I look into her eyes to find any trace of reprimand. She knows of my rebellion against our people, but all I see is love.

"Keep her safe." Grandmother's exhale is long, and her eyes fall shut. I wait. It's so long until she draws in a new breath.

I'm relieved she is still with me. "Keep Mother safe?"

She looks up and locks eyes with me. The name emerges like an exhale, "Alouette."

My breath catches in my throat, shock sending my heart into an uneasy rhythm. I say, "I would never put her in harm's way, Grandmother. She too is cautious when Balfour is awake." I stroke her hand and continue, "She gave me this last harvest." I pull a piece of fabric from my pocket. It isn't white anymore. A grimy brown color, really. I guess I don't keep my hands very clean.

I put it in Grandmother's hand. "Dove-down silk," she says, surprising me. I never told my mother about the fabric.

"How—"

"Oh sweet boy, there are so many things I know." The candle reflects in her midnight eyes. "I shall tell you about them someday, but that tonic is making my memories distant and unreachable."

"Another day, Grandmother." I kiss her cheek and tuck her hand under the blanket.

"Tell me of Alouette's family," Grandmother whispers into the night. "I may fall asleep, just keep talking, it brings me solace to hear your voice."

"Yes, Grandmother," I agree. "Alouette's father is advisor to the King of Ellery. She said he doesn't have a trade because he is so smart they don't need him to waste time on wearing down his body or hands when his mind is so brilliant. She described her mother much like I would have described you, Grandmother, in your more active years: intense and powerful. She manages the women of Ellery in childbirth." I pause to check on her breathing. A small smile wrinkles up one side of her face and I continue, "Alouette is an only child. Apparently, they are only permitted to have one child now. She said it wasn't always that way, but Ellery is quite full of people and they had to slow overpopulation. But she has several friends." I decide I don't want to share about her friends and skip to the story she told about the king's family.

"King Halcyon of Ellery has two children. He is the only one permitted to have more than one child, to ensure an heir to the throne. It doesn't matter male or female. But he has two girls. They are as different as night and day. The king himself can't figure out how to handle them because they are so different. Alouette said there is much talk about the fact that they may end up in a duel for the throne after their father dies." I quietly chuckle to myself. Grandmother looks as though she is sleeping now. Her face is limp and expressionless. I take the opportunity to talk about Alouette. "I don't know what to think about what she means to me. We have been friends since I was twelve and each year I see her, she brings my mind to life. It's like I'm not alive the rest of the year until I see her. But she must always depart too soon and I have no power to bring her back. There's no way I'll ever be able to come to her world. There's no way our village would ever receive her. But I want her with me all the time."

I notice the corner of Grandmother's cheek push back in a small smile and I realize she has heard every word. With a sigh, I kiss her cheek. I notice movement outside the window beside me. The festivities must be over. I wonder if they finished telling the history of Balfour.

Grandfather enters the cottage with a whoosh of cool spring air. I inhale its sweet scent and meet him near the door. "She is nearly sleeping," I whisper.

"Thank you, my boy," he embraces me in his long bony arms. "Sleep well."

I exit and walk around the side of Grandmother's cottage toward home, grateful I get one last peek through her window as I go by. I turn the corner. There is Hollis. Her mouth is gaping, and her eyes are wide. Wild violets fall from her hands. I pause for a moment, unsure of what to do as the flowers hit the ground. She looks down at them and back at me, then runs off. Did she hear me talking about Alouette?

I want to hit something. I want to run away. I want to fly. But I am stuck. With big feet on the ground, my heart is in the sky and there's no way to reach it.

7
CASTLE IN THE SKY

The leaves are changing to beautiful brilliant yellows and reds, signaling the return of harvest, the Sky People and Alouette. In the workshop, I'm tinkering with my newest contraption. It has taken a lot of time to get it just right, and I haven't had time to test it. I pump the bellows to liven the fire, insert the metal rod and wait for it to glow. Between each harvest my dreams and thoughts are filled with her. I have taken her many places on our land, but hers is still a mystery to me. My flying machine is nearly complete. I have tested several different designs and I am certain this will be the one to join her in the sky.

I lose sight of what is in front of me, as the light in the shop grows dim. A shofar sounds to the west, then another, and another. My heart leaps in my chest. How could she be so late? I have been on the Protection four harvests now and it felt as if she is always late. But this time is excessive. I toss the metal into the water, swipe the coals away from each other in the furnace and dash from the workshop.

"Ledger!" my sister shouts across the path. "Father is

looking for you."

I race into the cottage and find Father in a heated debate with Tolliver. I catch only the tail end when Father shouts, "No. We are your family. This is your village. You'll do your duties, or I'll have you thrown in the stocks!"

Tolliver's face is beet red as he stomps past me out the door. He leaves the tension hanging in the air like a cleaver over a slaughtered ram. I am wary of it dripping on me.

Father's armor is massive, and Mother has difficulty lifting it. I help her heave it to his chest and Mother cinches his breastplate tightly, wrapping an extra leather band across his chest to keep it secure. His brows press low and his eyes are dark.

"Ledger, you are coming with me today," he commands.

"Father, I'm not a warrior."

"I know, but your brother is a horseman now and my aide has taken ill. I need the extra hand."

"But, Father—"

"Why are all my children defying me?" he bellows. His eyes bulge and a vein pulses in his neck. I cringe at the conflict I've just walked into. Bile rises in my throat as I apologize. It seems like I'm apologizing for whatever Tolliver said before me.

Father is a border commander during the Clash and has been in direct combat. I think of Alouette. She rarely comes the first night, especially since I joined the Protection. My job is usually to supply arms and deliver messages. I am an errand-boy of the lowest order. The only other positions beneath me are the meal suppliers.

If I am on border duty, I will not get away until nightfall

every night while the Sky People are within range. Usually, I'm able to check on each unit and duck out to meet Alouette without anyone knowing or caring.

"Yes, sir," I agree against my desires, not that there is a choice in the matter.

Father doesn't acknowledge my agreement and straps on his sword.

Mother lifts a chest piece and places it over me. I look down at it and notice the scrollwork. It is the one Father has been making for months in the workshop. He wouldn't let anyone touch it or work on it. I remember the sweat rolling from his brow and sizzling on the new armor as he worked the metal. My heart aches at the thought of him doing this for me and yet I feel betrayed because he never told me that I would have to be on duty with him until this very moment.

"Why didn't you tell me when you started making this, Father?" I look into his intense eyes and see the sadness in them. Mother continues to dress me.

"I wasn't sure it was going to be necessary. I know you desire to be behind the lines supplying arms." He put his hand upon my metal-covered shoulder. "I know you are not your brother and I will not ask you to do as Tolliver would do. But I need your help, son. We are outnumbered every year and without my aide—"

A sound rings in the distance and we both look to the east. It is not a battle cry. It is the bell calling us to the village square. Father's eyes widen with curiosity.

"Secure the house," he tells my mother and she gathers the children toward the cellar.

We each pull the shutters closed for her and I follow him

out the door, father and son fully armored. We walk side by side to the village square. He walks with intensity in his eyes and power in his step. We pass each cottage of logs and mud turning left around the last into the square. My armor restricts my movements and collects my body heat like a furnace.

Many men in armor encircle the center columns. Only a few women and children from the nearest houses are present, curious to hear why in Balfour there is a meeting as the Clash approaches.

"Their scouts are absent!" Thelonious shouts rushing into the square. His armor is black and a little rusty near the bottom as though he leaves it in the dirt. He stomps up the steps between the four columns. Though most meetings are held by the council in one of the homes of the members, some meetings are held out here in the open. "Our long distance Protection has sent news that the Ellerians are not descending upon us." Many of us look to the south. Ellery looks like a jagged knife thrust through a cotton ceiling. "We have waited to sound the battle cry, because there is no battle to be had."

The puffy cotton-like clouds shield the full glory of Ellery from sight. As the wind blows, Ellery peaks and hides as it approaches. And yet, Thelonious is right. There are no Ellerian Guardians flying down in groups of six to attack our men in the fields.

"What do they want?" my father inquires.

"We do not know. There has been no contact," Thelonious replies.

"Are they waiting until they are closer to attack?" another

man asks across the square.

The question wafts into the wind as the clouds clear before Ellery. The island floats in its usual path, yet the skies are calm, and nothing stirs upon its surface.

“I am calling you to arms anyway.” Thelonious details a plan to do the same as we’ve always done. Stand ready and armed to fight no matter their strategy. Lock down the village as a precaution. And we wait.

Something is wrong, very wrong. My throat constricts and my head pounds as I think of Alouette.

***

I am out of my element following my father toward the border. I do not belong here, though I do wish to see Ellery up close. The briars make up the border and Father is shouting orders to his men. My body is not obeying him. I stand and gawk at the enormous rock floating beyond the briar. I have never been this close to it. It is massive and ominous.

“Ledger!” my father calls. I snap out of my trance and follow his directions to walk thirty paces east and stand ready. “Watch the sky. Watch the ground. Watch anything in between. If you see anything—anything at all—call out to the next man and pass the news along!”

I follow orders.

Standing for hours.

Nothing happens.

All day.

With only a six-hour respite each night.

The rock approaches one field length per day.

Closer.

And closer.

No one stirs.

For three days.

Each evening when the night duty takes over, I run to our secret meeting place. I wait and watch the skies. Spyglass in hand, I scope out any movement in the trees or clouds. For three days, she doesn't come. Alouette is gone.

I cannot leave the fate of my Alouette in the hands of five elders who see her as the enemy. After morning meal, when my father is long gone down the path toward Thelonious's house where the five Elders gather, I make up my mind.

"I'm going to make sure the workshop is tidy," I tell my mother as I heave the large door open, grasping for any excuse.

"She is gone, Ledger."

I dig my nails into the door and turn to meet her gaze. She isn't angry that I'm leaving. I see nothing but sadness. "I have to find out."

"What can you do?" she pleads. "You are only one boy with a heart after an unreachable winged girl."

"I don't know, but I can't just do nothing."

I step into the morning sun and drag the solid door shut behind me with a loud boom. I didn't mean to be so dramatic, but I cannot contain my frustration. I race to the end of our path and dash around the corner in a blink. My long legs carry me all the way to Thelonious's door where I stop. My hand poised, ready to knock.

Voices inside catch my attention.

"By tonight they will be fully over the lake and we will

not have to care what happened to them," Thelonious says. "But for today and maybe even tomorrow, we stand ready to fight."

"The men are weary of waiting. I think we can reduce our numbers to two thirds and allow them to go home," a low voice says. "Waiting three days is more tiresome than fighting for one."

"I agree with Thelonious. No one rests until the threat is gone. Same as every season," a raspy voice commands, probably Espen, the head of the frontline battalion. His men are all positioned beyond the briar and are always the first into battle.

"What are you doing?" a voice booms behind me. I jerk back from the door, spinning to face my seeker. Tolliver, with his hands on his hips, steps closer. Angus follows. "Well?" Tolliver demands.

"I, um, nothing." I can't tell him what I want to do. I don't even know what I am going to do.

"I am apprenticing on the council, not you."

I flinch at his statement and realize what he thinks I'm doing. "No. I just… I had a question for Father," I say.

"Sure you did," he says and barrels past me, pushing the bulky wooden door open. Angus forces me into the room with the most important men of our village. They are all seated at a roughly hewn table with four wide benches around each side.

"What is Ledger doing here?" my father asks.

"He was spying on you," Tolliver announces and laughs loudly.

The men laugh together as if there is some sort of inside

joke going on that I don't know. "Son," Father says to me, "Go home with the women and children."

The words hit me like a punch in the stomach. "No," I object. "I have an idea."

"We don't need ideas, son. We need answers." My father's brow furrows low over his eyes and the twist in my gut pulls tighter.

"But that's my idea. To get answers."

"Stop being cryptic and tell us what you want so we can get on with this meeting," Thelonious is loud and pushy. The pressure makes it hard to speak coherent words. "Now!"

"I just, umm, I want to go up to the island."

Silence.

No one says anything until Father bursts into laughter. The room follows his chortle. But I stand my ground and yell above the laughing, "I have a way to reach the floating island. I want to go look around, see if they are actually gone."

Thelonious rises from his seat at the table. "There is no way, unless you've sprouted wings, boy!"

"I built something that can fly. It hasn't flown yet, but I think it can and if I could—"

"No," Father spouts, pounding his fist on the table. A lampstand and a mug bounce, nearly falling over. "There is no way to get up that high. There's no way I will allow it even if you thought you could. They might attack if we trespass on their land."

"But—"

"Enough," Father says with a jolt and stands as though he is about to come after me. The tight lip and death in his eyes, remind me of a beating I received a couple years ago when I left Mila at the river by herself. I back down for fear of a thrashing.

I take a step back and bow my head. "Y-y-yes, sir."

With a whisper that is thick and airy, Father says, "Go home." The words fill the room and push me toward the door. My feet shuffle backward, and it takes every bit of strength to pull the beastly door shut. I stand outside for a few woozy moments. No one is speaking behind the door. It is silent.

Moping away, I collect the last bits of dignity I have left. I must find Alouette. Thinking of her pulls me out of the pit of despair. If I don't have my Father's blessing, I'll do it by myself. Each step inflates the courage within me. I look to the sky where the clouds are glowing red and pink. I cannot let this opportunity pass me by. I don't need them. The thought of flying again fills my resolve. Full of bravery or bravado, I don't care which, I walk home, and then run with my mind made up. I must get to Ellery.

EMPTY 8

With Mother and the children hidden away in the house, I round the workshop and bound up the ladder to the roof where my project is stashed. I forged a metal box to hold the fire and mounted a bellows on one side to pump in the air. The fire needs to be hot. Severely hot. It is hard to find enough fabric, because I only had one quilt from my bed. Fortunately, several weeks ago, I found some treasures in Grandmother's loft. She was delighted to give me something of hers, a small hammock and a quilt. After removing the front from the backing of each quilt, I sewed all four pieces together edge to edge. I am not fast or good at stitching so I kept the sewing project on the roof of the workshop. It is the only place Father rarely goes.

The fall air streaming across the workshop roof is chilling, even though I am sweating as I light the fire in the metal box. I tie short lengths of rope from each corner of the blankets to the metal loops on the makeshift forge. Propping up the four sides of the blankets with several staffs takes finesse and a steady hand. If it falls it might hit the fire and go up in flames.

Stoking and feeding the fire, the hot air fills the space between the blankets. Pumping the bellows that are the length of my arm, I make the fire hotter and hotter. It takes some time until finally the hot air fills the blankets exactly the way I imagined. The staffs fall away as it floats above the tethered box. It is a huge version of the papyrus lanterns we release into the sky on Delineation Day.

I add more coal to the fire because it burns hotter than wood. Hopefully it will be enough to soar across the village and up the rocky side of the island. I face the wind. Excitement pumps through my veins when I realize the wind is blowing directly toward Ellery.

People notice the floating blankets above the shop. I untie the box from the roof and it lifts several feet into the air. I had removed some length of the hammock so it is perfect for sitting. I connect it with hooks to the underside of the box and quickly sit in it. The hammock cups me perfectly within reach of the bellows. The whole thing bobbles for a moment adjusting to my weight. Leaning back, I reach above my head and pump the bellows several times to get the fire hotter and hotter. I can hear the flames snapping above me as it lifts me into the air with each puff. I gasp, realizing it is working. The pain from my last attempt to fly hangs in the back of my memory.

The contraption drifts higher and higher and I hear my mother scream my name. The wind carries me toward Ellery. Grinning widely as I rise into the sky, I think to myself, my contraption works. I am flying! I can hardly believe it as I laugh like a wild man.

Puff after puff of the bellows, my village begins to look like a shrunken version of itself. The people scramble like rats toward the village square following beneath me. I see my father's red face and his mouth shouting something, his arms flailing wildly.

I regain my composure and puff the bellows again. My course is set, the sky is clear, and the rock is nearing. Halfway to the island I waver. What if my father is right? What would I do if all of the Ellerians are just hiding and ignoring us? The thought throws my heart in an intense rhythm and my resolve plummets. Would they kill me for attempting to board their island?

Ellery has cleared the concealing clouds and hangs out in the open. The underside is like a cluster of dangling stalactites. To avoid the jagged rocks, I puff the bellows over and over again. The heat lifts me higher and higher. I miss the squeeze of Alouette's hands around my waist. I would feel safer with her this high in the sky.

Nauseous with panic, I approach the floating island. I really should have thought about how to land the flying contraption, but I didn't know if it would even get off the ground. The wind is my invisible friend guiding me toward the ledge where the castle stairs begin. I hold my breath and continue to glide through the air. The steps on the side of the floating mountain come faster than expected and I hit them with force. I land on my knees and the box topples to the side. A few red coals leap out. The hot air disperses, and my blankets quickly lose their air sprawling up the stairway. I scramble to my feet and kick the coals back into the box so I don't lose their blaze.

My heart beats wildly, standing on the steps of Alouette's home. I breathe for a few moments to get myself under control. Slowly, I realize I have succeeded.

Descending to the last step, I wave to my people standing on the outskirts of the village. They all scramble about like little ants. I don't know if they are glad I came, but I am sure they are glad enough that I survived.

"I made it," I shout and wave.

I realize after a moment that there could be people on this rock, lying in wait, ready to remove my head. So I fold up my blankets and tuck them down on the last step. That way, someone would have to come all the way out here to find it.

Now, it is time to find her.

There are so many sandy stone stairs leading up to the castle. The air is thin, and I am gasping for breath as I heave myself up each crunching step. It takes me a long time to climb them. The front of the beige stone castle has a wide archway, but there is no door or gate. I guess they don't need doors to protect from wingless enemies. The front hall of the castle is more like a giant carved cave. The walls are smooth and the ceiling bears carvings of winged people. Halfway down are two smaller hallways heading to the north and the south. I stop and look down the southern hall. I wait and listen. There is no noise, no movement, no one.

When I reach the end of the grand hall I step out into an enormous circular courtyard. All the way around are doors and windows. Looking up, I see a railing swirling all the way up with more doors. I count sixteen floors above the first before I start feeling dizzy. My body sways to the side, forcing me to inhale deeply.

"There is no way I can search this whole thing in one day," I say to myself. The sound of my voice bounces about the courtyard on the breeze.

"Hello?" I yell. The echo wraps around me. "Anyone here?" My voice swirls up the many layers above my head.

This silence is so strange. Dead and heavy. There aren't even any passing gnats or bees disrupting the nothingness. But I'm not sure if that is abnormal or not.

I walk straight through the empty courtyard, past an enormous carving. It is an Ellerian man with bulging muscles and wings poised aggressively. It intimidates me. The statue stands on the top of a stack of tan stone basins. Like a fountain, except it is dry.

I walk to the biggest of all the doorways off the courtyard. It is arched like the first doorway of the castle. I enter the room. The taupe stone floors turn to a shimmery yellow color, as if paved in gold. The smooth golden tiles extend through the middle of the room from the doorway to a platform where two large sandstone chairs are positioned.

"Hello?" There is less of an echo in here but enough that I wait for it to stop before I enter. The walls are adorned with floor to ceiling tapestries. Sky People's figures are intricately woven into them with grandly reaching wings. I don't recognize any of them, until I get to the last one. She doesn't look like Alouette, but there's something familiar in her eyes.

I search the first floor of what must be the royalty's homes. They are quite large and beautifully furnished with heavy carved bedchambers, intricate fireplaces, high arched ceilings and metal shined into an almost perfectly reflective surface. I stand in front of the mirror and gape at myself. I am a man, but my features are angular and immature compared to the muscular, toned men of Balfour. I look away and wish I could go back to thinking I fit in with them.

I don't have time to look through all the houses. I find the stairs that lead up to more homes and another that descends into the ground. I find it odd that there are stairs on an island of winged people. It is dark and scares me a little. If there is someone here, they would have heard me by now. The realization hits me that my search is complete. My lungs deflate and shoulders droop. Every last flame of hope of finding her is extinguished.

Alouette is gone.

I collect a few bits of coal and wood from the fireplace in the grand dining room, just in case I don't have enough for my contraption. I race back through the maze of Ellery, through the courtyard, through the grand hallway onto the front steps. My feet feel like bendy, wet straw. I slow down so I don't sail off the edge.

The sun is rising above Ellery like a giant eye peering into my soul. It exposes the ground with light where the Balfourians are still gathered beneath me. I step to the edge and wave until someone notices. Only a few wave and race around, most have their arms folded across their chest or poised on their hips.

It is difficult to get the hot air into the blankets this time without the staffs to hold them up so I drag it to the side of the castle. I lift the blankets and drape them across the craggy rocks on the outside wall. They snag and hold. After a little bit of balancing and puffing the bellows, it inflates and rises into the air. The hammock loops beneath me and I pump the bellows until it lifts me as well. Looking across the surface of the island, I run toward the edge of the rock and jump off, attached to a furnace and a bubble of hot air. My heart sinks as I leave the castle where Alouette had lived all this time.

Blinking back tears, I careen off the edge of Ellery. I don't have time for tears. I have to think. I have to find her. The rocky underside of the island drifts higher and higher as I drop through the air. I pump the bellows every so often, but only enough to keep me from plummeting.

I have to find Alouette. I must report to my village the Ellerians are missing. Then, I will ride the island until I find her. As soon as I land, I'll gather food, clothing, spyglass, a few of my tools and sewing kit, just in case I need to fix the float on my contraption. I lean in an attempt to steer toward the workshop so I can take off from the same spot, but the wind won't let me sail against it. It stubbornly pushes me northeast and I land in the cow fields on the other side of the river where Hollis nearly drowned me. It is more of a crash landing and I leap from the hammock seat right before all the coals spill into the grass. I quickly stomp out the flames, scattering the coals. Heart in my throat from the ride, I take a deep breath.

Flint, I remind myself. I'll need to bring flint to relight the fire.

Finally, I hear the Balfourians racing out to meet me. Excited to tell them about my ride, I'm sure I am wearing that stupid grin Hollis hates, but I don't care. I can fly.

"Ledger," Hollis screams and races into me. She grabs my tunic and pounds my chest angrily. "What in blazes are you thinking? They are going to skin you!"

With that, all the joy within me collapses like the air from my contraption.

"But I had to see if they were really gone," I defend.

"The Elders are furious," she says out of breath.

Tolliver and Angus are not far behind. They have the same tone as Hollis. I am confused at their fury. Their hands are on me, their voices thunder. Their breaths are short and faces contorted.

The villagers descend upon me in anger and screaming and judgment. I am on trial and no one is listening to me. The only words I can comprehend are "Trespassing," "Flying," and "Trouble."

"No, please let me tell you," I scream over the din. "They are gone."

"Silence," a man commands. Their voices trickle off like the dying of a storm. Thelonious breaks his way through the crowd. "Let him speak!"

Shocked that it's my chance to speak, I momentarily fall short with words, stunned by the chaos.

"Speak, son, tell us what you saw," Thelonious prods.

"They're gone. All of them." I describe their homes and the absence of any living thing. I tell them about everything, except the most important—Alouette. I look at Hollis. Her eyes are scrunched together with worry.

9 HIDDEN IN THE HOLLOW

"This is cause for celebration," Thelonious exclaims. "Our enemy is gone, and our village is safe." The throng's heated anger deflates as they accept his declaration. One by one they shift to cheers, growing louder until the whole crowd is triumphantly yelling into the morning sky. The sound makes my ears cloud over and my mind bluster in the confusion. I grit my teeth and dig my heels against the swing of reactions that pulls my whole world in two directions.

"No!" I scream over the clamor. "Wait!" My voice is lost among the wind and voices. The ground below me feels as though it's shifting. I push my way through the crowd and away from the madness. All the faces I know and love cheer for the demise of my heart. I run away—away from them all. I hear my mother call my name but continue running back to the village.

I dash between the houses. The walls seem as if they are reaching out to stop me as I burst through. Hitting the workshop door, I grab a delivery bag and fill it with coal and kindling. I scamper through the back and heave the door to my house open. Racing up to the loft, I pull the box from beneath my cot and load the bag with what I might need. Candles, a tunic, my knife, and flint. Down the ladder with my necessities, I dig through the basket on the dinner table.

"What are you doing?" Tolliver asks, winded from running. My mother rushes through the door behind him.

Startled, I whirl around to face them. "I'm going to find her," I say, breaking Tolliver's unspoken rule of not talking about Alouette. I grab a baguette and a squash from the basket.

Mother pushes her way around him. "Ledger, she's gone. There's nothing you can do about it."

I grit my teeth and yell, "Yes, I can. I can ride the island. Find out what happened."

"No, that's not a good idea. You don't know what happened to them." Hysteria creeps into Mother's voice as she realizes I am serious. She grabs my hand protectively. "You'll starve. You could be killed by whatever killed them."

"She is not dead," I snip and yank my hand away. Nearly hyperventilating, I take a deep breath and whisper, "I have to find her."

"Thelonious confiscated your flying thing," Tolliver interjects. This becomes another storm throwing my plans into chaos.

I look at both of them—one knows my heart and the other knows my fears. I close my bag and stomp between them. I'm unsure if I'm running toward or away. Scrambling out the door, around the house, I run toward the Hundred Harvest Tree, my mind races faster than my feet.

Reaching the clearing, I fall to my knees. My screams

and tears are a torrent of pain and anger. I pound the dirt and rage at the heaviness of my limbs. Everything is holding me back, resisting my good intentions. My head hangs and the dust of the earth clings to my hot tears.

Now there is no way to use my contraption to get back onto Ellery before it is unreachable beyond the lake. I am so stupid. I should have foreseen this. I should have known they'd never see Alouette and her people as anything more than their enemy.

I wipe the mucus hanging from my nose. Startled by a noise, I notice Hollis and Tolliver approach. Preparing myself for ridicule and rejection, I try to read their judgments.

Hollis looks at the dirty tear streaks on my face. "Boy, you're a mess."

"Let's go before Ellery is too far away," Tolliver says.

My breath catches in my throat, shocked by his words.

I look at Hollis.

"Let's do it," she agrees.

Does that mean she did hear me talking to Grandmother? I can't wrap my mind around why in the wild world either of them would want to go. Am I dreaming? Did I hit my head? I wipe my eyes with my dusty hands, smearing the grit on my face.

"Really?" My voice wavers.

I hear more footsteps on the path. "What are we doing?" Angus pants. His round face is red as he bends over to catch his breath.

Tolliver fills them in on what's happening. Angus agrees, "Let's do it."

I want to cry again, but for an entirely different reason.

I can't believe this is happening. I'm going to make it back to Ellery.

"—and if we hike around the lake that will give us time to get off the ground." Tolliver finishes whatever he is explaining.

"Why?" I ask still sitting in the dust. "Why are you helping me? You don't have to do this. I could just go by myself and do what I have to do."

"Does it matter?" Tolliver puts his hand on his hip.

I am stunned, gaping at them.

"If we keep standing here debating, we'll lose the opportunity." Tolliver turns to the others. "We're riding Ellery around the world to find out what happened to them. Who's in?"

Hollis and Angus say, "Me," at the same time.

A panicked cackle escapes my lips and I pull myself out of the dirt. Standing among them, my brain takes a while to grasp the reality of the situation. For whatever reason, they are willing to risk their lives to help me. It confuses me to my core.

Tolliver leads us into the woods around the north side of the village. The path is spread with bright orange leaves interspersed with fallen pine needles. I follow quietly, regaining my composure. Arm around Angus, Tolliver explains how they will steal the contraption.

As I dig through my mind to unearth a way to get us all up there, I assess how many people my contraption can carry. I am sure it can lift several people, but four? I don't know. Even if it could, how would they hold on? Hope erupts within me.

I have a bag of supplies hanging from my shoulder, but taking four more people changes everything. As we approach a fallen log, I say, "I'm going to need a few extra things to get us all up there."

Angus leaps over the log in one bound. Tolliver mounts the fallen tree and looks down at me. "What do you need?"

The power in his voice frightens me and I fill with jealousy. Attempting to stuff the feelings of inferiority, my words stammer, "I – I – I need another blanket to make the float bigger, including a needle and thread. We will need a lot more coal."

"Anything else?" he asks, still standing on his perch.

"I need to figure out how to lift all of you. I only have one seat. I have no idea—"

"A ladder," Hollis interrupts.

It is like a lightning bolt hitting my brain. "Yes," I say with a hiss. "I need a rope ladder." I pat Hollis on the back. She smiles as though she's won a prize.

Tolliver divvies out the tasks to each person according to who has access to different items. "Grab whatever food you can find," he tells us. He has always been good at telling others what to do. He looks down at me from atop the log. "You are to stay hidden, Ledger. I can't have you dragged off to the stocks."

"What? No," I blurt.

"You are to get in there and hide until we come get you." I look where he is pointing and recognize where we are.

We used to play in the northern woods as little kids. He is pointing at the enormous hollowed out tree. We had built a door to keep girls out of our fort. I remember a time when we were pretending to fight for the Protection. The girls were the Sky People and Tolliver, Angus, and I were the sentries. We fought with sticks as swords. One time I accidentally whipped Hollis's arm with my makeshift sword and she punched me in the ear.

It looks as though time and weather were not kind to the little wooden door. Tolliver grabs the rope handle and yanks it open. It creaks as he rips it out of the opening. "Get in there." He drops what's left of the crumbling door.

I want to protest, but he is right. He is always right. My head hangs in shame as I step inside the hollow. It is smaller than I remember. The smell of something decaying stings my nostrils.

"We will be back to get you before sunset. You have enough in your pack for midday meal?" I nod and watch them walk away. Hollis's yellow hair ripples in the wind, while Angus's heavy step thunders through the woodlands. Tolliver walks with his shoulders back and head held high. I realize I need him. I need all of them. I cannot do this without them.

***

Though I only must stay hidden for a couple of hours, I can barely sit still, let alone stay put. I sit cross-legged in the hollow tree, bouncing my torso and twiddling my thumbs. Standing and tapping the inside of the damp trunk, I can't stop thinking about the fact that I need to say goodbye to someone before I go. This is my only chance.

I leave my bag in the tree and sneak through the forest

to the edge of the village. Grandmother's house is on the northern side on the outer row of cottages. It takes me only a few minutes of weaving between trees and a moment of paranoia of being found to reach her back door. I sneak a peek through the back window. She is preparing midday meal, slowly moving from the hearth to the table in her small cottage with a bowl and ladle. Perhaps she is not as well as she seemed yesterday when I saw her in Mother's garden. There is a sadness in her face that wasn't there before.

I step quietly through the back door and whisper, "Grandmother?" She is visibly alarmed—eyes wide and hands outstretched.

"Oh my stars, you startled me," Grandmother exclaims and places a hand on her chest.

I scuttle over and help her sit on a bench at the table. "You have caused quite a stir, Little Edgy."

"Shhh, Grandmother. Please whisper. I cannot be found out."

"Oh, yes," she says with a wink.

"I am going back to Ellery," I say. She gasps, and I continue, "I will ride the island until I find them."

"Why would you risk so much?" She grabs both of my hands in hers. They are bony and frail.

"I have to make sure she is okay," I explain. "Tolliver has agreed to go with me."

She nods. "Good, good. This is good." She grabs my face with her wrinkly hands. "Trust your brother and remember who he has always been to you."

I feel as though she is speaking in riddles.

"There is much you do not know and have never seen."

Letting go of my face, she says. “You must be careful.”

“I will.”

“Listen to me child. There is danger in this journey, unknown peoples, beasts, even the cold could kill you.” Grandmother drifts off and mumbles for several moments. She gets up from the bench, shuffles around the room, and stops as if forgetting what she is doing, then scuffles to her bed.

She opens the chest at the foot of her bed, pushing blankets and clothing aside. She pulls out grandfather’s thick brown wool cloak. After grabbing a few other items, she lets the lid slam and hobbles to my side.

“Put this on,” she heaves the cloak into my hands.

“I can’t take this, it is Grandfather’s.”

“You will take it,” she says sternly, frowning a little. I acquiesce and put my arms through the sleeves, surprised that it fits. Could I possibly be the same size as my Grandfather now?

“Thank you.” I stroke the scratchy collar and marvel at how well made it is.

“Here, take these,” she says and pushes what looks like mittens into my pocket. Then she holds up a small black purse. Putting a few fingers in the opening, she pulls out a glistening trinket.

“I bless you in your travels. I command safety be around you always and thwart threats you don’t even know about.” She lifts the trinket from her closed hand. It is a leather strand with a silver bird dangling from it. Its wings are outstretched, and in its mouth is a twig with small silver leaves. I cannot conceive how anyone could fashion such delicate and intricate metalwork. Grandmother ties it around my neck. She looks into my eyes for a few moments and I hug her.

"Thank you, Grandmother."

She smiles an old crinkly smile.

"You never told me all the things you know about Ellery."

As she opens her mouth to speak, we hear voices outside the cabin. "Grandfather and Roan are coming," she says. "You must go."

Grabbing a piece of cloth from her mending pile she wraps a loaf of bread, a raw potato and a handful of dried meat and ties it closed. She joins me at the back door and puts the sack in my hands. Grandmother pushes me out the back just in time for the front door to open. I race straight into the woods with the weight of the cloak and a handful of treats. Grandmother looks frail. I may not see her alive again. My chest aches at the thought. I have to breathe deeply and bite my tongue to keep the premature tears at bay as I climb into the hollow and hide.

10

OFF THE GROUND

The forest is silent for a long time. I eat some of grandmother's bread and several strips of deer jerky from home. To pass the time, I count the un-cracked acorns on the floor of the hollow. They've been gone so long, I worry they have given up on me. My feet are losing sensation from sitting for so long. Then I hear it. A crack of a branch. The wind stirs the orange leaves in front of the opening.

I hold my breath.

Another crack. Leaning out the opening, I peer among the trees. Suddenly something small and hard bounces off my forehead.

"Ow!" I squawk.

A streak of gold blazes through the doorway knocking me backwards slamming my head into the pile of thirty-eight acorns. I scramble to my knees in the small space. Hollis giggles and loads another acorn in her slingshot.

"Don't you dare," I yell and put my hands up to shield my face.

She laughs again and shoots it anyway. It hits me in the

shoulder and I scowl. She tucks the slingshot into her satchel.

"So, what do you think?" she twirls and directs my attention to what she is wearing.

"Did you steal your brother's clothes?" I scrutinize her white tunic, brown trousers tucked into lace-up boots and a blue over-dress. With the pants, the over-dress looks more like an apron.

"Actually, I did," she says and adds, "I couldn't go flying through the air with a dress on. That just wouldn't be lady-like."

"And dressing like a boy is?"

"That's why I put on my favorite over-dress and cut it shorter."

She giggles and adjusts the belt that holds her water pouch, a leather sack, and what looks like a small dagger in a sheath. I worry about her having a knife but avoid saying anything. She might pull it on me for asking.

Footsteps approach our hiding place and we both peek out, finding Tolliver and Angus approaching with Kava following close behind.

Tolliver and Angus are loaded down with bags and bundles. Angus carries the burn bin for my contraption. It hits me that I might succeed, and my heart leaps to an enthusiastic rhythm as I smile wide. I will get back to Ellery. I will find Alouette.

Hollis and I attempt to exit the hollow at the same time, elbow to the ribs, pushing and shoving until we are free. Her hair gets in my mouth and I try not to spit on her. We squeeze through the small opening like twin calves being born. She comes out standing up and I plop to the ground like the weaker one.

I peer up at Kava, "What is she doing here?"

Kava glares at me.

Tolliver speaks for her, "I asked for her help and she brought a bag of medicines."

I snort and pretend to cough. Looking at her then at Tolliver, his hands are on his hips and his eyes tell me there is no challenging him. I look around at all of them. "Are you sure you all want to do this? It really isn't your fight."

"Yah, Ledger," Angus agrees.

Hollis shifts from one foot to another, "For sure." She looks at me with intensity in her eyes. When she looks away, I see a hint of something else. Fear? Anger? I'm not really sure.

"I'm in too," Kava answers. She doesn't know the full extent of why we are going. I don't understand why she would even care.

"You all realize we will be gone for an entire year? We won't be back until next harvest. Hollis, your mother might need you," I say.

"Your mama needs you, Ledger." Hollis balls her hands into fists. "I am going."

"Let's repack some of this and get on our way immediately," Tolliver intervenes, ripping us from the tense conversation. He drops a few bags on the ground and shortens one of the straps. His long sleeve black tunic shows sweat marks down his back. I feel bad that he's had to do most of the work. I scramble to my feet and help.

It takes a few minutes to disperse the weight of the contraption, blankets, coal and supplies between the five of us. We all strap on our loads, including Grandfather's cloak, which I shoved in my satchel because it is too warm for it. Angus's white shirt is streaked with black marks from the burn bin he carries, though he doesn't care. Kava has a rope tied around the float of the contraption and has it tied on her back, over top of a burgundy dress with puffy long sleeves and a black over-dress. Maybe Hollis has a point. Flying in a dress will be awkward.

Tolliver leads us out a good distance around the mill on the edge of the river. We follow him over the rockiest part, leaping from boulder to boulder to keep our leather shoes dry. Hollis catches me when I slip once. I bite my tongue to push back how foolish I feel. On the other side, we rest for a moment to fill several water pouches.

We follow Tolliver up the jagged bank of the river and head southward toward the lake. It is getting dark fast. I'm not sure how far it is but we should pick up the pace. Maybe I'm just anxious to get on the island. Tolliver and Angus walk ahead. Their hushed voices conceal their conversation. Hollis and Kava hike behind me in silence. Walking in the middle of my friends, I thank the stars for their help.

It takes all afternoon to reach the lake through the winding hills. Evening is upon us; the sun is behind the trees and soupy clouds streak across the sky. Cresting another wooded hill, I see shimmery dark blue peeking from between the trees as we descend the ridge. Excitement fills my body with an extra burst of energy as we all scurry down the embankment. I am out of breath by the time we dodge through the trees to reach the gritty shore. The lake fills a large basin with cliffs on the other side. It stretches eastward for what looks like a two or three-day hike. There is no way we can beat Ellery to the other end.

Above the blue expanse of water, Ellery drifts through the air. The sun hasn't set there, flooding the island with orange light. It is hulking and brightly lit. My heart aches at the thought of missing this chance. I must get up there.

We walk to the water's edge. Tolliver drops his things on the beach. "How long will it take to expand the float?"

My legs are numb from the journey. Relieved that we are done walking, I answer, "Maybe an hour?"

"If we can take off tonight, let's do it. By morning, Ellery will be well past the lake and beyond that ridge." Looking out across the glassy surface, I see Tolliver is right. It's now or never. "You get that thing ready to fly, I'll get the fire going."

***

"How did you get this thing off the ground by yourself?" Hollis asks as we finish expanding the float.

I am nervous because of its enormity. It's much heavier with the added fabric. *What if the extra weight prevents it from lifting?* I wonder. *What if it can't lift anyone else?* I just stand there, my guts grinding in worry. *I'll have to leave them all behind if it can't take off with all these people.*

A thunderous noise startles me. I whirl around ready to run away from the sound.

"I'm sorry! That was me," Angus says with a smirk. He pours the rest of the bag into the forge. The coal crashes down the metal sides, making another deafening bang.

"Angus, you scared the berries out of me," Hollis shrieks, stomping her foot.

"My apologies," he offers again and I chuckle.

Kava unplugs her ears and joins Tolliver in the dirt. He is bent over blowing on a scrappy pile of pine needles with little wisps of smoke seeping out. Suddenly a little orange flame lights and Kava cheers. Her voice carries over the water. Tolliver is as competent at building a fire as I am. Though he never really enjoyed smithing the way I do, he knows the trade and has the skills. I notice how dark it is getting as Tolliver picks up the entire pile of flaming scrub and dumps it over our coals.

"It may take a little while for it to get truly hot," Tolliver says. He installs the bellows to the side and pumps it several times, nursing it to life. "Get the float in the air, Ledger." I am annoyed that he is telling me what to do with my own contraption. He is helping me, not the other way around. I stare at him for a moment and realize there is no point in arguing.

"I'm going to have to hang it from a tree to get hot air in there. Maybe we should add a rope to the top," I say. "Bring me that rope." I locate the top of the float and cut two small slits. Hollis returns with an armful of thin rope. Threading it through the fabric, I tie it tight.

I assess the nearby trees to find a branch high enough to hold up the huge float. Finding one at the right height, I attempt to throw the rope up and over, but after three or four throws Angus tires of my failure and says, "Let me do it."

My cheeks flush, as I hand him the rope. He bunches the line in his giant hands, thrusts it into the air and hooks the branch on the first try. Seriously? He smiles through his thick orange beard and walks away. Why am I always the worst at everything?

A frustrated groan escapes my lips, as I position the float over the forge. My hands shake in irritation as I connect the ropes to the top of the metal bin. Tolliver pumps the bellows. The fire is not quite hot enough and needs more time.

I stomp off into the woods to relieve myself and clear my head. I think about the fact that it will be an entire year before I see Mother and Father again. My insides sink, full of sorrow from not saying goodbye. They will be so disappointed in me. I walk in several circles looking for mindyberries, little purple berries that ripen in the fall. They are sometimes hard to see in the shadows of the forest. Meandering from bush to bush eating the sweet berries, I am startled by voices shouting from the edge of the lake.

I dart through the trees stirring up the fallen leaves. The cold autumn air courses through my lungs making my chest sting. I reach the clearing and find everyone hurriedly packing.

"What's going on?" I ask out of breath. I notice the coal fire is burning nicely and the float is almost fully inflated.

"They're coming," Hollis says.

"Who?" I look to the sky at the floating island. With hope, I search the clouds.

"Father, Thelonious, our people," Tolliver shouts as he pumps the bellows. "Angus spotted them from the top of the ridge."

NEAR MISS 11

I pump the bellows over and over, heating the fire exponentially. Bigger puffs of hot air fill the float and it lifts slightly off the ground.

Everyone scrambles about packing their bags. Hollis wraps her belt around the straps of her sacks to keep them secure then helps Kava tie her long skirts between her legs.

"Add the rest of the coals," I tell Tolliver but Angus dashes for the bag of coals and dumps it in, accidentally dropping the whole thing on the fire. The float loses some of its heat as the bag blocks the flames.

Angus reaches in to pull it out, but Tolliver and I shout, "No!" at the same time. We both know it can be hot enough to burn the skin off his whole hand and hot enough to burn the bag to ashes in moments.

The whole contraption rises again as we hear men's voices in the distance.

"They're coming!" Tolliver warns. He takes over the bellows. The float continues to drift into the air.

Pump, pump, pump.

It's inches off the ground.

Pump, pump, pump.

It's at the height of my chest.

Pump, pump, pump.

I attempt to remove the rope from the top of the tree branch. It's stuck. It won't snap free of the branch. "Angus, help me free the rope!"

We see the men crest the ridge and descend the hill toward the lake. They are calling out to us.

Angus gathers the rope and throws it several times back over the branch. The whole contraption is rising into the air. It is enormous. A patchy bubble of woven fabric. Tolliver puffs the bellows a couple more times, but it won't rise beyond the tethered limb. Angus gathers the rope one more time and heaves it up and over, freeing us from the branch. The contraption bounces upward, and I grab the hammock seat, just before it sails out of reach. Tolliver and I exchange wide-eyed looks of panic.

Hollis and Kava unroll the rope ladder and hand Tolliver the ends. We quickly tie each side securely below my seat. I have to leap a little to get into it. "You'll have to get on one at a time as I rise into the air," I explain to Tolliver and he nods.

I lean back in the seat and take over puffing the bellows that are now over my head, pumping as many times as it takes to lift me above my friends. Hollis climbs the ladder first. It drops slightly with her weight, so I pump wildly as each person mounts the ladder.

Next is Kava, then Tolliver. I keep pumping and we keep rising. My arms are aching. Angus grabs the last rung of the ladder and runs down the beach. His momentum flings us out over the water. I pump and pump as hard and as fast as I can—until my arms are numb with exhaustion. We sail out over the lake as Angus struggles to hold on, toes dipping in the water. Using his powerful arms, he pulls himself up a few rungs until his feet can rest securely on the last one.

The men come scrambling out of the woods, shouting my name. Father sees Tolliver and shouts his name and mine.

"Ledger, no!" Father commands. I hear the anger in his words. My chest tightens as if his words could cause my plan to deflate.

"Who is that?" a man asks from below.

"It's Angus," someone on the beach answers.

"And who is near the top?" It sounds like Kava's father but I'm not sure.

"Hollis? Is that Hollis?" Thelonious shouts from the front of the angry mob.

Tolliver yells down, "We will be back next harvest."

"Who else is with you?" Thelonious pleads.

"Kava," Tolliver replies.

"No," Another man screams. I pump the bellows and look down at the beach as Healer Clovis runs into the lake, flailing and splashing. "No, you bring her back," he cries.

I hear Kava shout from beneath me, "I will be fine, Papa!"

Her father yells her name over and over as we drift farther and farther away. They are becoming ant-size. The men of Balfour pull Clovis from the water and stand him on his feet.

I continue pushing heat into the giant float above our heads as we rise triumphantly into the sky.

Above the shadow of the trees, the sunset is so bright it hurts my eyes. We are all silent for a little while as the wind pushes us eastward toward Ellery. We drift close to the sharp underside of the island. I puff the bellows endlessly lifting us faster and faster. Cresting the topmost ledge, the wind pushes us from below and we sail up over Ellery's surface like an eagle toward a mountaintop. The castle, a tall round tower jutting into the sky, is rapidly approaching. In a flash, we skirt over the surface of Ellery and I must act hastily before we overshoot the island.

I grab the rope hanging from the top of the float. Maybe if I let some heat out we will descend. Nothing happens at first, so I tug a little harder. It goes slack in my hands and I fear I may have torn a hole in the top. Hollis screams as we fall out of the sky. I touch her white knuckles gripping the rope ladder. Her blue eyes are round with terror.

Plummeting toward the floating island alongside the castle wall, I pump the bellows hoping it will level us out. There is a scuffle below as Angus hits first. He rolls and is on his feet in an instant. Plumes of dust and stones swirl around him as he chases us. Tolliver, inches from the rocky surface, reaches his foot downward. I look up at the towers of Ellery. We are coming in fast and the other edge of the island is approaching. It's either hit the castle or dive off the other side, and there is no way I am missing it.

Still in full forward motion toward the island's edge, Tolliver leaps from the ladder and yanks it back. Angus catches up, grabs the rope ladder and helps tug. I pull the top rope one last time to release the hot air and the blankets deflate quickly. Tolliver and Angus are still being dragged across the loose rocks toward the cliff.

My arms shake, and my body is abuzz. I am terrified we

will not succeed, when suddenly a gust of wind pushes us back toward the castle. The float is flattening, and the fire is dying. I pull the vent rope one last time.

Tolliver reaches toward Kava and she leaps to him. I hear him say something and she helps pull the ladder in this dangerous game of tug-o-war. Hollis is whimpering and holding tight to the rope ladder as we dangle over Ellery's rim.

With one last tug, Tolliver, Kava, and Angus pull us back from the edge as the float folds in on itself and flops down the side of the island's rocky edge. I land with a thud on the ledge; pain shoots through me. The fire spills over the side and I lose most of my coal. Some of the pieces singe the blankets on the way down. I panic and pull the forge up the side of the cliff with all my might.

"Ledger, calm down! Let me help you!" Tolliver shouts. The cliff crumbles beneath me and I fall downward. A hand grabs my tunic and drags me back from the edge. I catch a hold of the forge and bellows as they go down.

"Let go of it!" Tolliver commands.

"No!" I argue. I make one last yank and we both go toppling backward. We land on the island's hard surface.

Tolliver is swatting his clothes and scrambling to his feet. I feel the burning too. My head whirls with pain. I can't hear anything but my own screaming. The burning is so overwhelming I cannot stay conscious. I see Hollis and the others come to my aid as the blackness drags me down into unconsciousness.

***

Day 1

I am cold and burning at the same time. My left shoulder and arm feel like they are in hell and my right side in the frozen lake. Opening my eyes, I see only a dark cavernous ceiling. I run my hand up to my left shoulder. My tunic is gone. A bandage is on the burn.

"Don't touch it, Ledger." Hollis commands from across the room.

"Tolliver?" I remember our mishap. "Is he okay?" I sit up and pain shoots through me, making my head dizzy.

"He's fine," she answers, nearing where I lay. Her face comes into view. Brow furrowed, she reaches and pushes my hair out of my eyes and then swats me on the head. "He only had one small burn. What in the name of sanity were you thinking? You almost went over that cliff!"

I take a deep breath and attempt to sit up. She holds me down with one hand.

"Don't move until Kava gets back!" I try again, and she puts both hands on my bare chest. "Ledger, no."

"Get off me, Hollis. I need to sit up. I need to get my bearings." I wipe her warm hands from my chest and prop myself up. Sliding back, I lean against a stone headboard.

We are in a bedroom with high ceilings, a massive fireplace on one end and large gaping windows on the other. The bed is the fluffiest I've ever felt. My head settles down from its swirl around the room, and I take a deep breath.

"How long have I been out?" I am heavy with sleep.

"Since last night," she replies.

"How bad is it?" I touch the bandage not wanting to look. I am probably burned to the bone and unable to use that arm again. I hear footsteps before Hollis answers.

"It's pretty bad," Kava replies. She stomps in briskly with a leather bag and a handful of clean rags. "If you weren't such an idiot, this could have been prevented."

"I couldn't lose my contraption," I mumble under my breath.

"Your brother is fortunate you aren't a bigger idiot and you let go of it when you did. You both could have been killed," she says and my heart sinks at the thought of losing my brother—and my contraption.

"Did we save it?"

"What? Your stupid floating thing?"

I nod.

She scowls. "Yeah."

I lean back on the cool stone. Kava unwraps my shoulder and arm. The bloody bandage is my old tunic ripped to shreds. My skin is burned pretty badly in spots. It is severely red in the middle and bloody around the edges. Looking at it makes it hurt more. A wave of nausea hits me, and I try not to gag.

"You should be glad Tolliver is a thinker. He asked me to pack all sorts of medicines. Told me to imagine the kind of trouble you would get into. So I brought some of everything. Aren't you a lucky boy?"

"I am not a boy."

"Don't you mean 'Thank you'?" She raises an eyebrow at me, chastising me like my own mother.

"Thank you, Kava," I concede.

"You're welcome." She slathers a greenish salve on the burns and I wince in pain. She rolls her eyes at my twinge and wraps a clean bandage around it. Huffing, she leaves me alone with Hollis. Unfortunately, Hollis is almost as angry as Kava. Wincing at the shoulder pain, I kick the blankets off my feet and follow Kava through the tall doorway into the hall. Her scuffling steps echo down the wide hallway. I could follow her with my eyes closed. Hollis is right behind, her boots tapping rhythmically on the stone floor. Kava's burgundy dress wafts through a brightly lit doorway. Her shadow gets smaller and smaller as I follow her into the circular courtyard. The sun is high in the sky. The wind is still as powerful as it was yesterday when I was here alone.

How do the winged people of Ellery keep from sailing off into the sky with the currents of air through this place?

Kava walks through the middle of the courtyard, her dress whipping in the wind. She breezes past the empty fountain. I pause to catch my breath through the pain, staring up at the winged stone figure on top. Then I follow her through a double doorway that leads into an eating hall. The stone tables are nearly chest high and there are wooden stools around each one. I am distracted from the cold by the presence of Tolliver and Angus talking loudly about the castle and the location of things.

DECAY 12

"There he is," Angus says. It sounds like an accusation.

"How are you doing, little brother?" Tolliver rolls the first "r" making me feel like a little boy who has skinned his knee.

"I'll be fine." I clench my fists from anger or pain, I'm not sure which, and change the subject. "What are you working on?"

Tolliver answers, "We're making a map as we search. I figure we will have to learn how things work up here since we are going to be here for a while."

"Good idea," I nod.

"How much did you get to see when you were here?"

I approach the table with a large spread of fabric on top. In Tolliver's hand is a piece of black coal sharpened into a point.

On the map are several circles that must represent various levels of this towering building. I recognize the main floor on which we are standing with the courtyard, throne room, and dining hall. Tolliver has many other rooms drawn all the way around including an inner hall I didn't get the chance to investigate.

"Not as much as you, apparently." I'm irritated that they explored without me.

Hollis joins us around the maps. She invades my space, with her arm touching mine. I sigh. I notice my bag beneath the table and carefully bend over to locate my extra tunic. I find it and stick my head through the neck hole. Pain shoots through me when I place my burned arm through the sleeve and takes my breath away for a moment. I may have gasped aloud. Embarrassed, I hold still as Hollis gently helps me put it on the rest of the way. I don't look at her. Retrieving my water pouch, I take a swig.

"Want some breakfast?" Hollis asks.

I can hardly believe I missed the first night on the island. Plugging the pouch and tossing it on the table, I can't force myself to answer. My face warms and my head aches. She hands me a hunk of bread anyway. Frustrated about missing the first exploration of the castle, I eat in silence, ripping chunks of the dense bread with my teeth.

"I think the most important or wealthy people of their community live in the lower levels," Tolliver explains. "The lower class lives near the top. Angus and I went to the topmost level. The homes have less stuff. But we couldn't stay up there for very long. It was hard to breathe." Tolliver points his thumb at Angus, "He almost passed out on the stairs. I wasn't sure if I'd be able to stop him from rolling all the way down." He winks at me, and my tension eases.

"I was fine," Angus protests. "The air is strange up there, but I was definitely fine."

Tolliver chuckles, "We have to find a water source. I think it's time to go underground."

We follow Tolliver down to what I call the Grand Hall that leads out the western side of Ellery. Halfway down the hall is an arched doorway with stairs leading down into darkness. I remember yesterday, standing at the top fretting over how dark it is down there. I am no fan of the dark and we are heading into it. The walls are adorned with torch holders, but the torches are missing.

Tolliver descends first then Angus, Kava and Hollis. My body is frozen in place, uncomfortable with the dark, the cold, and the fact that I'm last in this little procession. I reluctantly follow them. The stairs spirals down to the right. I slide my hand along the smooth wall as I come around the corner. The sound of flint striking steel echoes up the steps. A spark cuts through the darkness, thanks to Tolliver. I follow closely to ensure I am never outside of the bubble of light the torch throws around the stairwell.

Some distance down, there is an exit to the left. The stairs keep going and Tolliver decides, "Let's start here." We follow him through a hall with a low ceiling. Angus reaches up and runs his hand along it. Dust particles fall into my eyes.

At the other end is a metal gate with iron bars running from ceiling to floor. It is unlocked, and Tolliver lifts the handle. We enter another wider passage with a series of holding cells on either side. Each one is a cavernous room with barred doors. Tolliver lights a few torches hanging on the walls. Angus takes one and inspects the first room on the right. The gate is open, and the room is empty. Tolliver looks in the one on the left—empty.

Most of the cells are taller than they are wide. I imagine keeping a winged prisoner would take a uniquely shaped room. Each has a bed of dirty feathers in the corner, like a nest. We check each one all the way down the hall. I notice the cell on the end does not have a gate, but a solid metal door with a small barred window near the top. After Tolliver checks the last side room, he steps to the metal door and leans up on his tiptoes.

I hear him gasp. "There's someone in there." He pulls the handle—it is locked. Each one of us takes a turn peering into the room. There is a dark figure on the nest of feathers in the far corner.

"Hello?" Tolliver calls into the room.

Silence.

"Can you hear me?" He bangs on the door. "Hello?"

Nothing.

Tolliver drops his bag near the prison door and looks through the window again. "He is not moving. He's either dead or deaf. Let's find a key."

Angus looks at him with scrunched eyebrows. "Where are we going to find a key in this place?"

"Maybe in the King's quarters or where one of the guards lived?" Tolliver says.

Kava clicks her tongue, "That is ridiculous. We'll never find keys."

"Maybe we can break the hinges," I chime in.

Tolliver and Angus inspect the door. It has external hinges but none like I've ever seen. A metal pin traverses the full length of the door. When Tolliver hands me the torch,

I wince at the pain in my burned shoulder. He pulls out his hunting knife and pries at the top of the pin. Sweat gathers at the nape of his neck and wets his black tunic.

Kava states in a monotone voice, "I am done being down here in this filthy prison."

Hollis nods.

"Ha!" Tolliver blurts after a few moments. The pin pries loose a little bit. He wraps his fingers around the top and pulls upward. "Angus, grab my leather gloves from my pack."

Angus digs through Tolliver's bag beside the door and retrieves the black leather gloves with years of gray ash ground into them.

"And find me something to stand on," Tolliver says.

"Did we come down the same hallway? There is nothing down here," Angus says coolly. His eyes light up, and he gets down on the floor on his hands and knees. "Here, get on my back."

"Thanks, cousin," Tolliver smiles, pushes his blonde hair out of his eyes and steps on Angus's back. He gains the leverage he needs to pull the long metal pin out, yanking and yanking until it is free. Tolliver leaps from Angus's back and they both pry the door open at the hinges.

We all pour in as the light of the torch floods the room.

"Hello?" Tolliver says approaching the heap in the corner. As we draw nearer, we smell it.

Decay.

Tolliver steps on part of its wing and it crumbles beneath his step. He puts a hand on what looks to be a shoulder and pulls the body over. The head lolls to the side and we see the absence of eyes—skin and hair falling from bone. Hollis shudders beside me and gags. I put an arm around her to shield her from the gruesome sight.

"Dead," Angus says.

"Probably starved to death," Tolliver adds.

"How long has he been dead?" I ask, hoping to get an idea as to when the Ellerians went missing.

"I would guess over a month, maybe two being in this cold cellar," Tolliver looks at me for a long moment.

"How long does it take to starve to death?" I ask.

"It's not the starving that matters," Kava replies. I look at her stern face. Twisting a handful of her skirts in a knot, she is still captivated by the dead winged man. "You can't live without water. There is no water source in here," she says looking around. There is an empty bowl near the door. "Seven days, maybe ten."

"So it's possible they went missing between one or two months ago?" I ask no one in particular.

"We'll be just as dead as him if we don't find water on this rock." Her voice drifts off.

Tolliver takes the torch from my hands. Exiting the rotting cell, we follow him in silence down the halls and back to the stairs. He pauses for a moment not turning either way, up or down. Anxiety weighs heavily in the pit of my stomach. I hope he goes right, up the stairs and out of the darkness.

"Shall we keep going down?" Angus asks.

Tolliver nods and descends the stairs. My heart pounds as I hurry to keep up with the light. Hollis and Kava are right behind me. I look up at Hollis. She is solemn. I catch her eye and her expression doesn't change.

We are stopped by another gate, this time in the middle of the stairwell. It is locked, and the hinges are on the other side. Angus and Tolliver try to pick the lock without success.

"End of the line, for now," Tolliver says. "We need to find some keys."

My stomach loosens, and I sigh in relief.

Tolliver ascends the stairwell faster than he descended. I struggle to keep up. By the time we reach the top, I am winded, and my shoulder is throbbing. Daylight floods the Grand Hall where I stop and lean on the cold, stone wall. Tolliver, Kava and Angus head for the dining hall. Hollis hovers nearby saying nothing. She runs a hand slowly along the wall. I look up at the ceiling, catching my breath. The stone carvings in the ceiling are of winged people dressed in knee length tunics like the one Alouette wore. Dove-down silk. The sculptures are menacingly poised with bows and arrows. Their muscular bodies are well defined, male and female. I fear encountering them.

If we catch up with them, will we be killed? If they find us trespassing on their island, will we be sent to die in their prison? The ache in my burned shoulder pales in comparison to the ache in my chest.

STICKY SPIT 13

Day 7

We have found plenty of food in the homes of the central tower, but our trouble has been finding water on this lone floating mountain. I am beginning to think they don't have water up this high. Maybe they kept it in the fountain at the center of the courtyard that is now dried up. We found buckets in the homes, but they too are dry. My lips are cracking at the corners and it hurts to talk. I ache inside and slowly swallow small amounts of my own saliva.

"Let's split up," Tolliver directs. "Angus, take the west side. Kava and Hollis you take the north. Ledger, the south, and I will check this side. Look everywhere, even if it doesn't look promising. There has to be water somewhere."

Angus nods scuffling off toward the north hall. I see doubt in Hollis's eyes. Kava tiredly takes her arm and pulls her toward the far side of the courtyard. I watch them walk in a steady pace around the empty fountain. The wind blows and pulls more moisture from my skin.

When the girls are far enough away, I plead with Tolliver. "Please don't make me search alone." I am tired of the eerie sounds of the wind through the castle. Each day, I am beyond relieved that I am not alone on this drifting rock.

He sighs and says, “Come on.” I follow him down the Grand Hall. The cold wind pinches at my cheeks. Tolliver seems unfazed by the frigid temperatures. He takes a left down the inner hallway that circles the castle. The royal chambers are on the opposite side of the castle off the inner hall, but I’ve not taken the time to search this side. Tolliver opens the first double doors on the right side of the hallway. It is pitch black inside until he lights a torch on the wall. There are rows upon rows of beds with cloth screens hanging between each.

“A sick ward.” I pick up a bottle and inspect it. Tolliver doesn’t confirm. There is shelving on the entrance wall where bottles, drying herbs, liquids and powders fill the shelves.

He steps closer and says, “We’ll have to show this to Kava.”

We inspect room after room that branch off to the right and the left of the inner hall. I heave the last door on the outer wall of the castle open. The thick metal scrapes the ground causing my head to ache.

Gasping, I recognize the tools and crafts in this large blacksmithing workshop. The front half is partitioned off by a counter that butts out into the room. It is clean and neat with displays of swords, axes and other useful tools and weapons. There is an upper shelf with strange metal objects of which I don’t recognize. I want to touch them, but Tolliver says, “Come on.”

“Wait,” I say, peering into the cluttered workshop behind the counter. The spectacularly built forge centered on the back wall entrances me. It is an enormous rock edifice built in a half circle. There is a hole in the ceiling above it and there are two large bellows that protrude from either side. I imagine all the things I could make as I inspect the tools hanging on the wall, laying on the workbench and the few on the floor beside the forge. Some I recognize. Some I do not.

“Ledger, it’s time to move on,” Tolliver says. His voice is tense but quiet. Leaving the beautiful mess behind, I follow him out the metal door. We circle back into the center courtyard and enter the dining hall.

“Can I ask you something?”

“You may.” Tolliver searches my face.

“Why did you come?” He looks away, quiet for a moment. Tolliver pulls a torch from the wall, lighting it with ease. Maybe he is formulating an answer. Maybe I should already know the answer. “I am glad you did,” I offer to fill the silence.

“Ledger,” he stops me. “I know what it is to be in love.” My throat constricts. I want to deny my love for Alouette, but he continues, “Mother said you would go whether I helped you or not. She was worried you would kill yourself trying.”

I suddenly wish I hadn’t asked. My shame is now out in the open.

“She still thinks of me as a boy,” My voice echoes down the stale hall.

“I told her that,” Tolliver says with a half smile.

“Really?”

“You proved to me—to the whole village—that you are resourceful and inventive.”

I puff up my chest at his compliment and follow him

to the back of the dining hall down a stairwell to a large kitchen. There are three stone ovens, each on their own wall, with a large worktable in a horseshoe in the middle of the room. The room is roughly hewn, and the ceiling is jagged and cave-like. It arches upward with a hole in the center, probably a vent of some sort. Around the room are several rough openings that lead off the kitchen. We follow the first one, which ends at several storage rooms with grain and preserved meats and one with a rotten grain smell. My stomach churns at the sour stench. We walk down another hallway leading around the backside of the ovens. My body is tired, and my throat is cottony, but I press on down the passage. It tapers gradually to a sharp dead end. Tolliver abruptly turns and faces me.

"Why do you suppose everyone else came?" I ignore my thirst and sticky spit.

"I'm not responsible for their choices. You'll have to ask them," he waves me off and tromps past me.

He used to be quick to tell me his opinion. Then I realize he derailed me with his compliment. There is something he's not telling me. I analyze each person aloud, hoping he'll open up. "Hollis will follow me anywhere," I analyze.

Tolliver chuckles lightly, "She is like a lost puppy. Remember that mutt you kept feeding outside the garden gate and mother commanded you to deny it?" I catch up, walking beside him.

"Yes." I shake my head at the sad thought.

"Father made you drag it in the woods and kill it," He laughs loudly, and it echoes off the stone walls.

I halfheartedly laugh as I think about the fact that I didn't kill it. I hid it in the hollow for a few weeks and kept feeding it. One day I returned, and it was gone. I imagined that it moved on and found a new home.

"I found it living in the hollow," Tolliver stated, "and put it out of its misery for you."

I jerk as he disrupts my pleasant delusion. "You did?" I stop in the middle of the kitchen with a hand on his arm.

He nods and winks at me. My mouth hangs open as he walks away.

I dismiss the thought. "So why did Kava come? She can barely stand my presence. I don't understand." I stop mid-thought, remembering that he admitted being in love. "You love Kava."

Tolliver doesn't say anything to my bold statement. He walks through the last opening in the kitchen wall nearest the stairs. This passageway is wider than the others.

"Do you think we will find the Sky People?" I hope he is as optimistic as I am.

"Maybe," he replies, lifting the torch above his head. "Maybe not."

"Don't you care if we find them?" I am annoyed that he won't give me a straight answer.

He just shrugs.

"I don't get it then," I say. My voice bounces back in my face. "Why help search for them?"

"Not everyone has the same goal as you, little brother." Tolliver steps into a wider part of the tunnel. "Hey, look at that."

I push him out of the way to see what he's found. It opens into a rounded cave. On the far side of the room there is a knee-high ledge holding back a pool of water. The light from the torch reflects off the surface and bounces around the room.

He laughs, and I join in, reveling in the joy of our find. Water. Beautiful water.

We waste no time scurrying to the water's edge. Getting on my hands and knees, I stick my face in and suck the cool liquid. I guzzle it, satisfying the lack in my body. It's been three days since the last drop from my pouch.

Tolliver, with torch in one hand, scoops the water with his other hand, scoop after scoop. He splashes it on his head and wets his face. His light curly hair darkens and stretches to his shoulders. He shakes it off like a dog and a relieved laugh escapes his lips.

"Here," Tolliver tosses my pouch and dunks his own into the pool. I do the same and watch the bubbles trickle out of the opening.

"We will survive," I encourage. "We will find them, and we will bring them home."

Tolliver sighs. His eyebrows pinch together with seriousness. "Your contraption has one flight, maybe two flights left before it falls to pieces or goes up in flames. You will not go searching the ground to find them and risk not being able to get back on the island. We barely made it last time."

He replaces the lid on his water pouch and heads back down the hallway. My heart sinks as the reality of what he is saying hits me. I want to argue. I want to blurt out some ingenious idea, but I have none. I am flying blind on this wandering island.

14

FINDING SOLACE

Day 18

The chilly morning air wakes me, wafting down the stone walls. Even though I have the king's bed curtains drawn, the cold air still seeps through, sinking deep into my bones. I haven't been sleeping well and wake unwillingly each morning with numb fingers and toes. It is shifting to winter sooner than I expect, maybe because we are high in the air. It is always colder the higher up the North Mountain Alouette and I flew.

Pulling back the curtains, I blink several times adjusting to the light. The sky is clear outside the tall gaping windows. I should close the shutters to keep out the cold and the light, but I don't. I kick the blankets of silk and stretch my tired muscles. A pain shoots through my arm. I wince trying not to tear my scabs again. I think of Alouette and wonder where she lived on this frigid island.

I snap out of my daze, throw on my boots, and Grandfather's cloak. I head for the dining hall to check the maps. We still haven't drawn out every level. Tolliver found it to be a waste of time after the tenth floor of living quarters that were exactly the same as the last. But I am keeping a tally of how many floors there are and place a stone on the location of the last dwelling on the map I visited so I would remember where I left off in search of Alouette's home.

I grab my pouch and descend into the kitchen to get water. There is a noticeable water line about four hands above the surface. Tolliver thinks that their water source may be drying up and it's possible they left on their own. But Alouette would have told me if they were planning on leaving. She would have said something.

I drown my empty pouch in the pool, filling it to capacity. Without Tolliver, Hollis, Angus or Kava, I will continue my search in the upper floors. I avoided Hollis at breakfast so she wouldn't follow me. Tolliver and Angus have taken it upon themselves to unload the spoiled grain from the kitchen storerooms. They've already hauled several bags from the kitchen, through the Great Hall, down the front steps and pitched them over the side of Ellery. I pass them as I ascend the kitchen stairs. They nod as we scoot around each other.

From the courtyard, I ascend the main stairwell that circles the inside of the castle tower. I climb to level twelve and walk along the stone railing on the left side overlooking the courtyard below. The doors are on the right, usually around twenty homes all the way around.

I search for any sign of Alouette. Each dwelling is made up of a series of rooms that extend to the outer wall. Heading toward the back is a narrow hallway with several rooms leading off it. In the sleeping quarters, richer families have real beds, but the poorer families only have sacks of feathers on which to lay. Some of the rooms have a window with shutters.

There is not much difference in the ninth, the tenth, and eleventh homes on this level. After searching the twentieth home, I am bored. My mind is numb and I'm tired of seeing nothing but the same thing over and over again. I want to quit but there isn't much else for me to do.

When I ascend to the thirteenth level, my lungs labor over the air. Lightheaded, I draw deeper breaths but it doesn't help much. I stop by the railing overlooking the courtyard thirteen levels below. I am a little over halfway up the tower. Shaking my head in disgust, a distant squawk disrupts the tedium. I look all the way up into the blue sky and wait as the sound gets closer.

Geese. I don't see them, but I can hear them approaching. There are no animals on this entire rock in the sky and I am yearning to see life. Dashing into the first home, I run straight to the back hoping for a window to see the birds in flight.

I sprint down the hall to the back bedroom, reaching the window in time to see a perfect arrow of geese streaking across the blue heavens. I inhale the crisp air and listen to them calling to each other in the sky, all following one leader.

The birds disappear over the southern horizon and I explore this home in reverse. There is an ornate bed with four wooden posts. I run my hand along the beautiful craftsmanship. On the headboard is a carving of a woman with a winged child in her hands that looks like a cherub with chubby cheeks and little wispy wings. A small table stands on the far side of the bed and something catches my attention. I recognize it in an instant. I gasp as I step around the end of the bed and approach the bedside table. It is my small metal windmill—the trinket I gave Alouette at our first meeting. I pick up the precious object.

This is Alouette's home. I look around at the stone walls, the black and green woven rug on the floor. Finding it brings relief. It's almost as though I have found a part of her. I hurriedly look around for any other signs of her life here. A large box in the corner holds clothes and blankets. Not much else.

The storage room has mostly the same food items as all the others. The front room has a table near the hearth with a cushioned bench. On the opposite wall is a long seat with padding along the entire thing, large buttons along the back, and a footrest at one end. It is leathery, yet soft to my touch.

I sit. Alouette sat here. I leap from the seat and sit at the table. She sat here too. I rush to the hearth. She probably stirred stew in this pot. I grab a ladle and stir the empty pot. Dropping it with a clang, I run my hand along the mantle.

My heart is racing, stomach churning. I want to find her so badly it hurts. I pound the mantle with my fist and growl into the empty echoes of this cavernous tower. I have fooled myself into thinking I had gotten closer to her, but now it feels as though we're even farther apart.

I hear a scrape on the stone floor and look up. Hollis is in the doorway peering at me with a quizzical look. We stand in silence for a moment.

"Hollis." Embarrassed that she may have seen my silly antics, I look away to avoid telling her about Alouette.

"I found keys," she says eagerly. She must have run up the stairs to find me because she is out of breath.

I snap to attention and realize what it means. The belly of the island is yet to be discovered. We found several stairwells leading downward, one led to a grinding mill, none that went as far down as the one past the prison, and only one that had a locked gate. Hollis holds up the dirty metal keys.

"Where did you find them?"

"Level six," she says panting. I try to remember searching level six, but they all blend together in my mind. Truth be told, I was not looking for keys. A smile plays at the edge of her mouth, "Let's go!"

Looking around the room, I don't want to race out this door. I want to savor the moment. I want to find solace. I want to sleep in her bed, eat at her table. But what I really want is to eat with her and talk with her. Yet, Hollis is hurrying me along. She jogs into the room, gets behind me and pushes me to the door. I linger for another moment.

"Ledger, come on! I have got to see what is down those stairs. It has been killing me for weeks," she says with another shove.

Heat rises in my neck and face like I am a pot she has placed over a fire. "No," I balk. "I can't. Not yet." "Why?"

"I just—"

"Why?" she pesters.

"I just can't leave this one yet," I snap.

"This room? Why? There are hundreds exactly like it." She tilts her head to the side and looks around.

"No, there aren't." Realizing I've said too much, I shut down. In an instant, I decide I should just go with her. With a deep breath, I rush out the door toward the stairs, releasing the tension a little.

She races after me and turns up the heat again. "What makes this one any different than any of the other crazy Ellery dens?"

I whirl around and boil over in an instant. "They aren't crazy!"

She pauses at my outburst and laughs. "They are our enemy, Ledger. Most of what they do is crazy."

I force myself to stay silent and bottle it the way I always do. But I can't put back in what just came bursting out. I want to walk away but a small voice inside me tells me this conversation is bound to happen.

"Not all of them." I wring my hands.

"Not all of them are our enemy or not all of them are crazy?"

"Both."

"And how would you know? Have you ever met them?" Hollis stops and crosses her arms; doubt is all over her face.

"Yes."

Her eyes widen. Her mouth opens, but nothing comes out. Hollis is never speechless.

"I met her when I was twelve." Heat reaches my ears and my head aches.

She lets her arms drop. Her eyes dart around, considering my words. "Who?"

"Her name is Alouette. She has visited me each year." Once the words start rolling from my mouth, they won't stop. "And when she didn't return this year, I couldn't go a whole year wondering if she is dead."

Her shock explodes into a fiery question. "So this isn't some ridiculous diplomatic mission to make peace with the

Sky People so they stop stealing our crops every year?"

"No." I look at her, pressure building in my head, waiting for it to sink in. "Who told you that?"

"No one. I just thought," she interrupts herself with another thought. "Are you—is she the one you were telling your Grandmother about?" Reality simmers to the surface, and then gradually, seething anger.

I look away. My mouth spouts on its own, "Yes."

"I thought you were talking about someone in the village. I thought we were leaving whoever it was behind in Balfour." Hollis is breathing hard, and I sense her agitation rising.

I stare at the ground as the truth of this expedition erupts full force. She stomps her foot. When I look up, her lips tighten into a line, and she speaks in a strange semi-growl ending in a violent scream. "We are spending an entire year away from our families in search of some girl?"

15

IN THE DEPTHS

Day 21

For three whole days Hollis ignores me. Not a single word. The best I can get out of her are angry eyebrows and flared nostrils of disgust. She hasn't even told anyone about the keys she found. We sit in silence in the grand dining hall eating the strange porridge Kava prepared in the main kitchen. My stomach is grateful for this odd gray mush, but the flavor is repugnant. I find myself gagging several times attempting to make it go down. I swish with water after every bite.

"We need to find some honey to put on this before I lose my appetite and stop eating permanently." Dropping a clump back into my bowl, I laugh and say, "It's like feces dropping into a hole in the ground." Tolliver swats me on the back of the head.

"I found some keys," Hollis blurts without her usual fanfare.

"Really?" Tolliver asks. "Let me see."

She tosses the metal ring of keys nonchalantly over the table and Tolliver catches them right before they land in his mush. His eyes brighten, and he takes off running. The rest of us look at each other for a moment and dart after him, fumbling to catch up.

We find ourselves standing at the closed gate down the prison stairs. Tolliver tries key after key in the lock while Angus holds the torch over his head. As we stare beyond the bars, a low rumbling sound emerges from the dark.

Straining my ears to hear over the jingling keys, I whisper, “Do you hear that?”

Tolliver tries another key with a disappointed grunt.

Stepping closer to the gate, I hear it again.

A guttural hum.

“Got it,” Tolliver exclaims, startling me. The latch lifts freely and Tolliver pushes the door open. We follow the spiraling staircase into the depths of the floating island. As we round the last corner there is yet another gate.

“What the—?” Tolliver shouts, pulling out the loop of keys again. The jingling echoes down the dark stairwell. He inserts the same key from the previous door.

I hear the sound, louder this time.

Guuuuuurrrrr.

“Yes,” Tolliver says as he unlocks the gate and flings it open.

“Wait,” I say, grabbing the door and yanking it shut. “I hear something.” We stand in silence for several moments.

“I don’t hear anything,” Angus declares and pushes past me, opening the gate. He plunges the torch through the doorway, followed by Tolliver and Hollis.

“But I heard—”

“Come on, Ledger,” Kava says, passing through the gate. I look back at the dark stairs, and then down at my friends and the fading torchlight. Choking back the anxiety rising in my throat, I clomp down the stairs against my will, joining them at the bottom.

"What is it?" I step through a tall arched doorway into an enormous cavern. We are standing on a round balcony overlooking a dark cavity. Iron bars protrude from the ledge in an arc connecting to the wall behind us. The enclosure stretches in both directions beyond the reach of the torchlight. In this dark cave, our small flame is like a single star in the expanse of the night sky.

Tolliver takes the torch from Angus, approaching the wall to the left.

"Here we go," Tolliver says and lights torch after torch along the wall. "Angus, grab one of these and light the other side."

Angus obeys and the two shed light upon the deep dark pit. I shiver, not so much at the cold, but at the sound that emanates from the depths below. I attempt to hold back my rising panic. My body jolts and the hair on my neck and arms stands on end.

"I heard it that time, Ledger," Tolliver says.

"There's something down there," I whisper.

"Found stairs," Angus declares loudly and tromps back to where we are transfixed.

"Shhhh," Tolliver silences him and steps to the back wall, grabbing an extra torch. He is calm, reaching his hand through the bars and dropping it.

We all watch as it descends into a stone-walled pit. A shadow moves in the back corner. Instantly, my stomach is in my throat. A hiss comes from below and Tolliver throws his other torch in the direction of the movement.

The flame lands in front of a mass of brownish-red scales and teeth. The jaws snap at the light and the creature recoils.

"It's a giant snake!" Angus exclaims.

"No. Give me your torch, Angus," Tolliver demands.

"Surely not!"

"You can get another off the wall!"

I scramble to the wall and grab one as Tolliver pitches Angus's torch into the cavern. This time it lands behind the creature. It lights up several other heaps behind it, but they do not stir. I toss one more beyond the hissing, gurgling animal. It becomes more defined as our eyes cannot believe what we are seeing. The scaly creature stands on four legs with sharp claws. Wide papery wings protrude from its back. The head, spiky and full of teeth, snaps at us.

My chest aches, and my body tells me to run, but I'm paralyzed with fear.

"Dragon," Hollis gasps. At the sound, the beast thrusts its body toward us. Leaping back from the edge, our screams fill the cave. The dragon hits the side of the pit and slides to the ground below. We wait for it to rear up again but nothing happens. Tolliver approaches the bars. One after the other, Kava, Angus, and Hollis join him at the ledge. It takes me an extra moment to start breathing again. My skin prickles as the darkness presses in on me. I grab another lit torch and join them.

The dragon's head lolls to the side. The guttural hum begins again followed by an airy whimper. I shiver at the sound.

"It's dying," Hollis says. She leans toward the edge

pressing her body against the bars. “How could it still be alive?”

“There’s probably water down there,” Kava adds.

Hollis nods, watching the dying beast below. “It probably doesn’t have enough energy to fly either.”

“Should we put it out of its misery?” Angus asks.

“What? No,” Hollis whines. “Why would you do that?”

“It’s going to starve to death anyway,” Tolliver says. Hollis protests again, as they walk away. Tolliver grabs a glowing torch from the wall and heads back upstairs. Angus and Kava follow him.

I linger with Hollis who is peering into the cave. Walking along the bars, she searches for a new angle to inspect the beast. My racing heart and dizzy head tell me not to follow, but I do. She grabs a torch and heads to the stairs descending into the dark cave.

I follow the glow of her torch and golden hair down to a landing. The safety of the iron bars continues down the steps, protecting us from the claws and teeth on the other side.

I hear heavy breathing. Turning toward the cage, it is there, following our flame. Claws scratch on the stone. Warm breath surrounds us.

Hollis steps near the bars.

“Don’t get too close,” I say in a sharp whisper.

Hollis shoots me a scowl and hands me her torch. She kneels on the dusty ground, opening her bag. Rifling through it for a moment, she pulls something out. She approaches the cage and tosses something through. We hear scuffling to the spot where it landed.

"What did you do?"

"Jerky," she says, sounding like an insult.

"You're feeding it?" My heart palpitates. "We can't keep that thing alive. There's no way—"

"No way, what?" Hollis snaps at me. "No way Papa Tolliver will approve?"

"That's not what I was going to say."

"Then what, Ledger?" she challenges.

"There's no way we have enough food to last a year for us, let alone a dragon." I hang my head, hating my logic.

Hollis tosses another piece of jerky to the monster in the shadows. It scrapes in the dark to get it.

Drawing nearer to the cage, I hold out both torches for a better view. It looks at us through the bars, dark eyes blinking slowly, jaws chewing frantically. There are spikes jutting from nose to brow. Its skin is scaly and dry. The wings that dangle limply at its sides have a barb at the tip.

Hollis tosses piece after piece between the bars. After it chews up every bit, she snatches her torch from my hand. Hoping we are done, I grunt with irritation when she walks down the rest of the stairs—ground level with the beast.

I light a few wall-mounted torches on the way down, so it's not so horrendously dark. We walk along with a stone wall on one side and bars on the other. Following us around the enclosure, it seems the dragon could simply reach between the bars and eat us. I peer up at the enormous dragon. Hollis could be standing on my shoulders and might not be able to reach the top of its head.

"Where are we going?" I light another torch on the wall.

"I don't know. Just like you, I have never been here

before." Her tone is full of acid.

"I know that," I say, embarrassed.

"What the skies is that?" Hollis rounds the back side of the cavern and there is a strange pile of flesh pushed through the bars. "Ugh, it's another one," Hollis groans. The smell of death hits me full in the face. A splash of bile stings the back of my throat and I cough several times.

It is grayish and gooey on our side of the cage, but only a pile of bones inside the dragon's enclosure. As we get closer, it smells worse than the corpse in the prison above.

"It's dead," I state, holding my nose. We continue around to the end of the tunnel of bars. There are a few more torches toward the end. I light them. On the cage side, there is an enormous locked gate and to the right, is a large gaping tunnel.

I hear the sound of trickling water and Hollis says it first, "Water and look," she says. "A third one. But it's mostly bones." Her shoulders droop, and she looks back at the scaly creature following us with quiet eyes. "She ate her friends to stay alive."

"Oh lands, that is disgusting." My stomach continues to churn at the smell, the cannibalism, and the horror of this dying beast.

"What else could be down here?" Hollis wonders aloud. I catch a glimpse of her curious eyes as she turns down the large tunnel. I jog, catching up with her. After a few hundred paces, I realize it's getting colder. Hollis is shivering too. The torches flicker in our hands as a frigid wind whistles through the tunnel. We round a corner and see light radiating from the next bend. Picking up the pace and shuffling our way around the corner, we come to a sudden halt, standing on the edge of Ellery.

Alouette had told me she would sneak out of a cave in the base of the island. This must have been what she was talking about. Down here we are much closer to the ground that drifts by at a decent rate. We are over a forest. There is a flock of small birds swirling about from tree to tree.

"Oh, a spyglass," Hollis says behind me. She steps up and peers through the gray metal telescoping spyglass. She takes a long, long look.

"Can I see?" I ask.

She responds with silence as she continues to swish back and forth viewing the landscape.

"Can I please see?"

I wait a couple more minutes.

I see what might be a herd of deer at the edge of a meadow.

"Hollis, can I—"

"Fine," she shouts, slamming the spyglass into my chest.

I gasp at the blow. She crosses her arms and stares down at the passing countryside. Grasping the spyglass in my cold hands, I have no idea what to say. She has never held on to anger this long. When we were little, she usually forgot what she was mad about by midday meal and we were playing again in our fort behind her cottage.

I extend the telescope and look for the herd I had spotted. Sure enough, there are five doe and a buck picking their way through a meadow of golden straw. Craving meat, I wonder how to get down there to hunt. I look from tree to tree and each opening in the forest for any signs of human life below, but only find a couple of rabbits hopping around a thicket.

"Hollis," I begin.

"Don't," Hollis says, crossing her arms. "Just don't."

I want to say I'm sorry for dragging her up here. I want to say I'm sorry for not telling her about Alouette, but I fear saying her name will set her off. I've never felt so distant from Hollis, my best friend. She is always the one who encourages me and lightens me up. Now her face is dark with pain. Her arms are wrapped tightly around her. I want to tuck her in my arms to make her feel safe and comfort her the way I always did, before it meant something different than I intended.

"I'm sorry," I say. It doesn't cover it all, but I can't talk about feelings, let alone plans and marriage.

She sighs deeply and drops her hands to her sides. She looks at me with pain in her eyes. "I thought we were running away together."

I am frozen with guilt and the blood drains from my face. My heart sinks at the thought of such a huge misperception. I don't know what in the world I can say to make it any better. So I simply stand there like a fool.

Her eyes are so blue and the daylight from the opening of the cave reflects in them brightly. Tears are welling, but she looks away before they fall. She kicks loose rocks as she saunters back through the cave. My thoughts are whirling as I follow several feet behind her, like a chastised child, through the tunnel. We pass the sleeping dragon, whose belly is a little more satisfied than it's been in a while, and tiptoe up the stairs. I don't close the gates behind us. They hang wide open like a gaping wound, black and festering, unwilling to let me forget it's there.

16 COLD DISTANCE

Day 42

The flurries begin at dusk and fall all through the night. The next morning, I wake to drifts of snow in the courtyard. It is actually quite beautiful, like a stone garden full of white grass and icicles hanging from the fountain at the center. The wind whips through the courtyard, picking up the fluffy flakes and spiraling them into the air in little glistening cyclones. I reach in, catch a handful, and wipe it on my brown wool cloak while kicking my way through the drifts. The chill permeates my thin boots and I shiver crossing the frosted courtyard.

I'm not fully prepared for the freezing temperatures of winter on Ellery and living up so high makes it even colder. My grandfather's cloak does its best, but periodically I dream of the large leather boots Father had acquired for me back in Balfour. I should have thought ahead. Instead, I have taken to scavenging the homes above for any animal skin to cover my body. I hit a jackpot in what looks like an avid hunter's home. There are several animal skins I don't recognize, among them striped skunks, a wild cat, and something that is probably a bear or other large beast. I made a pair of furry leather pants and strapped the skunks to my feet with a couple of lengths of twine. They drag at my heels because I didn't cut the tails off. At least it made Hollis laugh for a moment. Other than that, she avoids me like I have a skin disease.

As I kick the snow from the path, I notice Hollis standing on the east side of the courtyard. I pause midstride. Her face is turned skyward, catching snowflakes on her tongue. She must have gotten the animal skins I passed along to Kava. She has the wild cat wrapped around her shoulders with a thick black pelt hanging down like a cape. Her boots are laced to her knees and snow sticks to the toe. She leaps a little to catch the next big fluffy flake. This is the Hollis I know. Joyful. Carefree, finding delight in any little thing.

There is a pain deep in my gut. I am hungry to talk to her.

She closes her mouth and looks around, catching my eye. Her demeanor descends into irritation.

"Hi." My voice squeaks. Clearing my throat, I try again. "Hello."

She doesn't say a word as she walks away, abandoning me in this icy place. I'm not sure what to do about her cold shoulder. She has been ignoring me for so long, I feel invisible. Weeks have passed without any acknowledgment. My sadness is being eaten away by frustration and now it boils like acid in my stomach.

The cold bites at my fingers as I ascend the stairs to the overlook where I sit every day. The snow-covered hills with their green peaks poking through the white surface remind me of mother's creamy potato and kale soup. My belly growls in agreement. I draw a spyglass to my eye and scan the landscape, watching for any sign of Alouette, the Sky People, or anyone who can give us a hint of their whereabouts. I expect the same old nothingness. Leafless trees interspersed with evergreens dot the hills. To the east, the sun blinds me for a moment. A pillar of smoke rises wistfully from a grouping of spiky pine trees.

My breath catches in my throat. I've finally spotted signs of life. Leaning out over the edge of the stone rail hoping to catch a glimpse of someone among the trees, I wait and watch through the spyglass, my heart thrumming harder and harder.

Then I see it. A figure with dark hair and dark skin wrapped in something tan, probably deerskin. Without thinking, I wave and yell for several minutes, before realizing they can't hear me. I need my contraption to get down there and talk to them.

Slamming the spyglass closed, I race back down the stairs, around the castle, through the north hall and courtyard into the room that houses my contraption. I push the old wooden door open and snow wafts in with me. There is a fireplace to the left and a room full of tall wood tables stretching as wide as the grand dining hall, but the ceiling is lower and there are rugs dispersed throughout. On the far end is a long bar with stools sidled up to it. Ellery's version of a tavern.

Around the fireplace are auburn plush chairs and beside them sits my contraption. I lift the edges of the float. It is burned in several spots. I consider how long it will take to repair and whether the blacksmith shop will have enough coal to fill the burn bin.

The door thuds open behind me. I whirl around finding Tolliver standing in the doorway.

"Hey, little brother, what are you doing?"

"N-nothing," I stammer, not sure what to say. The snow lashes around him, sticking to his black hooded cloak, his face in partial shadows.

"I saw you run by in a hurry. What are you excited about?" Tolliver swipes the hood from his head.

"I saw people on the ground," I admit.

"And you think you're going to fly down and talk to them?"

My head pounds with frustration, "Maybe." I don't want him to ask me questions. I don't want him watching my every move. I think about how nice it would have been if no one had come with me on this trek, so no one could stop me from doing what I must do to find Alouette.

"Don't bother," he says. "Let's survive this, Ledger. We can't do that if you're going to take unnecessary risks. Going down there right now is pointless, even if that stupid thing is functional. We calculated they went missing eight weeks before reaching Balfour."

I want to argue with him, but his logic is flawless. "I'm just sick of being up here, doing nothing for weeks on end," I blurt.

"If you want something to do, I can give you a task. There are plenty of things you can do to make life easier as we chase your wild dreams around the world." His blunt words hit me like a fist to the face.

My anger flows in a torrent of complaints. "I'm sick of you telling me what to do," I yell. "Hollis hates me. Kava hates me. You keep acting like Father, and Angus is like your personal mule. I've got no one and nothing—not even hope! You are snatching that away and I'm sick of it!" Out of breath, I stop, instantly regretting every word. I wish I could reach out, grab the words from the air like fluffy snowflakes, and put them back in my mouth.

Tolliver is taken aback, eyes wide and mouth open.

My head hurts as if it might burst. My eyes sting, but I refuse to let any tears fall. I brace myself for the lash back.

Tolliver inspects me. I hate the way he looks at me, concerned. Ready to fix it all. But he can't. No one can. I'm stuck here on this frigid island and all I can do is wait.

I'm done waiting. I can't take the impending conflict and to avoid more judgments and commands, I stomp past him out the door. I race back to my post on the lookout tower with defiant tears and clenched teeth. The pillar of smoke is nearing. We will probably pass them by sunset.

I don't care what Tolliver thinks. I will fix my contraption and I will get to the ground. I've been in a holding pattern my whole life. Since I met Alouette, I've had to wait month after month for her to return for a few days of satisfaction. I am forced to be passive and powerless.

My hands shake with cold and fury as I hold up the spyglass again. Beyond the smoke, I see water. Lots of it.

17

LEVEL THREE ANGER

Day 51

I push the hulking metal door open. The wind sneaks in around my feet, invading my privacy dusting the floor of the blacksmith's shop. Muscling it shut behind me, I feel the wall for the torch. Panic over the dark ignites in me as I strike, strike, strike the flint. The little orange flame saves me from the creeping darkness, and I sigh in relief.

At the back of the workshop, I stir the coals in the forge from yesterday. I pile them together and blow on them. Small red spots glow amongst all the gray ash. Adding more jagged bits of black coal around the pile, I pump the bellows until a flame flickers from the ash. I am a champion of fire, watching my creation come to life. It lights my face and I stare into it as if it can tell me the future.

I consider my life in numbers. It has been fifty-one days since we left Balfour behind. Twenty-four days since I made Hollis so mad she refuses to acknowledge my existence. Four hundred sixteen days since I've seen Alouette. I remember one harvest when she arrived at Balfour; she was sad but tried to cover it up. She had brought me a small sandstone carving of a bird. A lark.

"My name means lark," Alouette explains as we sit together atop a large boulder high above the mountain path.

I nod and run my thumb along the smooth surface.

"I like blue larks the best, so I painted it for you." Brush strokes show across the blue wings and tail. The head and beak are black, and the chest is white.

"Thank you," I say, watching the sadness return to her eyes. "Are you okay?"

"I will be fine," she answers. "But let's not ruin this visit with talk of trouble."

"Are you in trouble?"

"No, not me. Ellery has been in disarray lately. There's too much to explain and I'd rather not." She sighs and leans back on her elbows with the setting sun on her face. I touch her hand and lay back, enjoying her presence.

Remembering how easy it is to be with her, there is no chaos, no confusion, no struggle. I miss her. It's been ten days since Ellery started out over the ocean. I don't keep a lookout anymore on the east tower. I still check every couple of days for land, but there is nothing except endless water in all directions.

The contraption's burn bin sits on the table, void of coals, ripped from the float.

After Tolliver and I found the smithy shop, I stashed my contraption in here. If he comes around to pester me again and tells me not to bother fixing it, I can quickly hide it and pretend to work on something else. It's been eight never-ending days of inspecting and repairing the float made of quilts.

Tolliver is stuck in a routine of exercising by running the stairs in the morning and playing cards with Angus until midday meal. Most days he spends the afternoons with Kava in the sick ward while she thumbs through the Ellerian medicine books and experiments with different herbal remedies. Hollis has disappeared among the castle walls and corridors and I'm too afraid to ask Kava where she is.

I pull a chair close to the forge and stitch closed a burned hole in the quilt. At first, I considered adding patches, but it might be simpler to sew the holes shut so that I'm not adding extra weight. It is the thirteenth hole I've sewn so far.

I stitch and stitch until I hear a commotion. Looking up from my tedious work, I wait for the sound again. Shouting comes from outside, not in the hall but farther away. My heart leaps into my throat and I fear we are being invaded.

I whip the contraption to the side, poke the needle into the wood counter, and quickly head for the door. It opens with a hideous creak and I drag the door shut, wishing it had a lock and key.

I follow the sound of Angus's voice into the courtyard and find him racing about with a handful of dark feathers.

"Yes! You're brilliant!" he shouts, face to the sky.

I follow his gaze. Tolliver is on the topmost ledge poised with a bow and arrow. He waits for several heartbeats and shoots. A squawking, flapping bird falls all the way down the center of the open tower.

Angus cheers again as the bird lands with a thud in a snowdrift.

Tolliver lets loose another arrow and misses. Without skipping a beat, he whips out another arrow and shoots again. Squawk, tumble, thud.

Putting his bow down, his laugh swirls down with the wind. I smile at his fearlessness and join his triumphant laughter.

"We will have a feast today!" Angus announces.

Kava is standing right outside the dining hall and moments later Hollis emerges from the Great Hall. Her wildcat cape is open in the front and flaps as she walks. She is wearing black pants, black boots and a white shirt. My stomach aches to say hello, but my heart can't handle her sour reactions, so I say nothing. Angus hauls the three birds through the dining hall and down the back stairs to the kitchen. I follow behind Hollis and Kava.

Angus tosses the birds on the worktable and yanks out feathers, throwing them haphazardly all over the floor.

"What are you doing?" Kava crosses her arms.

"Making supper," Angus says with a goofy grin.

"Of course, but don't make a mess. Let's dip them in boiling water. Defeathering them will be much easier and cleaner," she explains, as if he should know.

"Oh, really?" Angus defiantly jerks another fistful of feathers from the carcass. "It might be easier, but it's not faster," he says and tosses the plumage over his shoulder.

Kava whispers, "Bonehead," under her breath and shuffles to the hearth on the back wall. "Ledger, can you start a fire while I fetch the water?"

It didn't really sound like a question. More like a demand. I can't obey. Everything inside me wants to stick out my tongue and walk away, but Hollis is here. She isn't avoiding breathing the same air as me. Without waiting for a reply,

Kava heaves the cast iron pot down the corridor toward the spring. Grumbling under my breath, I strike the flint on the steel several times before it catches. It will take a while to heat up, and Angus might have the geese fully defeathered by the time the water boils.

Hollis plays with the feathers, tossing them up and watching them drift gently to the tabletop. Kava struggles from the corridor to the hearth and I refuse to help her. She bosses me around too much, I think, crossing my arms. It feels good to watch her struggle and nearly drop the heavy pot as she attempts to hang it on the hook over the flames. Her burgundy dress gets dangerously close to the fire. Regret jolts me because it felt good to watch her almost catch on fire. I reach over at the last second and help her loop the heavy pot over the hook.

Kava grabs a large blade from beneath the table. She squints her eyes at Angus and slams the knife down on the neck of one goose. He narrows his eyes back at her while stripping more feathers. Kava hacks the head off the next bird and grabs the third from Angus's hands. She pulls while he rips out more feathers. I take a deep breath to relieve the tension. Rolling her eyes at him, Kava ties their feet together and hangs them over a bucket in the corner. I wrinkle my nose at the smell of blood.

It takes Tolliver a while to descend the tower and join us in the kitchen. He emerges through the dark stairwell and Angus cheers loudly as he approaches.

"Thank you, thank you," Tolliver bows dramatically. Angus slaps him on the back as if he has done something heroic.

"I kept seeing the geese flying over and thought it was about time to have some meat again," Tolliver explains. The longbow in his hand is taller than he is and curves ornately at the ends. Ellerians definitely make beautiful weaponry.

Tolliver and Angus toss ideas back and forth on how to prepare the birds. I don't much care. They aren't the mushy grain we've been eating for weeks. Even if they were boiled with cabbage, I would be happy. Tolliver has always hated boiled dinner. There was a time we ate boiled potatoes and cabbage for three weeks at home, which does not compare with how long we've been eating the grain muck from the storage rooms of Ellery. My mouth salivates at the thought of pulling a leg from the side of a roasted bird and biting it between my teeth. Seasoning, or no, it will be magnificent.

I look at Hollis, wondering what she is thinking. Her eyes never meet mine, but she doesn't look angry. Just tired and cold. She tosses another feather watching it drop to the ground.

"So, Hollis, what have you been busying yourself with?" Tolliver places the bow and quiver on the table.

"This and that. Freezing to death and missing home." Hollis meets my eyes for the first time. Her gaze fills my body with a strange sense of relief, as though I'm finally eating after days of starvation.

"I haven't seen you much lately. I thought maybe you locked yourself in a prison cell and started decomposing," Tolliver chuckles.

"So why didn't you come looking for me to make sure that wasn't true?" Hollis gives a half smile and excitement rises in my gut, anticipating a full grin. It doesn't come. She glares at him instead.

"Maybe I should come see what you're up to," Tolliver nods and raises his eyebrows at her. It's as if something is happening of which I am unaware.

She places her hands on her hips and says, "Maybe you should mind your own business."

"Kava told me what you've been doing."

I assess Hollis wondering what everyone is talking about.

"Like I care what you think," Hollis crosses her arms and stomps her foot. In the past weeks, I've come to know the levels of Hollis's anger. First Level: the seething underground anger with dirty looks. Second Level: the blatant I'm-mad-at-you anger that will blurt anything so you understand how mad. And the Third Level: the screaming anger that ends with her stomping away or tiny pointy fists flying in your face. I can tell she is moments from stomping out or swinging. I step back in anticipation.

"Stop feeding that thing. You are wasting our food storage." Tolliver's voice grows louder. "And by the tenth month, we will be out of food. Then what, Hollis?" His voice echoes around the stone room.

"Then I'll let it go," she says with a rebellious head bob.

"Good, let it go now. Then we don't have to feed it. It can find its own food, away from us."

"Fine," Hollis says.

"Fine," Tolliver replies, looking satisfied.

"Fine!" Hollis screams. She shoots a pained look in my direction and stomps out of the room.

Balfour's Ledger would go after her, give her comfort. I don't know if I can do that, but before I can stop myself,

I'm heading up the stairs after her with a growing pain in my stomach.

I catch up with her as she exits the dining hall.

"Hollis," I call.

"What?" she whirls around. Realizing it's me, she throws her hands up and keeps walking.

I look across the courtyard, down the hallway that hides my contraption. Fixing it will have to wait. In a moment of panic, I state the complete opposite of what I actually believe, hoping to reach Hollis. "You are right to feed it."

"What?" she says facing me again, rage rising in her fists. Level Three anger impending. It's like intentionally approaching a rabid wildcat.

My heart races now that I have her attention. I think what Tolliver said is logical. We can't spare the food. But maybe I do think it would be wrong to let it starve to death.

"But we don't have the food to spare," I state, wishing I didn't say it. She growls and looks away. "But," I continue with no idea what I'm going to say. My head is a jumble of miscellaneous words and I can't seem to say the right thing in these moments when she is actually looking at me and actually talking to me, feeding my hunger for her attention.

Her face contorts at my conflicting statements. "Get to the point."

With a pause I consider what I should say to keep her from stomping off again. "I think it would be a good idea if you release it. Is it strong enough to fly yet?"

A small hint of a smile sneaks onto one side of her mouth. She quickly wipes it away and scowls. "Maybe," she says. "What do you care?"

“Really? Can I see?”

The smile gains more ground and her little pearlescent teeth peek from between her pink lips. “I can’t guarantee she won’t kill you if you get too close.”

I worry that she is referring to herself more than the dragon. In an attempt to douse the flaming tension between us, I say, “I bet she is amazing.”

The smile spreads across her face. My gut wrenches at the glorious grin but it doesn’t reach her eyes. They are still angry and full of pain. My whole body says to hug her, but all her signals are spiky and standoffish.

She nods toward the Great Hall and takes off running. I rush to catch up as she ducks around the corner down the dungeon stairs toward the dragon.

18
HINT OF MISCHIEF

Hollis neither takes a lighted torch nor waits for me to get over the fact that it is pitch black down the stairwell. She darts out of view. I can't waste a moment, or I will miss the opportunity to befriend Hollis again.

The thought steels me momentarily against the darkness as I race after the sound of her footsteps. Keeping myself oriented, I run my hand along the wall as we descend around to the right. Suddenly, I hit the gate doorway with my shoulder and stumble down the steps. Pain shoots through my sensitive skin. I touch my arm to see if it ripped my healed burn wounds. There is no wet blood coming through my tunic, but I hold my arm as I continue on. As panic swells in my chest from the absence of sight, an archway comes into view at the very bottom of the steps. Relief washes over me and I realize I've been holding my breath most of the way down.

Her silhouette races through the door and around the corner. I can't believe how she navigates the dark staircase with such ease and familiarity. Following her into the torchlight, I catch up with her on the stairs circling the dragon's cage. Somehow she managed to light up most of the room with torches on the walls. The massive animal follows her small form down the stairs and around the cage.

"Tristeh!" Hollis yells. "Tristeh, fly!" She waves. She reaches the bottom step and stands in front of the beast. It hulks over her several feet. Its wings are poised in the air, looking more like an attack position than anything.

The panic in my chest is right at the surface and I hear myself howl, "What are you doing?" My feet carry me to her side in a flash.

"Fly, Tristeh, fly!" she calls.

The beast shrieks beside me. I whirl around to face it, hurling my body against the wall. Heart pounding in my chest, panic is replaced by adrenaline. My arms tense and my fists rise.

Hollis continues to flap her arms and shout.

The shriek arises louder this time.

The beast flaps outstretched wings. It pumps them several times and lifts off the ground. With another screech, it bounds into the air. It flies to the upper part of the massive cave and takes one lap around the ceiling.

Its bellowing call is answered by Hollis mimicking its noise, "Weeeehaw!" She beams at me. "See? She can fly," Hollis says out of breath.

I am confused by her warm smile and bubbly laughter. Even her eyes are smiling. I have the urge to kiss her in this moment. My reactions to her always seem wrong, backwards, upside down.

Catching my breath, I realize my fists are still poised to

fight. I loosen my stance and fake a smile. "Why were you yelling 'Tristeh'?"

"That's her name." Hollis says, as if I am the biggest idiot. Her new pet dives low around the room and swoops by, blowing Hollis's golden hair out of her face. I jolt and press against the cold stone.

"You named it?"

"No, that was already her name." She shrugs.

"How do you know?"

"It is written on the cage," she points out. "Over here." I follow her around the cage a few paces, along the rough stone floor are three plaques. "Tristeh, Bijou, Gaetan," she reads aloud.

Remembering there were three dragons in this enclosure, I look around for their corpses. The one shoved through the cage is gone. I peer through the bars in search of the one near the water trough finding none. I look at her, readying myself to ask where they went, but at that moment the one living dragon lands directly in front of me with a loud thud. I leap back gasping aloud.

Hollis snickers. "She likes you, Ledger—for dinner maybe."

The sound of my name on her lips snaps me back to the reality that I am winning her back by pretending to be interested in this chilling beast. Her sarcasm worries me because she could lash out at any moment.

Braving a glance at the dragon, I say, "She is amazing." It terrifies me, but I am thankful it is bringing Hollis back to me. "How did you figure out which one is her name?"

"Watch," Hollis says. "It's in the small movements." She

steps to the cage, curling her small pale fingers around the bars. "Bijou," she calls.

The dragon doesn't move. It stands on all fours watching us, making me a little uneasy.

"Gaetan." Her voice echoes across the shadowy cave.

Nothing happens and I'm starting to doubt anything will happen.

"Tristeh," she says finally and the dragon's eye twitches forward and nostrils flare slightly.

"That's it?" I shake my head in disbelief.

"Yes, did you see how she looked at me? She even nodded a little."

Peering up at the reddish dragon, I whisper, "Tristeh." Its eyes shift to meet mine and I swallow hard. It is nauseating to be in the sights of such an intimidating creature that could rip my throat out in one swipe of its claws.

"Yes, you saw it!" Hollis bounces. She pulls something from her pocket. It is a goose head. She pushes her hand between the bars and I gasp.

"Hollis!" My stomach lurches, imagining the beast ripping off her arm.

The dragon slowly creeps forward while inhaling the scent of the bird. It slowly opens its scaly lips and takes the head out of her hand without even grazing her skin. She drops her hand with a smug look.

"You okay?" she asks with a single raised eyebrow. "Do you need a minute to regain your manhood?"

An embarrassed chuckle escapes my lips. "I'm okay."

She pulls the other two heads from her pocket and offers, "You want to try?"

I shake my head. She raises her brows as if asking again and I decline even more vehemently. My dark curls fall in my eyes and I stubbornly refuse to move. Hollis shrugs and tosses the goose heads into the cage. The dragon scoops them up in its powerful jaws, chewing them like dumplings.

"How often do you come down here?" I keep her talking, easing the tension in the air.

"Every day." She wipes her hands on her black pants and we walk together around the cage. She pulls a torch from the wall and directs me to a low opening on the right side of the cave. It is a short hallway with piles of what looks like leather. She waves the light over them.

"They are saddles."

"What would they need saddles for?" I am confused. She stares at me. "They ride the dragons?" Taking the torch, I kneel to inspect the saddle. "Their infamous flying beasts are dragons?"

"I remember my Father used to tell stories about their beasts. But they haven't used them in battle for years. I wonder why," she says, her face full of consternation. The concerned frown is all too familiar. "I can't imagine they would need dragons with their enormous wings anyway. I wonder why in Balfour they would have dragons at all."

"What if you could ride one?" I instantly regret asking.

She gasps, "Yes! I've been dreaming about it for weeks. I've helped saddle Ol' Man Dudley's mule several times when his fingers started turning in on each other. It couldn't be that different, right?"

"Wait. It's too dangerous to even enter the dragon's cage," I state, hoping to deter Hollis, the risk-taker.

“Oh, I’ve been in there plenty of times.” She waves an unconcerned hand in the air.

“Really? Why, why would you do that?”

“How do you think those rotting carcasses got cleaned up?” She puts her hands on her hips. “She stands very still any time I’m inside with her. She is very well behaved.”

I stare at her. It sounds like she is talking about Ol’ Man Dudley’s mule.

“Can you please help me saddle her?” she begs so sweetly and folds her dainty hands together.

Her eyes sparkle, and I have a sinking feeling she won’t let me back out, especially because she knows I’ve saddled horses countless times. And besides that, I owe her. A lot.

I stand very still and look into her pleading eyes. My heart aches to be her friend again, to talk like this every day. I remember the many adventures we had in Balfour with her wild ideas, and all the times I ended up wounded or worse, grounded. This will get me more than wounded. Death by dragon does not sound fun.

“It’s not so much the saddling I’m worried about,” I explain, “It’s the riding.”

She smiles and places a hand on my shoulder. “You won’t be riding. I will. So let me worry about that.” Pushing out a pouty lip, she begs, “Please?”

Her blue eyes are full of life with a hint of mischief. I can’t say no. I can’t lose her again. Every smile she shares feeds my soul and I can’t go back to starving again.

I surrender with a nod.

FLY TRISTEH 19

She squeals, voice echoing out into the cave. Her dragon replies as she leaps and hugs me. My whole body tingles at her touch and I return her embrace. She hasn't touched me in months. I was an empty man and she has filled me back up with a simple hug that used to mean nothing between us. She lets go too soon and absentmindedly runs a hand down my chest as she selects a saddle. My breath catches in my throat at her caress. I let it be what it is to her—a mindless passing graze.

She hauls a saddle, straps and all, through the small doorway. With deep breaths, the ache in my body eases a little as I follow her out.

In the illumination of the open cave, I can see light green scrollwork pressed into the tan leather. The seat is thickly padded and the straps have metal buckles at the end. It is much like our horse saddles except for the size. The seat is normal size but the straps are long enough to wrap around the Hundred Harvest Tree.

Hollis heaves the saddle close to the cage and Tristeh

approaches sniffing.

"Is this yours?" Hollis asks the beast. Eyeing her strange way of communicating with it, I am surprised when it blows air out its nostril and walks away.

"Hmm," she grunts and drags it back to the storeroom, exchanging it for another saddle. "How about this one?" I have never seen a white saddle before. This one has embossed vines and reddish flowers down each white fender. The seat is burnt red leather.

Tristeh draws near again. She sniffs and doesn't walk away.

Ecstatic, Hollis shouts, "Yes, this one!"

"Seriously, you can't know that."

"She has a language, Ledger. You just have to take time to learn it, silly boy." Hollis lifts the white saddle and walks to the backside of the enclosure. I grit my teeth at her remark and the fact that she is still jabbing me even though I've agreed to help her.

The dragon follows her tiny figure all the way around the cage. I stand in awe for a moment when a revelation hits me. We could ride the dragon outside. We could search the ground. I won't need my silly contraption that may or may not fly anymore.

We could fly a dragon.

I snicker to myself at how ridiculous it sounds. I would first have to get over the fact that this dragon terrifies me to the core, and then muster the strength to actually touch it. Why can't I be as brave as Tolliver? Or as trusting as Hollis? Or as tough as Angus?

I use the idea to embolden myself. I resolve that I'll

pretend we are saddling a horse. Granted it is a giant scaly horse with talons and sharp teeth.

There is an enormous gate in front of the opening to the cave that leads outside. It must be how they get the beast in and out. Hollis slides the large metal bar that locks the gate closed. It squeaks loudly, echoing around the massive cavern. In an instant, the dragon stops moving. It may even be holding its breath like I am. Hollis pulls the gate open wide enough for only her and the saddle to squeeze through.

"Leave it open," she nods and walks toward the beast. I'm surprised by her caution with this thing. I don't remember her being so self-controlled. I thought she'd walk brazenly into the cage and slap it on its back. Instead, she slowly places the saddle on the ground in the center of the enclosure and backs away.

"Let's see if she rips it up." She smiles and inches her way out the gate pushing it closed, but doesn't latch it. She puts her face between the bars, cheeks flushed with energy, eyes ablaze with excitement. Usually those eyes lead us into trouble, but maybe she has harnessed their unruly nature and is capable of taking precautions.

We hear loud grumbling as the dragon circles the saddle. It inhales the scent of the leather, nudges it with its nose several times before coming to rest beside the jumbled pile of straps and pads.

"Yes," Hollis cheers. "She just might let us do this." She wiggles her eyebrows at me.

I chuckle nervously as anxiety cuts off circulation from my limbs and pumps it through my head and chest like a torrent.

“Come on,” she chides, entering the cage while holding the gate open for me.

I take one step through and the dragon hisses loudly, mouth gaping wide. It raises its haunches and I quickly step outside the cage.

“I don’t think she wants you to come in,” Hollis says.

The threatened creature calms down, rests on the cold ground and waits.

Completely okay with not going near the thing, I push the gate closed and encourage, “Be careful.”

“I will,” she agrees. I almost believe her as she gently approaches a dragon four times her height. It looks as though she could walk underneath its belly and not be able to touch it.

My body is throbbing even though I’m not the one who is coming within reach of giant jaws and claws. I have a bad feeling that I’m doing the wrong thing, again.

Hollis tiptoes to the saddle and unwinds the straps on the floor.

“Grab the straps that go over the far side and pull them up over the saddle toward you,” I coach, keeping my tone calm and quiet. “Then they won’t get caught when you slide the saddle over her back.”

Hollis nods. She takes an agonizing few minutes to organize the straps and lift the saddle. I worry her arms won’t allow her to lift it high enough to reach the dragon’s back.

The dragon slowly lowers its body to the ground, stone crunching beneath its weight. Its leg joints are more like a dog’s. Luckily, its back is void of spikes. Still, it is higher than Hollis’s head. She cannot possibly lift the saddle high enough. Before I decide I should help, it rolls its backbone toward her without instruction.

Hollis coos sweetly at the dragon as she places the white leather saddle upon its crimson scales. She pushes the straps and they flap over to the other side. I want to cheer for her, but decide against it for fear the sudden noise will disrupt their peaceful interaction.

Once applied, the dragon slowly rights itself and rises to its knees. Hollis stands there holding the straps nearest her. "Now what?"

I whisper, "Reach under and grab the front strap. Latch it to the front strap on your side." She nods and follows my direction. "Then do the same with the back strap. Tighten it as much as you can around the belly." The dragon winces as she pulls each strap taught, tying them through a metal loop.

She stands back and we both notice the weird way the saddle sits on the dragon's back. It is puckered up in the middle and sliding to the side. There is also a strip of leather that hangs awkwardly underneath.

"I don't think that's right," she says.

"Oh, wait," I ponder a different way. "Maybe unhook the front strap and wrap it around the front legs. Across its chest."

The dragon is getting antsy and is uncomfortable with the incorrect installation of the saddle. Hollis speaks gently, calming it momentarily. She unlatches the front strap and wraps it around the dragon's chest. It tightens easily, and Hollis hooks the strip of leather connecting the front and back. The saddle is finally snugly in place.

She giggles and the dragon leaps to its feet.

I am taken aback by the sudden movement and prepare to save Hollis. My heart pounds with every moment. The dragon bounds into the air with the white saddle upon its back. I can't decide if it is trying to rid itself of the binds or if it is enjoying itself.

Hollis stands in the middle of the room awaiting her ride. I fear for her life but refrain from calling out to her. I hear a barely audible whistle come from Hollis. The dragon dives toward her and I resist the urge to close my eyes. It lands in the exact spot it had taken off from. Hollis giggles again, placing a hand on the scaly shoulder. The beast kneels and leans to the side. It has been trained well. My only hope is that Hollis knows what to do.

She lifts her left leg and places it in the stirrup. She grabs the front of the saddle and heaves her little body up, swinging her right leg over the seat. She leans to the far side, probably inserting her foot in the other stirrup, while the dragon rights itself.

I'm not sure what the commands would be for a dragon. The same for a horse, perhaps, but horses don't fly. I am dizzy with the possibility of danger and all the unknowns.

Hollis settles herself into the saddle. She lifts a few unused straps that protrude from the back of the saddle. "What's this for?"

"I have no idea," I shrug, annoyed that I really have no idea.

She drops them and noticeably doesn't know what to do with her hands. "Am I missing something?"

I realize there are no reins or bit, nothing to control the dragon. My gut wrenches and I tell her, "Get off, Hollis. We need reins so you can direct it where to go."

"There weren't any reins in the storage room though. Maybe dragons don't take a bit."

"Please, please just get down and we'll figure something out."

She grabs onto the front of the saddle. When I think she will swing her leg over and dismount, she actually kicks with her heels and says, "Fly, Tristeh!"

"Hollis!" I shriek in a very unmanly way. But it is too late; the dragon rises to its feet and springs into the air in one smooth motion.

She howls joyously as the beast soars around the room with wings spread wide. As it makes a sudden upward thrust, Hollis loses her grip. She screams as she falls from her perch with one foot still hooked in the stirrup.

BRACED 20

The dragon reacts to her cry and descends to the ground. Hollis dangles upside down from the side of the beast, with her cape draped over her face.

Without thinking, I pull open the heavy gate and race to her lifeless frame. Instead of hissing at me, the dragon gently leans to the side, placing Hollis's limp body on the floor. Frantically, I yank and twist her foot free. I adjust her body so she is lying flat, but the shape of her lower leg doesn't look right. I hold Hollis's head in my hand. Tears blur my view.

"Hollis! Hollis!" I yell, hoping to rouse her. The dragon whines and I jerk back to the reality that I'm within inches of it.

I scoop up Hollis's slender body into my arms and run through the gate, slamming it shut behind me and sliding the lock in place with my shoulder.

With the strength of ten men, adrenaline helps me bound the stairs in the pitch black and avoid hitting the iron gate on the way. We reach the top before I am winded. "Kava!"

I call rounding the hallway, courtyard, and into the dining hall. I slide sideways to fit down the slender stairway to the kitchen.

"Kava! Help!"

Coming around the bend, I find Tolliver and Kava scrambling about, adjusting their clothes. I don't have time to care about their red faces and mussed hair. I lift Hollis onto the cleanest worktable.

"What happened?" Tolliver asks.

I lay her gently onto the wood, minding her limp head and sprawling legs. "I think she broke her leg." I pant, attempting to catch my breath but I don't remove my hands from her.

Kava inspects her shin and gasps. "She did."

I look away trying to stomach the odd angle at which it lays.

Kava touches Tolliver softly. "Can you fetch my bag?" He nods and darts out of the room.

"What were you guys doing?" She unties Hollis's left boot.

I am panicked for what to say. "I think the bigger question is, what were you and Tolliver doing?"

"Stars, Ledger. She broke her leg and you're judging me?"

A groan emanates from Hollis's throat.

"Oh, no. It would be better for her to stay unconscious for this part," Kava says.

Tolliver returns with the bag of medicines and herbs. She digs through it and retrieves a brown bottle with no label. My heart hasn't stopped pounding in my chest and with every passing moment it beats into my throat.

"I need to set the break," Kava says.

I know what that means. I've seen it done before. Juniper's father broke his arm and when they set it, he passed out from the pain. Kava quickly slides off Hollis's boot.

Hollis's moans grow into cries. "Ledger," Hollis calls to me. I lean toward her face and hold her cheeks in my hands, her tears streaming into my palms.

"It's going to be okay," I promise.

Kava unhooks the leather strap from her bag, folds it in half, and slides it between Hollis's teeth. "Bite down on this." Kava gives Tolliver some directions, but I can't look away from Hollis's frightened blue eyes. "Ledger!" Kava yells.

"What?" I reply with the same intensity.

"Hold her hands down," she commands. "And lay across her chest so she doesn't move. Tolliver, hold the other leg."

I nod without looking away from Hollis. Crossing her arms over her chest, I hold her opposite hands in mine. I lean over, nose to nose with her.

Kava counts and Hollis's body jerks beneath me. The leather falls from her mouth with a yelp. In the next breath, she gives a blood-boiling scream. I am startled having never heard her in this much pain. There is so much agony wrapped up in her wail that tears sneak their way out of the corner of my eyes and drop onto her cheeks. I hold her tight, even after it is over.

Hollis pulls her hands from mine and wraps her arms around me. She squeezes me tightly and cries into my shoulder.

I shouldn't have placed the idea of riding into her head. I shouldn't have volunteered to help. This is my fault. I don't deserve to be her friend. My thoughts punish me.

Hollis slowly releases her grip and I lean back to see what Kava is doing. Hollis's black pant leg has been pulled up and Kava is pouring clear liquid from a bottle onto her wound. Before long, Kava has her leg wrapped with bandages and braced with two wooden spoons on either side.

"We'll have to find more cloth to wrap it so it will be sturdy. We don't want it to move at all."

Tolliver pats Hollis's uninjured leg. "What in the world were you two doing?"

"We—" I start.

"We were climbing," Hollis interrupts. "The Rocks. Outside." She eyes me.

"Yeah, outside." I join the lie, realizing if Tolliver finds out she was wounded by the dragon, he'd kill me, or the dragon, or both.

"Yeah, right," Kava objects, "You two haven't said more than two words to each other in weeks. Now you're climbing together?"

"I wasn't climbing," I state, hoping to improve on Hollis's story. "Hollis was. I was walking by when I saw her fall. So I carried her in here." I look at Hollis with my eyebrows up.

"I guess now that he saved my life, we can be friends again." She smiles wryly, and I fake a chuckle.

Kava rolls her eyes and says, "Isn't that lovely."

Tolliver reaches over me and helps Hollis sit up. "You won't be climbing again for a long time."

Disappointment washes across Hollis's face. "I guess

not." She looks down at her leg. She winces in pain as she adjusts her position. "How long?"

"I think about eight weeks, sometimes ten or longer," Kava replies. Her brown eyes bounce from Hollis, to me, to Tolliver. "We need to move her to a bed."

"I can do it," I volunteer.

"I know you can, but her leg needs to be braced so we don't have to set it again."

Hollis shudders.

"Are there any boards lying anywhere? Maybe a small table top?" Kava looks around the room.

I draw a blank.

Tolliver thinks fast, unloading a shelf on the wall, tossing pots and utensils onto a worktable. He pushes the empty shelf up and down, up and down until it comes loose from the wall. Tolliver carries it over and we help Hollis lift her body onto the slat. Kava takes a few strips of fabric and straps her legs to the wood.

We lift the board, I on one end and Tolliver on the other, steadily lugging her up the stairs, through the dining hall and into the open courtyard.

"Let's take her down the royal hall," Tolliver directs. Hollis has been living somewhere on level two or three, but it doesn't make sense to take her there.

We carry her across the snowy space through the tall wooden doors that bears the crest of the royal family. It is a bird with a branch in its mouth. Tolliver leads the way into what must be the queen's bed chambers. With the exception of white fabric billowing from the middle of the ceiling, mounted to the walls and draped to the floor, the room is laid out a lot like mine. It was probably beautiful before inches of dust settled into its folds. The four poster bed has vibrant green drapes around the entire thing. There are woven rugs on both sides of the bed and a fireplace beside the door to a balcony.

We place Hollis on the soft bed. Kava pats the blankets, encouraging Hollis to slide off the board, but a puff of dust rises from the fabric.

Hollis slaps the padding. "Can we pull these nasty blankets off?"

"Boys?" Kava nods at us. We lift our wounded princess one last time as Kava peels the top blanket off, and folds back the rest to reveal clean sheets of crisp white fabric.

"Boys," Hollis mimics the command and points at the bed.

Tolliver and I set her down, and she cries out in pain as we assist her in sliding off the board. Falling limp on the fluffy feather filled mattress, Hollis is breathing hard as if it has taken all her effort.

Kava gives Hollis some instructions and then with a stern, motherly look says, "You shouldn't have been rock climbing alone, silly girl."

Tolliver pulls the door shut behind Kava and we are alone.

Hollis heaves a heavy sigh. "Thank you for corroborating the climbing story." She lays her head back and closes her eyes. Her words slur with exhaustion. "He would kill Tristeh in an instant, wouldn't he?"

I nod, even though she isn't looking at me. In the

fireplace, I construct a neat stack of tinder. I strike and strike the flint, but it won't light. Frustrated, I want to throw the flint and steel.

I finally have my best friend back and all it takes is lying to my brother.

"Ledger," Hollis calls weakly.

I strike it several more times, finally getting a spark. I blow and blow until it lights the scraps of wood.

"Please don't tell Tolliver about Tristeh. I can't lose her."

I come to her bedside. She is peering at me beneath droopy eyelids. She yawns and says, "Please feed her, Ledger."

"I will," I promise. "I will." Sitting, I put my hand on hers. She doesn't pull away. She surrenders to the drowsiness, closing her eyes and fading into sleep. My heart is full of her and my stomach is satisfied. I sit by her side for a long time watching her long lashes flutter.

After a while, I stoke the fire and add the last few logs. By the time the sun goes down, its warmth fills the room. I lay beside her peaceful frame on the bed and watch her sleep, until I drift into a dream about saving Hollis from a dragon.

Each day, I visit her and give her a report of Tristeh's status. Alive. Eating regularly. Tristeh is strangely sad, as though she misses Hollis. It took several times to unlatch the saddle by daring to reach between the bars of the cage. Keeping her alive is the best way to keep Hollis healing and keep my own hope alive to reach the ground in search of Alouette. My heart sinks each time I think about Alouette, as if I am betraying Hollis or I'm betraying Alouette because I am caring for Hollis, I'm not sure which. Trying to figure out which gives my head a deep ache.

MENACING GRAY CLOUD 21

Day 84

The beast doesn't growl at me any more when I descend the dark stairwell into the cave, torch in hand. I take a moment to relight some of the extinguished torches around the enclosure before I approach with her meal. Five weeks ago, Hollis gave me directions to prepare the mush in the kitchen and haul it down to the dragon. But I found a better way of mixing it once I've reached the dragon's cage. I keep a supply of grain in the storeroom and bring hot water with me when I descend the stairs. It is more efficient and less suspicious. Hauling water is a lot less strange than hauling a meal large enough to feed an army. At least I could say I am on my way to clean something, or fill something with water, like the fountain or some other rain trough. I am a terrible liar, so I need to be prepared with a logical response to any questions.

I follow my usual routine, pouring steaming water from the large pitcher into the basin outside the cage door. Tristeh starts her usual food dance. She prances on her toes and breathes heavily. I worry she isn't getting enough food each day because of how excited she is for feeding time. The click of her talons echo across the stone floor as I step into the storeroom and bring out the first scoop of grain. Two, three and four scoops. I stand over the sack that is now emptied of grain. I'll have to go scour the upper floors of the castle again for more.

I use an expired torch handle to stir the last of the mush together. The mixture cools as I stir and by the time it is ready, it has stopped steaming. I test a bite and Tristeh whines, blowing a puff of warm breath in my face for eating her food.

A couple of weeks ago I found a feeding door. It opens the bottom two feet of the gate, flapping up enough for me to slide the basin in without having to enter the cage and risk my life. I tied a rope around the handle of the basin so that I can pull it back when she is done.

Tristeh does one last prance on her toes and she sticks her nose into the mush. She eats much like a mutt. I laugh at her smart way of tipping the basin so she gets every last drop. I watch her eat the entire thing and lick it clean.

She usually curls her giant scaly body around the metal dish in a big hug, but this time her nose flares and her ears perk up.

I scowl. "What is it?"

Everything is quiet until she whines.

"Hide," I whisper.

She obeys and ducks into the dark far corner of the cave. She whines again louder than before and I shush her before ducking into the storeroom. Watching the stairs, I wait for someone to emerge.

Nothing.

Her talons tap, tap, tap nervously in the shadows.

I anticipate whatever it is she is sensing.

Nothing.

I wipe sweat from my brow.

Still nothing.

Tristeh growls. Surely someone is coming now. I wait and wait, wiping my face and neck from the sweat that is pooling. I realize the temperature is rising and inhale sharply, darting from my hiding place. Tristeh follows my lead and we race each other to the door of the cage. The bars halt her movement, but I continue down the cavern and around the bend to the opening out the side of the island.

The water spans out in all directions, choppy and ominous. There is nothing that explains the quick rise in temperature. I lean out to see around either side of the rocks. To the east, I spot it. We are approaching a giant cloud of smoke shooting out of bubbling, violent waters. My heart jumps into my throat and chokes my airway.

A volcano erupts in the middle of the expansive waters. The heat is rising and we haven't even passed over the top of it yet. Stepping back from the edge, I rest my hands on my knees and catch my breath.

I race back to the dragon's cage. "You're right, something's wrong," I say. "It's a volcano." She doesn't know words, but she gives a high-pitched whimper in response. "I have to warn the others," I state and bound for the stairs. Tristeh runs alongside me the entire way and takes to flight as I ascend the cave stairs. "I will return," I say. She flies up to the ceiling and replies with a loud shriek. Without a torch, I race up the dark stairwell.

"There's a volcano," I shout, sprinting into Hollis's chambers in a panic. She and Kava are shocked, either from my abrupt entrance or from my absurd news.

"What?" Kava is confused.

"We are approaching a volcano," I explain, out of breath. "The temperature is rising. Can you feel it?"

"No," Kava says, not really believing me.

Hollis sniffs and says, "I thought I smelled something burning."

I chuckle between heavy breaths. "You smell a volcano?"

"Yes, it's not like wood burning. It's," she inhales again, "something else."

"I have to see this," Kava says and heads for the door.

"I want to see it too," Hollis whines. I laugh because she sounds like her dragon today.

Once Kava disappears down the hall, I whisper to Hollis, "You're as whiney as Tristeh."

She looks at me quizzically and I explain, "She was whining and acting weird. So I ran to the cave opening. That's when I saw the volcano."

"I want to see it," she pleads again, with a little less whine in her tone and more excitement.

"What am I supposed to do, carry you?" I look at her wrinkled white man-tunic and black trousers with one pant leg pulled up.

"Yes please." She raises her arms the way my little brother, Killian, would do to Mother. I sigh at the thought of the family I left behind. The baby will have her name by the time we return. I think of her little blonde curls. She may even be walking by then, that is, if she survives her first harvest.

"Let me ask Kava if that's okay." I head for the door.

"No, please…just…please?"

The sound of her pleading and the scrunching of her blonde eyebrows transform my logic into mush.

She sticks out her bottom lip and says, "I have no more pain and I'm so sick of this room. It's been over five weeks. Even Kava said this morning that I can probably put some weight on it."

"She did not."

"Okay, she didn't say it quite like that. But she said I could very soon. So maybe you can carry me? Please?"

I cross my arms, hating being pressured into doing something, especially if it has the potential of getting me yelled at by Kava, or worse, Tolliver. I grit my teeth because I can't say no.

"It's a volcano, for sky's sake. I have to see this."

"Fine, fine, fine," I concede. "But we're wrapping your leg before we go."

Hollis directs me to the splints and strips of cloth Kava has available any time Hollis needs to use the privy. I wrap her leg neatly, but she swats me away because I'm not quick enough. She swirls and twirls the fabric around her leg and ties it messily at the end.

"There." Hollis reaches for me with a smile.

Quickly snatching her wildcat cloak from the chair near the fireplace, I drape it around her shoulders. She hooks it around the nape of her neck. With grave apprehension, I slide a hand behind her back and one under her knees. She wraps her dainty arms around my sweaty neck and I lift her. Her leg dangles and there is no sign of pain on her face. I brace her for a moment. Having not been this close to her face since the day she broke her leg, my heart pounds and my breath is stuck in my throat.

Giggling and pointing a finger toward the door, she shouts, "To the volcano!"

I follow her command. Regaining my sanity by the time we reach the royal hall, I carry her out of the castle to the east tower where Kava, Tolliver and Angus are gathered. Tolliver has a spyglass to his eye.

Halfway between the horizon and us is a spout of thick gray smoke and ash fiercely shooting out of the water. The smoke billows at the top like a giant mushroom. The ocean breeze pushes it toward the south but only slightly. From the top of the lookout tower, I can see black rock pushing up through the surface of the water.

"Wow," Hollis gapes at the sight, pulling her cloak tighter against the cold winter air.

Angus greets us with a nod.

Tolliver scowls. "She should not be out of bed."

Kava opens her mouth to say something when Hollis squawks, "Are you kidding me? And miss this? I've only heard about volcanoes in the histories."

"We know, Hollis. None of us has seen one either," Tolliver replies, inspecting the cloud of ash and smoke. The waters churn angrily against the black rocks surrounding it.

"Did you notice it is getting warmer?" I'm not really looking for a reply. "How long until we pass it, do you think?" Mild gusts of warm air blow in our faces, but it's not as significant as down below in Tristeh's cave.

No one answers me for a long moment and Tolliver says, "Probably tomorrow."

"Suppose we'll pass over top of it?" Angus asks.

I think of Tristeh, the one closest to its heat. Could she withstand this? Is this always spouting? Or is this extremely rare? My head spins with questions and Hollis voices a question for me, "Will we get burned?"

"Obviously, I have no idea," Tolliver replies. "But it is not out of the realm of possibilities. So maybe we should make a plan."

Angus nods to the lofty castle behind us, "Maybe we should take shelter on an upper floor."

"Good idea," Tolliver agrees as the plume of smoke and ash grows nearer, blotting out part of our blue sky with a giant menacing gray cloud.

ENDLESS OCEAN 22

Tolliver and Angus are hauling buckets of water up the fortress of Ellery for evening meal and drinking. That way we don't have to come down for any reason until we pass the volcano. I'm not sure it matters, seeing how high the plume of ash is in the air. It seems unavoidable.

I carry Hollis back to her bed and bend to lay her on the crinkled blankets.

"Can I go see Tristeh?"

Stopping shy of the surface, a pain shoots through my back. I groan. "Today?"

She nods looking into my eyes. My back gives out and I plop her onto the bed awkwardly. "Let me rest for a minute. We just walked the whole castle. I think I deserve a break, Your Majesty."

"Oh, really. My servants never rest." She joins my playacting.

"Yes," I rub my back and fall to my knees on the floor near her bedside. "Please, Your Royal Bossiness."

She waves laughing snobbishly, as I spasm on the floor

holding my back.

"Ready now? Or do you need an official reprimand?" she asks with a silly tone. I stand and stretch toward the high ceiling.

"I'm ready." I rub the knot in my lower back before scooping her up in my arms. The knot tightens again as I lift her slender body, but I don't show the pain. Hollis hugs me hard, choking me a little with her embrace.

I anticipate her yelling, to the dragon! But she doesn't. She faces the door in expectation. I carry her to the dark stairwell.

"Grab that torch," I say.

"We don't need a torch. Just go," she says, jerking toward the stairwell as if I'm some pack mule she has to prod.

"It's dark." I catch myself whining and change my voice to a manlier tone. "I need to see where I am going so I don't hit your head on the wall."

She looks at me unamused with one raised eyebrow. "Stop being afraid of the dark."

We have a staring stand off and I lose.

Taking my time, I feel for the first few steps before I gain a good rhythm descending into the depths of Ellery. I slow for the gate, being sure not to bump Hollis into it in the pitch black. We round the corner, coming into the light of the dragon's cave.

"Tristeh," Hollis whispers.

With a loud screech and gust of air, Tristeh bounds into the air before us and circles the ceiling once before following us down the rest of the stairs. Hollis wriggles in my arms, urging me to come near to the cage. She grabs a bar and yanks us close as Tristeh lands before us. My stomach wrenches standing this close to the dragon.

Tristeh pushes her body against the cage and Hollis places her small hand on the rough scales. She pets her shoulder and down her back as she slides past.

Panic rises in my throat. I worry she will smash her arm or hand against the bars. I really want to pull her away, but the two are reacquainting themselves. I stand still as a rail, holding my breath until it's over.

"Look at you," Hollis coos at her giant scaly baby. "You are such a big girl. Healthy and well taken care of." She turns to me with a big grin. I start breathing again as her smile disarms me.

The dragon makes another pass against the bars and nuzzles into Hollis's touch until I hear her low growl. I yank Hollis out of reach of the beast as Tolliver and Angus come traipsing through the upper doorway into the pale torch light.

I suddenly remember the mutt I kept in the hollow and how Tolliver admitted killing it. I'm not sure if Hollis knows what he is capable of. As they round the corner, I notice the bow in Tolliver's hand and the quiver on his back. My insides ache at the oncoming conflict. Surely Hollis will not let it die without a fight.

"What are you doing?" Hollis demands, lurching in my arms. I nearly drop her as she goes stiff.

"Something you should have done weeks ago." Tolliver pulls an arrow from the quiver and places it on the bow.

"What? No," she squawks.

The dragon echoes her cry and fills the room with a deafening shriek.

We all jerk away from the dragon as it nears the cage bars, except Hollis. She yells, "Fly, Tristeh!" She waves and the lizard leaps into the air with one powerful gust.

"It has to go, one way or another," Tolliver says, right eye trained on the swooping beast, the bowstring pulled taut.

"She doesn't deserve to die!" Hollis furrows her brows. "I'll release her."

"You said that before," Tolliver says, "And yet, it is still here eating our food supply."

"I'll do it right now then," Hollis puts both hands in the air in surrender. "Please, Tolliver, please."

Tolliver lowers his bow and eyes her with suspicion. "Then do it. Right now, so we can all see it," he challenges.

I open my mouth to interject about the fact that we are over an ocean and who knows where the nearest land is but clamp it shut. This isn't my fight. I don't have to choose sides.

"Okay," Hollis says lowering her voice, as though she is taming my brother. "Take me to the gate, Ledger," she murmurs. Her blue eyes are full of sadness.

I carry her to the tall metal gate at the far end of the cave and stop at the latch. She pushes away from my body and I set her on her feet. The dragon lands on the other side of the gate and whines at Hollis. She sighs and puts her weight on her healing leg. Taking a small limping step to the gate, she slides the latch. With drooping shoulders, she pulls the gate open several inches and hobbles backward. She isn't going to be able to open it the entire way limping like that.

"Get on my back," I say, kneeling beside her. She climbs on wrapping her arms and legs around me. Her hands pull the gate, as my legs carry us backward. The large metal door swings all the way open, blocking the dragon from entering the walkway and opens to the cavern leading to the outside. The gate clangs against the stone. Hollis whimpers as the dragon takes a slow step over the threshold of her prison.

Tristeh stops to look at us, or just Hollis. She sniffs the air and continues walking. With the click of talons, she warily tiptoes toward freedom. The scaly red dragon looks back at us several times, inhales the strong breeze coming from outside, then rounds the corner. We hear her talons several more times, then a loud whoosh and all is silent.

Hollis opens her mouth and weeps without holding back. I lower her to the ground and face her. I have no words that can help. I just hug her. Hollis goes stiff and screams at Tolliver. "I hate you! Now she will die, because there is nowhere for her to go over this endless ocean."

"I'd rather she dies than you," Tolliver says and walks away.

I can tell from the way he walks, shoulders slumped, head down, that he is affected by what just happened. He isn't a monster. He believes it had to happen. I do too, in a way. But Hollis can't see the fact that Tristeh needs too much. Her sobs echo off the walls. I am betraying her by thinking it, but it's true. We must survive at all costs.

As soon as Tolliver and Angus disappear from the dragon's cave, Hollis wipes her face and attempts to stand. I see her wince only once. She pushes the gate and limps weakly down the corridor following Tristeh's exit.

"Where are you going?" I follow close behind, reaching for her but not touching, just in case she falls.

She hobbles the entire way without a word, supporting herself on the wall and turns the corner with determination. She angrily wipes away her tears. Stepping beside her, I ask softly, "What are you doing?"

When we reach the opening in the rock overlooking the choppy waters, she lowers herself to the ground. She sits with her legs outstretched, shoulders drooping and breathes deeply. I stand and watch her for a moment unsure of what to do.

Do I leave her to have her sad moment? Or do I sit with her? Am I supposed to comfort her? I wish I could ask my mother what to do. She always has good advice. Hollis won't be able to make it up all those stairs her first time walking in weeks. So I join her on the ground and allow myself to feel the absence of my mother. My heart sinks at the thought and Hollis's tears agree. I resign to wrapping my arm around her and she leans into me. It is surprising how high we are suspended above the ocean. I get a strange dizziness looking down into its murky depths.

23 HUNKER DOWN

When we emerge from the empty dragon's cave, I hear yelling from the courtyard.

"Just make sure it is covered," Tolliver directs from somewhere far off.

"Got it," Angus replies in a booming voice.

"What's going on?" Hollis looks around.

I wonder the same thing as I carry her across the courtyard.

"Don't put her in there, Ledger," Tolliver commands from several stories up.

The sky is darkening because of evening and the advancing cloud of smoke and ash. Tolliver leans over the ledge, blonde hair hanging in his face. I realize it has grown long, nearly shoulder length. Without mother to cut it, his hair is shaggy and out of control. I wait for him to tell me where to go, because I'm too tired to use words.

"Bring her up here."

My head pounds. "I already carried her up two flights of stairs. I don't think I can do anymore," I groan.

He shrugs. "We will be on top of that volcano in a matter of hours, not days," he says and disappears from view.

"Angus," I call toward the dining hall. I nearly bump into him with Hollis in my arms. "Can you help me?"

"Why are you carrying her like a wee baby?" Angus pushes his orange curls behind his ears. "Set her on her feet and she can ride on my back."

I lean down placing her gently on her feet.

"Why are you guys talking about me like I'm just a sack of grain?" Hollis puts her hands on her hips, hanging her leg limply.

Angus laughs and kneels. Hollis grabs his shoulders and climbs on. He tells me to go in the kitchen and cover all the sacks of grain, making sure the open one is closed.

Once I complete my task, I ascend the castle steps. Unsure which floor they are on, I must listen for them before moving on to the next floor. I keep going up and up.

By level ten I'm winded. "Where are you?" I finally yell up the tower.

The wind tosses my hair around and sends a voice down with it. "Thirteen."

My head whirls and I brace myself on the stone wall. Alouette lived on thirteen. I take a deep breath as I walk past Alouette's home as if her ghost stares at me from the doorway. The evening is graying with twilight. Following the sound of Tolliver's voice, I find them five rooms down and enter the living quarters they've occupied. A fire in the hearth casts orange light around the room, along with several candles on the table and a sconce beside the door. Hollis is on the padded bench against the wall with her leg up. Kava sits at the table. Angus is across from her using a fat wooden ladle to eat his mush, and Tolliver stands over them talking loudly about shutters.

"What would you like me to do?" I take a seat at the table.

"Pick a bedroom on the western side facing away from the volcano and close the shutters. Take one of those pails of water and make sure you cover it. It looks as if we will go right through that cloud of smoke." Tolliver places a hand on my shoulder and says, "This may be a regular thing for Ellery."

I nod, feeling calmer with his hand on my shoulder. My heart slows, and I sigh. Thirteen flights are quite a hike. I've seen Tolliver many mornings run the stairs, as though he is training for the Clash. Maybe he's just bored. I wonder how many flights of stairs he runs each day.

Kava slides me a bowl of mush. I thank her and eat heaping spoonfuls. Tolliver helps Kava close up the bag of grain. Their hands brush and she glances at him, blushing.

"Thanks, Kava." Angus wipes his mouth. He tromps to the door, grabbing a pail of water. He walks out toward Alouette's home. I jolt upright and mimic Angus's actions in fast motion.

"Thanks, Kava." I wipe my mouth, grab my pail and dash out the door.

Angus hesitates in front of Alouette's door.

"I want that one," I blurt.

With a tired unconcerned look, Angus says, "I walked all the way over here, this one's mine."

"Please, Angus?" I am fully ready to fall to my knees

and beg.

Angus curses under his breath at the inconvenience. “What ya gonna give me?”

“I’ll—”

“You’ll fetch me another pail of water when I need it. That’s what you’ll do.” Angus grunts and heads to the next door.

Relief trickles down my back with a bead of sweat. I push the door shut behind me and shuffle my way to the table. The sun is already down on this short winter day. I light a chamber stick and carry it with me while I set my pail near the hearth. Pulling a small pillow off the bench, I lay it on the pail.

I head to the bedroom, to the tiny metal windmill on the nightstand. I lift it and blow into it. The small blades swirl round and round. I think of Alouette. Her wings. Her eyes. I chew my lip in worry about what might have happened to her. Is she dead or alive? A voice interrupts my thoughts.

“Why are you all the way down here?” Hollis stands in the doorway.

I gape at her, annoyed that she has snuck up on me twice in the same home.

She hobbles down the hall toward me gripping the wall, favoring her left leg. “Can I stay with you?” She reaches the bedroom door and waits for my reply.

“I don’t believe that would be appropriate,” I state, remembering the Balfour Code of Conduct and using it as an excuse to say no.

Hollis snorts and scrunches her eyebrows. “I don’t believe it would be appropriate to board an island circling our world. I don't believe it would be appropriate to feed a dragon." Laughing and limping to the four-poster bed, she sits and sinks into the fluffy mattress of feathers. "Oh, wow, this bed is soft."

My gut is in tangles. I want time with my own thoughts. I want Alouette's rooms to myself. But I don't want to create an argument. So I avoid it completely, lighting the bedside lampstand.

In truth, I don't want to endure this night alone. What if the ash cloud is so thick we all choke to death? Maybe we should all be in the same room, so we are safe and looked after. I decide to let Hollis stay, though she didn't exactly give me much choice. I open the trunk and pull out several blankets.

"What are you doing?" She watches my every move.

"I'm making myself a bed."

She scowls at me and I dramatically scowl back.

"You can lie on this bed with me, Ledger, I don't have fleas." She laughs. "Anymore."

It irritates me that she is so casual. I grit my teeth and refuse to laugh. Regardless, I finish piling blankets for a sleeping mat. Ignoring her pout, I head to the window. I scan for the volcano, knowing full well it is in the opposite direction. I pull the shutters closed.

"Is there a thorn in your paw, scary bear?" Hollis says with that irritating high-pitched giggle.

I lie on my makeshift bed feeling heavy and unreachable. "I'm a little worried we may choke to death," I say, hoping to shove her out of her chipper mood and drag her down with me.

She fake-giggles again and my skin crawls with irritation. "It'll be fine," she mutters. "Kava said we'll probably be just fine," her voice trails off.

Her eyes sadden as she looks away. I feel bad for scaring her. I frown at my rudeness and consider how I can make up for it. I look around the room and notice something under the bed. I reach underneath and pull out a small pillow. There is an embroidered bird on the front. I imagine it is Alouette's pillow and place it on my mat.

Hollis watches my every move. Her blue eyes are glassy with tears so I place my forearms on the mattress and my chin on my hands. "I'm sorry. I didn't mean to scare you."

"It's not just that," she sighs. "It's everything. Tristeh is gone. You're here, but still gone. Tolliver hates me and there is a volcano about to roast us alive."

"What do you mean I'm still gone?"

She looks down at her hands, wringing the sheets in her tiny fingers.

"You're not the same Ledger on Ellery as the Ledger I knew in Balfour."

I understand what she means. I don't really know who I am up here either. I feel lost.

"You're not carefree anymore. You're distracted and sad," she says. "And a little boring."

I jerk and meet her eyes. She cracks a smile. I sit back on my feathery mattress and gape at her, offended by the assessment of me.

I lie back on my mat resting my head on Alouette's pillow. I stare at the patterns of light and dark the candles create around the room.

"I can't help that you're bored, Hollis."

"No, Ledger, you are boring," she says again. "You rarely tell me jokes anymore. You don't play games. And," she puts a finger in the air, "You don't sing about your food anymore."

We laugh together and our voices echo in the shadowy room. The last time I sang about my food, my mother had packed me a lunch to eat with the men as we helped fix the roof on Angus's cottage. Uncle Roan was furious that it caved in before we had a chance to fix the rotting support beam. So we had to replace most of it. Hollis had arrived with her father's meal and stayed to eat with us.

"Oh little bread," Hollis began to sing from atop Alouette's bed. "Crunchy on the outside, chewy on the inside. Oh little bread."

My face grows hot with embarrassment as she sings my made-up song. "Okay, Hollis, I understand," I say, trying to stop her.

"Oh little cheese."

A laugh sneaks out of the deep parts of me. Hollis continues singing and laughing at the same time.

"Okay, stop it," I say with a smile. "I get it. I'm boring."

She yawns through another verse about berries. The last I hear from her is a long sigh. With eyes closed, her chest rises and falls at long intervals. Her mouth hangs open and I realize if the smoke does come in, she will inhale it. We all will.

Inching toward the chest at the end of the bed, I open it finding several sheets. I quietly drape it over the two posts on the headboard and down over Hollis. That way her head is beneath the sheet yet it isn't smothering her. I drag another out, lay down and drape it over my whole body.

Sleep doesn't come fast enough. I drift from wake to dream to wake again. I smell the smoke. If we aren't over it by now, we should be close. I don't remove the sheet, but drift back to sleep where I am hunting in the woods with my father. For some strange reason, he is wearing his full battle armor and we are quietly approaching our prey. His bow is poised, ready to shoot and right when Alouette comes into view, I jerk awake.

IN THE GRAY 24

Day 85

Tossing an arm, the sheet wafts in the air. Morning peeks through the shutters, shedding light on the dust drifting down around me like gray snow. There is a finger's width of ash on the floor. Hollis is still fully draped with her sheet. Tiptoeing to her bedside, I peer beneath. Still breathing. Still sleeping.

I head for the hallway, leaving big footprints through the powder. Outside, I look over the railing. Everything is gray. The tan stones of the castle have been blotted out by gray ash. I marvel at how it looks like a completely different castle. I touch the railing, wiping away a layer of dust.

Looking for Angus, I open his door and traipse to the bedroom. Angus is asleep on a mattress on the floor all by himself. Covered in ash, he looks like an old man. A dead man - gray, sallow, and still. My heart thuds at a nervous beat worried for my cousin. I rush over and jerk him awake. "Angus."

"Are you okay?" I wipe ash from his face as he wakes.

He sits up and rubs his face, hair, and beard. He coughs and coughs as the ash plumes from his head onto the dirty blankets.

"Why didn't you cover your head?"

He coughs again and says, "I didn't think it would make it past the shutters."

I scoot to the kitchen and gently lift the blanket off his pail of water. It sloshes back and forth until I reach his side. He takes it and drinks, and then splashes some on his face. The ash becomes gray mud as he smears it down his cheeks. The pounding in my chest slows as the red in his beard begins to show, looking like himself again.

At that moment, Tolliver enters and asks if we're alright. Kava is not far behind.

"We're fine," I reply. Looking at Angus I add, "I think."

"Angus, you look like death." Tolliver nods.

"I taste death," Angus retorts, spitting some ash-muck onto the blanket.

Tolliver looks as though he slept with a sheet over his head, as well as Kava. Only their feet are dusty.

Tolliver looks at me. "Where's Hollis?"

"She is still asleep."

"Did she breathe any of it in?" Kava asks.

"No, I don't think so. I draped a sheet over her last night." I expect a pat on the back from Tolliver or a "Good job, Ledger," but he walks away.

Kava and Angus follow him to number five. Angus shakes his head as he walks across the balcony and ash plumes from his head. I return to Alouette's room to wake Hollis. When I enter, she is already getting out of bed.

"Let me help you." I reach her just in time to lift her into my arms.

"I really should start walking on my own, Ledger." With droopy eyes, she smiles sleepily. "Kava said it is okay for me to put pressure on it."

"Oh," I say, leaning to put her down.

"But, maybe you can carry me this one last time?"

Kind of enjoying her embrace, I agree and carry her small frame to the fifth door. I hear the echo of Angus coughing as we approach.

"How are we going to clean up all of this ash?" Kava asks as we enter the room.

"We don't need to clean, really," Tolliver says. "If we open all the doors and windows, the wind will take care of it eventually."

Kava nods and I set Hollis next to her on a stool at the table. There is no fire in the hearth. No morning meal. Angus, seated across from Kava, coughs again.

Tolliver says, "I think we need to figure out how much grain is left."

I blink, trying to care.

He continues, "Let's search all of the homes, starting at the top and bring down all the rest of the grain and other edible items people stored. Then we can figure out how long we have until the food runs out."

I nod in agreement. "Are we going to have to lug each one down all these stairs?"

"I have an idea about that," Angus interjects and wheezes, holding back a cough. "I found a pulley and a bunch of rope. We could use it to haul the sacks however far down we can get it."

"Great idea," I say.

Angus coughs and hacks as he takes a breath, "I don't want to run down there to get it. I can hardly breathe as it is. Can you fetch it for me, Ledger?"

I agree without complaint as he hacks, spitting gray saliva on the floor.

"Ew, Angus, I do not need to see your mucus," Hollis moans.

Tolliver glares at her and she shuts her mouth quickly, eyes wide with caution.

I leave Hollis to fend for herself with Tolliver and hurry down the stairs to get Angus's pulley and ropes. Kicking little piles of ashes, I haul them back up thirteen tiring flights of stairs.

When I return, Tolliver has already gone to collect grain on the upper levels. I hand Angus the ropes and pulley. He ties them together while coughing more gray gunk from his throat. Kava eyes me with furrowed brows. Her medicine bag sits next to her.

"Sounds as if Angus is going to need you to make him some sort of concoction with all that hacking," I say smiling, needing things to be light and pleasant.

Kava retorts darkly, "I told him it sounds serious. But he thinks he can cough it all out."

Angus stops and looks at her sharply. He snorts, hacks and spits into a bucket on the bench next to him.

"I need to leave," Hollis complains. "I am nauseous from all the spitting."

Stifling a laugh, I wait for Angus to finish tying the ropes end to end. He double knots both ends, bigger than my fist. "The end knots are to keep it from dropping all the way to the ground, so make sure they don't come untied or you'll have to run down and fetch them," Angus says.

I agree, and we head to the upper floors to help Tolliver collect grain. Angus's breathing is labored as we ascend level after level. He stops and spits several times in each stairwell. I am concerned he won't make it back down.

"I can do this. You can stay below where we send the bags."

Angus looks at me and pushes his red curls out of his eyes. He is sweating even though the heat of the volcano is far behind us. "Okay, good idea."

I leave Angus behind. We work most of the day dropping the bags four levels at a time. I'm glad we don't have to carry them down one by one. By the time we get the first load to the ground floor, the sky is fading.

"Why don't you take a break and eat something," Kava calls.

"We'll eat when we're done," Tolliver answers.

"You'll eat now because you haven't eaten all day," Kava hassles him. She follows a worn path in the ashes to the dining hall.

Tolliver's face goes a little red and concedes with a nod. I am a bit surprised by the power she has over him. I choke back a laugh when Tolliver looks at me sternly.

Angus sits down by the railing and hacks up another chunk. After counting all the bags, Tolliver helps Angus to his feet. Angus is slow on the next stretch of stairs. I put my arm under his as Tolliver does the same on the other side. We practically carry him down a full stairwell when his legs go limp. Almost toppling down the last steps, we take on the full weight of Angus's hulking body. Tolliver lifts his right leg and I grab the left. They are as heavy as tree trunks. We haul him down and around the corner to the dining hall.

"Kava," Tolliver grunts. "Help, Angus stopped moving."

We lay his limp body on the floor. Kava hovers over him, pulling his eyes open. They are bloodshot and not focusing on us. She puts her fingers to his neck, pauses and puts her ear to his mouth.

Tolliver paces behind me, rubbing his sandy hair into a wild frenzy.

"Can you get my bag?" Kava places a hand on Tolliver.

"Ledger?" He defers the task to me.

"No, you Tolliver," Kava commands. "Quickly."

Tolliver runs off to find her bag of medicines and Kava looks at me, "Tolliver is losing it."

I agree, but Angus starts coughing again. Kava pushes his heavy body to the side. Gurgling comes out of Angus's throat with another mucusy glob of ash.

"Is he going to be okay?" I ask.

"If he had let me give him something upstairs, he would probably be better off."

When Tolliver returns, Kava shakes a small brown bottle and dabs her finger in it wiping it under his nose. She directs us to put him in the smallest room we can find with a fireplace. Tolliver builds a fire as Kava creates a mixture in a small pot with water and several tree oils. It smells like eucalyptus and possibly juniper.

Tolliver and Kava work alongside each other, caring for Angus. They come and go from each other's side. They remind me of Mother and Father, working wordlessly in tandem. Sadness fills my gut as Angus awakens with a coughing fit. I feel the weight of the blame. It's my fault he is here. If I hadn't taken us on this journey away from our home, Angus wouldn't be sick. Hollis wouldn't have broken her leg. I wouldn't be completely lost.

STAY TOGETHER 25

Day 113

A shofar blares somewhere in the castle. Three long blasts. I am confused momentarily. In Balfour, three long tones means Ellery is approaching. But we're on Ellery. Turning from the forge, I raise my eyebrows at Angus.

"What the straw mattress?" he blurts. He holds back a cough.

I shrug.

Laying down his hammer, he heads for the door. I push the short rod of iron into the red coals and lay the tongs aside. Angus is out the door and around the corner by the time I race after him and reach the hallway. I catch up as another series of three blasts fills the courtyard.

"Where is it coming from?" I ask.

With a determined look on his face—brows low, lips pursed—he barrels down the north hall. We round the outside of the castle and see Tolliver on the east lookout tower looking out over the ocean. I follow Angus's lead and race to him.

I am out of breath. "What's going on?"

"Look," Tolliver exclaims and points. With a wide smile he says to me, "Land, little brother."

Angus grabs Tolliver, wrapping him in a bear hug. They release and laugh together, pumping their fists in the air. I am jealous of their closeness. Tolliver and I will never be as close as they are.

Angus grabs the spyglass, pointing it east. I notice that he is wheezing and bracing himself on the stone railing but pretends to be fine. He spent several weeks in bed, until one day he was up and helping me in the smithing workshop. I asked him during his first coughing fit in the shop if he was okay. He just spit in the furnace and kept working. So I didn't mention it again.

"I have an idea of how to find more food." Tolliver says with a wicked grin, rubbing his palms together. Angus returns the smirk, eyes lighting up.

I clench my jaw and brace myself for his wild scheme. The look on his face means it is challenging and probably dangerous. I'm not sure I want to know but the fact that he didn't say it to me means I'm not included in his plans.

Angus takes another look out over the blue-gray waters. I grow impatient to see the dark sliver of land cresting the horizon in the afternoon light.

"Can I see?" I groan hoping to get Angus's attention. He ignores me. Frustration rises from my belly. I hate it when everyone disregards me as if I don't matter.

Kava comes running from the castle, out of breath and asks what the alarm meant. Hollis isn't too far behind, hobbling toward us.

"We spotted land." Tolliver puts his arm around her and

escorts her to the view. He points and says, “Have you ever seen anything so magnificent?”

She squints at the horizon while her brown hair whips in the wind, caressing his face. Tears well in her eyes and she bites her lip.

Her emotion makes me uncomfortable, so I say, “It seemed we’d never get away from this ocean.”

“Too right, little brother, too right,” Tolliver says.

Hollis reaches the overlook, winded from the walk. With a brilliant smile she looks out at the scene.

I look out at the perfect line where the dark waters and the light blue sky meet. I can barely see the stretch of green. It feels like a dream and I look around for something strange to happen. But it doesn’t. The wind just presses on my skin.

As Tolliver and Kava embrace, I turn away abruptly. Feeling awkward, as if my head is filling with needles, I walk away.

***

Day 116

Ellery drifts over the sandy beach, through the wrinkly hills and is approaching high mountains that seem as if we could crash into them. I sit on the ledge of the tower watching our approach. In another couple of days, it will be a new moon. It will be the second new moon since winter solstice. That means it will be my day of birth. I remember the day I turned thirteen, all of the village gathered to celebrate. I was the first of the season to turn thirteen, so the feast was special. But this was my banquet, which made it extra special. I remember slipping my small feet into my leather boots and walking out the door where the village welcomed me into manhood. All I had to do was walk over the threshold of our cottage door. I froze. I was overwhelmed at the attention of every man, woman and child I knew. But I was also terrified of messing up. I had seen plenty of boys become men. They performed just fine. I wasn't sure I'd be able to fulfill what was expected of me.

When I took that first step out the door, cheers filled my ears. Hands patted me on the back. Mother had tears in her eyes. Father stood proudly. And all I did was walk through the same door I had my entire life. That time I stepped out as a man of Balfour. I didn't feel different. I didn't even look different.

The sliver of moon hangs in the morning sky. The heavens are streaked with orange and blue clouds. One by one, Hollis, Angus, Tolliver and Kava join me, watching us drift closer and closer to the mountains like a log floating down stream. Will we hit the side? Will we scrape it as we go by?

"Should we brace ourselves?" Hollis's slender brow pinches together in concern.

Kava, standing with her hands on her hips, says, "Don't be ridiculous. There is probably a perfectly carved path for us."

Angus sits next to me on the ledge, legs dangling off the other side. He coughs and clears his throat a couple of times.

"I'm just wondering if we can get off," I say.

Tolliver laughs, and Angus gives a short chortle to keep from coughing. The moments crawl by as the cliff comes nearer to our rock. The wind picks up and it sounds like we are in a cave. Rocks crunch below and tumble away as our island drifts alongside the mountain. I look up at the gray rock and white snow above our heads. I marvel that it towers over Ellery. I couldn't have imagined anything being higher than this floating fortress.

"I want to see how far we are from the edge," Tolliver says. When he heads around the castle, we all follow. Hollis isn't hobbling much anymore. She only rarely uses the cane I made for her. We've been walking around the castle each day to build up her strength. I smile at her beside me. Returning the grin, she reaches for my hand. I let her take it for extra support. We all exit through the enormous front entrance of the castle. When we round the corner heading north toward the mountain, Tolliver halts and puts a hand out, stopping us in our tracks.

"Oh my lands, we are being boarded," he gasps. We peer out around the corner. A group of men stand in line to leap the gap between their world and ours. My heart shoots into an uneasy rhythm. I can't believe what I am seeing.

The men wear brown baggy fur pants tucked tightly into boots of stretched leather. Their jackets are all different, one with gray fur, others with tan or dark brown. Some wear hoods concealing their faces and some do not, revealing the orange paint smeared across their eyes and bridge of their nose.

Tolliver shoves us back around the corner to hide from the intruders.

"We don't know if they come in peace or hostility." Tolliver's hands are balled into fists and he is pushing them together making the vein stick out the side of his neck. My stomach rolls with his intensity and the impending invasion.

"Good point," Angus agrees. "Let's hide."

Tolliver nods and we run back inside like our life depends upon it. He leads us to the throne room where we all scramble for a hiding place behind tapestries. I hide behind the one of the girl with the kind eyes at the back of the room near the Ellerian thrones.

Shortly we hear voices speaking words I do not understand. They sound as if they are asking questions and are confused. Probably confused about the missing Ellerians. My heart is racing out of control and I am having trouble breathing quietly. Then the voices grow nearer and enter the throne room. They are talking hurriedly and one of them is getting angrier, yelling at the other men.

They abruptly stop. It is silent for a few moments. I hold my breath, trying not to give away my position. They erupt in shouts and I hear Hollis screaming. Peeking out from the side of the tapestry, I see Hollis being dragged from her hiding spot. A burly man with head shaved smooth and a tan jacket with black fur jutting out of the shoulder seams holds her down with one hulking hand entangled in her blonde hair.

I freeze. I don't know what to do. I must hide, but I must make sure she is okay, and my body will not make the choice between them so I remain stuck.

At the next breath, Tolliver leaps from his hiding place and races to Hollis's aid.

"Let her go," Tolliver demands.

The men rush toward Tolliver. As the first one approaches, Tolliver punches him in the face and he goes down hard. The second man exchanges blows with Tolliver and a third kicks him in the stomach while he is distracted. My gut wrenches at the heavy hit as he falls to his knees. The kicker drags Tolliver by his hair to where Hollis is held. He forces him to the ground with a fist full of his hair.

Another group of six men enter, one of them is wearing a gray fur hood with a wolf's head on it. Sharp teeth crown his forehead. A shiver runs down my spine and I can't catch my breath.

The wolf man is yelling at his men in questions like he is their leader. They are answering with heads bowed and choppy syllables. They speak to their prisoners: my brother and Hollis.

Wolf Man asks them something in his strange language. He waits a moment and then screams the same phrase at them.

Hollis cries. I should be there. It should be me instead of Tolliver. He reaches for Hollis's hand and the man restraining him kicks him away. He winces in pain and I'm not sure I could handle what he is enduring. I am not strong like Tolliver. I wouldn't have gotten even one punch in.

Wolf Man demands an answer and Tolliver speaks, "I don't know what you are saying. We do not know where the people of Ellery are."

Wolf man tips his head and speaks in a strange accent. "Ellery?"

"Yes," Tolliver replies. "Ellery is gone."

The man asks more questions in his fast-tongue language including the word Ellery, but Tolliver looks at him quizzically. Wolf man points at the tapestry closest to the door and yells at Tolliver.

"I don't know," Tolliver says shaking his head and putting out his hands.

Wolf man mimics him and says something to his men. They yank Tolliver and Hollis to their feet by their hair. Hollis whimpers. My stomach rolls with nausea watching them as they are dragged away. As the voices and footsteps grow distant, Angus emerges from his hiding place. I follow him staring open-mouthed at the empty room. Angus puts a hand on my shoulder and I start breathing again.

Crying comes from the other side of the room. Angus and I approach the weeping tapestry and I pull it back to find Kava on the floor holding her knees, tears streaming down her face. We stand gaping at her for a moment, both unsure of how to deal with a crying Kava. She is always so strong. Seeing her this way makes me angry. She should be bossing us around right now.

So I say what she should be saying, "We have to go after them."

"Yes, let's do it," Angus agrees, running a restless hand through his hair. Since we've been on this island, it has grown to his shoulders in a tangle of untamed red curls.

"What if we get captured with them?" Kava wipes the tears from her eyes.

I imagine for a moment what it would be like if we return home without Tolliver or Hollis. Balfour's rage would be more intense than when I landed my contraption in the field. My head aches at the thought.

"Then at least we will be together," I say. "The biggest thing is to stay together." I am surprised at how confident

I sound. I'm completely faking it, of course. Chewing the inside of my cheek, the taste of blood floods my mouth.

"Maybe Kava should stay here," Angus suggests. "So at least she will be safe."

"No," Kava and I say at the same time.

"We need to stay together," I say. "Kava, gather a few bandages and remedies, just in case they are wounded when we find them. Angus, we need weapons."

GOLDEN TRADE 26

Hurrying to the kitchen, I fill several water pouches. I shuffle back out to center court and call for the other two, "Kava, Angus, you ready?"

Kava comes jogging down the stairs with a bag over her shoulder. Angus steps out of the armory door and yells across the courtyard, "Kava, you any good with a sword?"

Kava just laughs, and Angus shakes his head. He approaches with two swords, a bow and two quivers full of arrows. He hands Kava a small knife in a sheath and gives me a quiver to carry knowing full well, I am no good with a bow. But a sword, I can probably handle, seeing that I make them.

We head out the front of the castle and across the rocky surface of the island. The mountain is one good leap away. Dread rises in my throat. I don't think I can do this. I step closer and look down between the rocks, which is not a good idea. Panic drains the blood from my limbs and my head is reeling.

"Okay," Angus says. "The person who will be the worst

at this goes second. So at least the last one can throw them across and the first one can catch them." He looks right at me and a terrified laugh sneaks out of my mouth.

Angus steps up to the edge, breathes deeply, puts his big foot out and leaps across with ease. I am bolstered by his success and step up. Angus walks alongside Ellery as it moves along its path.

"Come on, Ledger," Angus encourages.

"Okay, I can do this." My heart hammers in my chest and my tongue is dry. I put my foot out like Angus. If I lean forward my foot will land on the mountain. One, two, three, go! But my body does not obey. I can't breathe, and I am dizzy.

"Ledger, look out!" Kava screams. I look up just in time for an overhang from the mountain to hit me in the face and throw me backwards. The next thing I know, I'm on my rear end and my vision is blurry.

Kava helps me back to my feet. She is obviously holding back a laugh and I decide not to think about it. Just do it. I'm simply going for a walk. I face the mountain; the cliff side is level with Ellery again and I leap forward, landing flat-footed on solid ground. Sharp pain shoots through my feet, but I don't care. I made it. I hear Kava land beside me.

I take a deep breath and she slaps me on the back of the head as she walks off to find Angus. I am such an idiot. I touch my face where the rock hit me to see if I'm bleeding. It's only bruised a little.

We climb the rocks and meet up with Angus, then trek west some distance to find the spot where the Wolf Man exited the island. Angus locates boot prints, many large and one small set heading north. I worry for Hollis. She can't handle this sort of thing. I grind my teeth as we hike the rocky paths up the mountain. I look back at Ellery as it drifts slowly by as we enter a large cave. My world is leaving without me and frustration eats at my gut because we might not be able to get back on the island.

The cave is dark for the first several paces, and then we see a light at the other end. It looks to be an opening out the other side. Less of a cave, more of a tunnel. We reach the end and hide on the left side of the opening. I peek around the rock and look out across a valley of large round huts with smoke emerging from only the hut in the middle. People are coming and going from their homes. There is no sign of Hollis or Tolliver. I don't know what to do.

"What do you see?" Angus steps round me and peers out over the village.

Kava grows impatient and says, "Well?" She steps around me to the cave opening.

It's as if nothing happened. ¬There is no racing about. There are no prisoners. They must be hiding them. I am at a loss for what to do now, as if I expended all my fake brilliance on Ellery.

"Let's sneak around that side," Angus says pointing to the hill rising on the west.

I follow Angus around the village through thick brush and trees. Thorns pull at the skunk pelts wrapped around my feet. I'm glad I had cut off the tails a couple days ago. When we hear voices in the strange language, we stop abruptly and quickly hide behind a pale green juniper bush.

We sit watching the small village, waiting for some

sign of where our friends are. Finally, I see Wolf Man exit a smaller hut and enter the larger hut in the center of the village. "They're in that one," I state. The roof is covered with layers of woven straw. The walls are some sort of orange clay, with a strange zigzag pattern etched all the way around. It stands out from all the other buildings. More and more people enter the center hut and I'm nervous they'll eat them or something worse.

No one stirs in the village for quite some time. No one comes or goes. "Let's go," I say, nodding toward the center hut.

"We cannot just walk in there," Kava says.

"We can't just sit here," I reply.

"Let's do it," Angus agrees. "Kava, where is your knife?"

She pulls it from her satchel and unsheathes it.

"Good," Angus says.

Angus nods toward the hut and we run from the brush toward the center of the village. I feel a wave of terror being out in the open. What if we're running into a trap? We reach the building with zigzag markings and sneak our way around to the door. There is a thick pelt hanging over the doorway. We hear voices. There is no yelling, no threat of death.

Gently pushing back the curtain, I peer inside. There are many tan faces. Everyone is dressed in fur all the way around the room. It is surprising how many they have squeezed into this hut. Kneeling in the center is the girl with golden hair next to my brother. They are alive. My hand shakes as I hold the curtain and strain to hear what they are saying, when someone notices me. I drop the pelt and pull out my sword. Angus does the same and we step back, braced for a fight.

Kava is frozen in place, dagger ready.

Inside there are raised voices and strange words of surprise. Then the curtain is pulled back and Tolliver is standing before me. Unharmed.

"Tolliver, let's go," I whisper reaching for him.

He swings his hand away and says, "No."

It confuses me so I try again. Tolliver grabs a fistful of my cloak, dragging me inside where all the faces stare at me. Some old, some young, all dark skinned with smooth black hair.

The bald men with the long black hair spiking from their shoulders and orange paint across their faces kneel around the inner circle. Three rows of men, women and children sit in silence with their legs crossed. My skin is itchy from all the focused attention.

"Welcome," a high-pitched voice with an odd accent says. I walk cautiously to the center of the hut. Angus and Kava follow close behind.

"Come, sit."

Locating the voice, it belongs to an old lady with deep bags under her piercing black eyes. She is seated at the top of the circle next to Wolf Man. "Welcome in Jikuni," she says with her old twisted fingers held out. Her deerskin robe hangs limply from her bony arms. She wears a necklace of small bones with strands of curly brown hair dangling between each. It must be human hair, because I've never seen an animal with fur that long or curly. Following Tolliver to a mat in front of them, Angus, Kava, and I kneel beside Hollis. My chest aches for air, and I can't help feeling we need to run away.

"We talk," the old lady says slowly. "Where Ellery?"

"They are gone," Tolliver says, kneeling on the other side of Hollis.

"Gone," the woman repeats. "Where gone?"

"We do not know." He puts his hands out and shrugs. "We are searching for Ellery," Tolliver explains.

"Searchy?" she imitates looking at Wolf Man. "What is searchy?"

"Search. Look," Tolliver clarifies, putting his hands to his eye like a spyglass. "We are looking for Ellery."

Peering around at the strangers, I notice there is only one person standing, a guard with spiky shoulders and crusty orange face paint. He is poised with his hand on his sword and the other behind his back. He wears a necklace of little white teeth—human or animal, I can't tell. Either way it makes my stomach splash bile into my throat, and I hold back the urge to cry.

"Yes," she nods and speaks in her native tongue to Wolf Man. They chatter back and forth a few times in their quick-syllables. To all of us, she says, "Help you need?"

I struggle to understand her accent. I have never heard anyone have such difficulty with my language before.

Tolliver hesitates for a moment and responds, "We need food." He motions lifting food to his mouth and chewing.

The Wolf Man belly laughs, "Yah." He nods in understanding or agreement or both.

"We help you food," the saggy old lady says.

Tolliver nods and the old lady nods along with Wolf Man. Soon every head is nodding, including Hollis and Angus. I'm not. All I want to do is grab my friends and run out of here.

“What you pay?” asks the lady.

“Pay?” Tolliver scowls.

“You trade, need food.” She nods again leading the whole room into nods.

“I thought you wanted to help. We don’t have anything to trade,” Tolliver says.

Her face goes sour and Wolf Man whispers to her. Her old eyes light up as she says, “Yellow girl trade.”

My gut wrenches and I shout, “No!” The whole room of dark eyes looks at me.

“No?” The old lady’s eyes harden.

“She is mine,” I blurt.

Hollis looks at me, eyes full of pleading and horror.

“Oh, she is you.”

All heads nod again. Wolf Man grows impatient to strike a deal. He jabbers to thc old lady again.

“Food,” he says and points aggressively at Hollis.

“No,” I reiterate. The guard with the teeth necklace steps behind me.

As Wolf Man argues with the old lady, I whisper to Tolliver, “Let’s get out of here.”

“Thank you,” Tolliver says to Wolf Man and the old woman. “We must go now.”

He gets to his feet and bows slowly. Hollis, Kava, Angus and I do the same and head to the door at the same time. Teeth Collector blocks our way with crossed arms.

Wolf Man gives him a curt command and he grabs Hollis by the hair. Her eyes bulge, and I lunge at him with all my weight. Unmoved by my scrawny body, he pulls a knife from the belt around his waist. In one smooth motion holding Hollis's hair, he slices it short.

A terrified scream comes from Hollis. Tolliver jabs at Teeth Collector and Angus pulls out his sword. Hollis is released and falls into my arms. Her hacked hair is falling into her teary eyes. The hulking man ignores Tolliver's punches and hands her hair to Wolf Man.

Squeezing her tightly, I hold her as she shakes and cries. Wolf Man smells the clump of hair, satisfied with the trade. He says something in his language pointing at the door.

Teeth Collector walks to the doorway and pulls back the curtain, allowing us to leave. With arms wrapped protectively around her, I lead Hollis out the door. He tells another hairy-shouldered guard something. The guard leaves and returns with a bulky burlap bag. Tolliver doesn't look in the sack and accepts it. We follow closely as he walks swiftly away hand in hand with Kava.

My insides wrench as we hear shouts from behind us. Several guards come after us as we head for the tunnel through the mountain. They shout strange things and point to the east side of the mountain. Tolliver seems to understand their meaning and points upwards.

I bite my tongue and guide traumatized Hollis up the embankment. She wraps herself around my arm, making it hard to climb. But it doesn't matter. I'll keep her safe. I'm just glad she is alive.

The cavernous path between the mountains is consumed in shadows. Ellery looks so small among the massive mountains, like driftwood floating down a forest stream.

With Angus in the lead, we run along the ridge as if drawn back by a force. It's strange to be homesick for Ellery.

Hollis and I make the leap together. I barely think about falling to a bloody death between the cliff and the rocky island.

THE HUNT 27

Day 120

Relieved to be safe and together again on Ellery, we all sleep in the same room for several nights. Angus and Tolliver on the king's bed, Hollis, Kava and I sprawl out on mats around them. Each night is darker and darker approaching the new moon. I appreciate the company and the conversations.

The day of my birth comes, and Tolliver makes a plan to go hunting. We are still within reach of the mountains and he thinks we have time to hunt before we reach the end of the range.

We all stand on the surface of Ellery. It is surprisingly warm, and we've left our cloaks and furs behind for our adventure in the woods. Hollis and Kava found more clothes in one of the royal chambers of either the queen or her daughters. They stand in the bright morning light wearing long beautiful dresses.

Hollis keeps swishing her yellow dress back and forth, staring into space. Her choppy hair hangs at a sharp angle on her cheeks. I should ask if she is okay. Instead I watch the silver trim on her long sleeves shimmer in the sunlight.

"I wish you would have thought of this sooner," Kava says with her hands on her hips. She is wearing a light blue Ellerian dress with a rounded neckline and draping sleeves. A silver chain link belt hangs from her waist and drapes to the ground. "It's stupid for you guys to jump off and run the risk of not being able to get back on, especially after what we went through," she complains.

Hollis and Kava look out of place in contrast to Angus, Tolliver and I. Angus and Tolliver have collected piles of tunics and slacks left by the Ellerians so they never have to wash clothes. They are both wearing all black: boots, pants, and shirt. I look down at my dirty white shirt and brown slacks. I wash them every couple of weeks. I tip my head to smell my armpit and gag. I need to wash again.

"That's where you come in," Tolliver explains. "We have the rope, just in case we are far from the ledge and can't leap across." He finishes hammering a large metal stake in the ground and fastening the rope to it.

"Fine, fine," she shakes her head.

"Besides," Tolliver says, putting the spyglass in her hand. "It looks as though we will be in the mountains for another couple of days."

Angus, Tolliver and I gather our weapons and empty canvas bags. Tolliver leaps first and then Angus. I take a few steps back and jump across. My heart is thumping wildly, but it feels good to succeed and land without hurting myself. I think of Alouette's wings and wish I had a set of my own. It would make life much easier.

The rocky ground pokes through my skunk skin shoes. They are worn away in several spots and the craggy ground tears them all the way through. We walk up the side of the mountain together and head east. Tolliver picks up the pace so we are walking faster than Ellery is drifting.

The mountain slopes down in front of us and is no longer level with Ellery. We follow it down into a small valley of evergreens and leafless trees. Tolliver halts us with a hand in the air then points down into the ravine. There is some sort of beast traipsing through the brush below. I'm not sure what it is from up here, but it is quite big with brown fur.

"Angus head north down that slope," Tolliver whispers. "I'll go straight down from here as soon as I see you in position."

"What about me?" I am armed with a sword.

"Stay here," Tolliver says as Angus walks away.

"I can do something," I whine.

"We only have two directions in which we can approach. Angus and I are better shots than you. Stay put, brother." Tolliver whips out an arrow and tiptoes down the mountainside. I see glimpses of Angus's red hair through the trees as I lower myself to sit on the sharp rocks. Tolliver descends out of sight.

Sometime later, I hear a shout. A loud roar rips through the valley and I jump to attention. The beast is probably attacking them. I pull the sword from the sheath and shuffle down the mountain. The ground is covered with crunchy dead leaves at the bottom. I hear another roar and head north toward where I imagine Angus bloodied and mauled. I tromp through the brush and crinkly leaves, not worrying about being loud.

Pushing my way through a thorny bramble, I trip and fall

out the other side. I land with my face in the leaves. I look up to see Tolliver and Angus standing over me.

"Do you have a wild bird in your head?" Angus laughs. He has a bloody blade in his hand and Tolliver has proudly shouldered his bow. The fight is over.

"I thought—"

"You thought we invited you to this party and we didn't," Tolliver says.

"What?" I shriek. "It's my birthday."

His eyebrows raise as he retorts, "I mean, we didn't call you down the hill."

The pressure of sticking up for myself builds in my head. I want to explode on them and demand they take me seriously and treat me like a man. But I did just stomp loudly into the middle of their hunt. Luckily, the animal is already dead. I grind my teeth as Angus snickers at me.

Angus puts his knife back into the guts of the beast and rips upward towards its head. It looks like some sort of small bear with tusks. Its tongue lolls to the side as Angus and Tolliver handle it. With a sticky sloshing sound, he yanks out the parts we don't eat and tosses them into the weeds. Tolliver ties the front paws together with a rope, which he tosses up over a tree branch several feet above his head. When Angus is finished cleaning the animal out, he signals Tolliver who pulls the carcass up and ties it off on a nearby sapling. Tolliver holds the carcass still as Angus strips off the hide. Angus uses his knife to saw off each of the back legs. This amount of meat could last a long time.

"Give me your bag," Angus holds his red dripping hand out to me.

I hand it to him and he loads it with the two back legs. He packs the front legs into another and quarters the torso. He can only get three of the quarters in the rest of our bags.

They discuss how to haul it back to the island and resort to wrapping it in its own skin as a makeshift bag. Angus ties it closed with a strip of leather from his quiver. They each grab a bag and leave two for me.

"Two? Why do I have to carry two?" I yank one onto my shoulder.

"You said you wanted to help." Tolliver gives a playful wink, eyeing the second one. I lug the heavy bag onto my other shoulder crossing it over the first, pushing the weight to my back. We head up the east side of the valley to catch up with the island. Halfway, my legs are burning, and I am out of breath. I have to stop several times to gulp down air that isn't reaching my lungs.

When we crest the top, Ellery is a short sprint away and Tolliver prods us to run. I trot like a mule with a load that is too heavy. It bounces and hits me in the back at every step. Reaching my arms back, I hold my load tightly, attempting to make it a little less painful. My brow is sweating, and the cool breeze is icy on my face.

There is another smaller valley in front of us before we reach Ellery. Easily running down, I worry I might die on the way back up.

"Stop, I can't," I plead, out of breath.

"No, you knew we'd have to run to make it back. Come on," Tolliver demands.

"I can't," I say gasping for breath. My legs are about to give out.

"Yes, you can," Tolliver prods. "We are almost there."

"Wait," Angus says, stopping us. He is scoping through the trees ahead and pulls out an arrow. Mounting it on his bow he takes a shot and then another. He smiles wide and pumps a fist in the air.

We follow Angus to his kill.

"Nice shot, brute," Tolliver says grinning. He lifts the rabbit from the place where it died with Angus's arrow sticking out of its eye.

"I've still got the skills," Angus says with a happy jaunt.

They laugh together as I kneel in the dirt to catch my breath. As I unload the bags from my aching back, Tolliver urges, "Let's go."

I groan and follow them the rest of the way. Every step is excruciating. The sharp rocks under my feet. The extra weight that drags me down and strains my back. The burn of my legs and chill on my face. By the time we reach the moving ledge of Ellery, my body is numb. Swaying with exhaustion, I peel the bags from my shoulders and heave them onto the ground. I don't complain so the girls won't know how much of a wimp I am. Kava and Hollis are sitting near the edge waiting for us. There is a little pile of fur in front of them.

"What is that?" Tolliver shouts across the chasm.

"We may have done some hunting ourselves," Kava replies. They each hold up a squirrel.

Tolliver laughs and shows them our dismembered kill. Hollis is confused. She probably can't tell what it is.

The gap between the mountain and Ellery is widening with every moment, while we stand around chatting. Looking ahead along its route, it will only get wider.

"Tolliver, let's get over there. Looks as though our leap will get more difficult the longer we wait," I say pointing at the cliff.

Tolliver nods and throws his bag across the gap. Angus tosses his and one of mine. I heave the last one over to the girls.

"One, two, three," Tolliver yells. Side by side, we all take a flying leap across. I land and steady myself. When I hear a scream and rocks falling, I whirl around. Tolliver is barely holding onto the surface of Ellery.

Angus and I scramble over to him. We each grasp an arm and drag him up the side of the cliff. As soon as he is safe, Kava's knees hit the dirt even though she is wearing a beautiful clean dress. She wraps her arms tightly around him while we all sit panting in the gravel.

"What happened?" My heart is pounding.

"He landed and the rocks gave out underneath him," Hollis explains with her hand on her racing heart. "He nearly slid right off."

My stomach aches at the thought of him falling down. It would be like getting ground in a grain mill. I'm never doing that again.

We grab our kill and head to the castle. The front of Tolliver is covered in dust particles. His black tunic is ripped open and blood speckles his chest. His expression is serious with tight lips and lower teeth protruding. Kava doesn't release him the entire trek inside.

PRESERVATION 28

Kava ignored the meat we hauled in for most of the day because of her concern for Tolliver. Instead, she has tended to the scratches on his chest and a gash she found on his forearm. After bandaging him, she forces him to lie down. Tolliver protests, telling her he is fine, but eventually he concedes to her will.

When I approach Tolliver's room to ask how much of the meat we should dry, I find they have fallen asleep together. Deciding not to wake them, I amble back to the kitchen. Angus, Hollis and I work in the kitchen all day. Stripping meat from bone, salting some of it for drying, boiling some for stew, and looking for more ways to store it for later use.

"Can we talk about Kava?" Angus breaks the silence.

"Okay," Hollis replies. "Why?"

"She doesn't seem like herself lately. She seems," Angus pauses, deep in thought.

"Lost?" Hollis fills in his blank.

"Yes," Angus says. "She is losing it."

"What can we do about that?" I doubt we can do anything.

"I think they need to get married," Angus states.

I burst out laughing, but Hollis nods. His statement is ridiculous and unnecessary. Marrying Tolliver will not heal her. "I don't think so," I say. "Maybe they need a break from each other."

"No, son, she needs him."

"Don't call me that, Angus. I'm not your son!" I snap.

My father claws his way into my mind and pats me on the head. Anger rises in my throat, my hands ball into fists. I'm sick of being treated like a child by anyone who is even a day older than me.

"Sorry, Ledge," Angus replies with his hands in the air. "I didn't mean anything by it. He made the contract with her father over the summer. They were supposed to be married at the Harvest Festival. They need each other."

My teeth clench, and my head throbs. "She's just being dramatic! Tell her to take one of her tonics or something," I shout.

Angus's eyes are wide with shock and Hollis is uncomfortably looking at the floor.

I can't listen to this. It's just crazy. I head out the door.

Stomping up four levels in a fury, I think about Tolliver and the fact that he became of marrying age last summer. It hits me hard. He was supposed to get married after the Clash. When the Sky People weren't there, I made a mess of their lives, everything changed. All their plans were ruined… because of me.

***

"This is disgusting," I say, nearly gagging over the slimy sea snail.

Alouette digs through her basket and pulls out another delicacy. "Okay, sorry. I should have given you this one first," she says, handing me a small bowl of yellow chunks. "This is a pineapple."

Warily, I pick one out like it's a dung beetle. I bite into it carefully. It is juicy and sweet. Delicious. My eyes widen as I chew faster, taking two more pieces and shoving them into my mouth. "Oh, that's much better," I say, juice dripping from my lip.

Remembering Alouette's smile and how her brown eyes sparkle in the sunlight gives me a drop of what I need. Hope. She is the reason we are on Ellery. I realize Kava doesn't need Tolliver for sanity's sake. They belong together and I'm standing in the way. It's time for me to get out of the way.

***

Day 142

As we make our way across the sky hovering above fields and forests, hills and lakes, the skies blow in a relentless storm. Day and night for three days it has been raining. Water is pouring in through the windows and doors, landing in the center courtyard and washing through the grand hallways. I notice a gentle slope to them, guiding the water out of the castle, down the steps, and off the edge of Ellery, finally washing away the last of the volcanic ash.

Now I know why there is a step up into any of the rooms on the ground floor of the castle. It is plenty high enough to block water from flooding those rooms. I stand in the doorway of the dining hall, looking across the courtyard. Rain is overflowing the fountain, pouring over the sides of each bowl, one successively larger than the other all the way down into one large pool. It is quite mesmerizing.

The rain is cold, but each day is warmer than the last. Spring is coming. I head down the back stairs. The loud pounding of the rain diminishes as I reach the kitchen. Kava is making a stew in the large pot hanging in the hearth. I watch her chop a few of the tubers we got from Wolf Man. They taste like potatoes. Weeks ago, I was shocked when Angus said Kava needed to marry Tolliver. As I watch her care for Tolliver the way Mother takes care of Father, it seems as though they are already married.

"You don't have to wait," I state, interrupting the silence.

"Wait for what?" Kava doesn't look up from her chopping.

"To marry Tolliver," I say.

Her head jolts up and she looks at me. Her eyes, full of pain, scrutinize me. "Yes, we do." She goes back to chopping. The knife slams loudly on the wood slab and echoes around the room. Her lips pinch angrily.

"We could," I start.

"No, Ledger. It would be dishonorable to break tradition."

"I was going to say we could do the whole ceremony," I explain.

She pauses and sets down the knife. "The whole ceremony?" Her eyebrows reveal anger directed at me. "What about my father? What about our families? Where would they be for this ceremony?"

"We can do the ceremony exactly the way it is supposed to be and we can fill in the parts that your family would have."

She looks down at the vegetables in front of her. I see a droplet land on one of them and then another. "I don't know, Ledger. My father..." She cries for a moment. Kava scoops the pale yellow vegetables and dumps them into the boiling pot. She sniffles and wipes another tear.

Uncomfortable with her emotions, I leave to fetch what I came for. I pull out my pouch ready to fill it in the pool. Without thinking, I walk right into a big puddle all over the floor.

"What is this?" I say, realizing my feet are soaking wet. Our water supply is gushing out onto the floor and heading for the door.

"Kava?" I call.

She hears the panic in my voice and gets down the hall quickly. "What's the matter?" She stops short of the waterline. "Oh."

"What do we do?"

She stares at it and doesn't answer.

"Is there a way to stop the flow?" I consider that it is rainwater. "It must come from outside."

I run out in search of Tolliver.

I find him in the throne room sitting on the king's throne. He does not look very royal with his leg draped over the arm of the chair. But he does look older. And tired. His pale hair hangs over his eyes.

"Tolliver, the pool of water in the kitchen is overflowing from all the rain," I shout. My voice echoes off the wall and by the time it returns, Tolliver is on his feet. He is wearing a clean white shirt with a black thick fur vest.

"Really?" He saunters to my side, "Suppose we can close it off?"

"I looked for something in the water room to use, but there is nothing. We'll have to find where it goes into the kitchen from the outside."

"I might know where that is," he declares and steps into the rain. Out the front entrance, we exit left, following the outer wall for several paces. The rain beats down on me like many hands slapping me on the head and back. The droplets are huge and heavy.

"Look," he yells above the hammering rain. There is a huge pool of water filled all the way to the top. At the base of the wall there is a slight whirlpool where the water could be draining into the kitchen. "Find something to block the drain."

We look around and find plenty of large rocks to use. We each grab one of a different size. Both of us are drenched from head to toe, so stepping into the pool of water doesn't quite matter anymore, though it sends a chill up my spine as the water level reaches my knees. I lead the way to the center of the whirlpool looking for the drain. The dark clouds block the sun and the spattering rain blurs the surface of the water making it difficult to see.

"We'll have to figure out how big the hole is," I say loudly. He nods. I kneel, and the water is up to my waist. I pant at the sheer iciness and reach a shaking hand into the frigid water. "The rock is too small," I shout. "Give me yours." We trade, and he tosses mine into the storm. The wind whips around us and my body is convulsing from the cold. I place the rock down over the opening, but it is too small as well. "It needs to be twice this size."

"Okay," Tolliver agrees and splashes off to find another. I stand and lob Tolliver's rock. The rain is rushing down the side of the castle into the pool. It really is quite genius the way they built it to collect drinking water and drain into the kitchen basin.

I hear a voice in the wind. I find Tolliver through the graying sheets of rain. His hair is soaked and sticking to the sides of his face. The clean white tunic is translucent, and the fur vest is a matted mess. "Ledger," he yells again, waving me over. He directs me to a rock that has been hewn into a rough rectangle. "This one looks as if it was carved."

I nod and decide to share what's been on my mind. "Why don't you and Kava get married?"

We lift it together and Tolliver laughs and snorts. "I would, but she won't."

We wade into the frigid pool together, stopping just over the hole and I ask over the wind and rain, "Why doesn't she want to marry you?"

"Ledger, one thing at a time. Can we put this down, then talk?" he groans. We let it down easy. It lands on the bottom and the whirlpool stops. The surface is hammered with circles everywhere the rain hits.

Tolliver slaps me on the shoulder and shouts, "She wants to marry me, but she wants to do it at home."

"I don't get it, why did you two come if you already had a contract to marry?"

"I had to. Don't you see that now?" he shouts over the

pounding torrent.

"No, I don't see," I say, wiping the rain off my face, only to have it replaced by more. My whole body is shaking from standing in the icy pool of water and the intensity of our conversation. There is a deep chasm between us like there are things he's not saying. I am to blame. Why doesn't he just say it?

Tolliver grunts and walks away. I follow his wet footprints through the castle. We slosh to the kitchen where Kava is stirring the stew.

When we enter, she gasps at our sopping wet clothes and hair. "Oh my stars, what did you do?"

"Come see," Tolliver waves her over and she follows us to the side room. The water is not rushing anymore. It is only a trickle. We stopped it just as it reached the doorway.

"Wow, good job," Kava exclaims. Beneath his soaking wet hair Tolliver smiles mischievously. He reaches out his wet arms to hug her and she squeals, "No, you're all wet!"

She pushes him away and races up the hall. Tolliver scuttles after her and whines for her to give him a hug.

I wander into the warm kitchen. Dragging a bench near the fire, I sit and peel my skunk skin shoes from my feet while Tolliver taunts Kava, chasing her around the kitchen. There are several holes along the bottom of my worn out shoes. I had added pieces of leather, but now the shoes won't even stay together enough to keep the pieces inside. "I can't wear these anymore," I say, flinging them into the flames beneath the pot of stew.

"Ledger," Kava scolds. "Why did you do that?"

"I can't wear them anymore. They were crumbling off

my feet," I explain.

"No, why did you throw them in the fire?" Her intense brown eyes stare me down. "Now our food is going to smell like your feet."

29
WILD FLOWERS

Day 193

The first full moon since spring equinox is coming soon. It is glowing brightly off the balcony outside the king's chambers. In Balfour, Delineation Day is usually on the first full moon when spring starts. Sighing, sadness spills out of me as I think about our families celebrating without us.

I wait for the sky to darken fully to see the expanse of stars on the clear night. The breeze blows through my fresh clean tunic. I have retired all my ratty furs from the winter and wear one of the king's shirts. They are a little big on me, but it's good to have new clothing and a new season to enjoy.

"Ledger?" Hollis enters the chambers.

"Out here," I call.

She finds me sitting on the wide stone railing along the balcony edge.

"Delineation Day is in three days and Kava is planning on accepting your brother's proposal." She looks at me with a dreamy smile. The bluish-gray tunic she is wearing makes her eyes look bright blue. She is back to wearing pants again.

"Really? Did she tell you that?" I try not to think about

how strange I feel looking at the shape of her slender legs in tight black trousers.

"Yes." She climbs up next to me. "I'd like to do something special for her. I want to collect some flowers."

I laugh, sounding much like a goose, and inspect her face to see if she is teasing. She has a worried look on her face with eyebrows pinched together and lips pushed to the side.

"Oh, you're serious."

She nods and continues, "We aren't too far from the ground and the wild flowers are so beautiful in the fields below. I thought you could lower me out of Tristeh's cave with the rope and pulley."

I think for a moment and wonder if it's possible. "I don't know if we have enough rope." Since we left the mountains, we are gliding over a high prairie in full bloom.

***

We spend a good part of the morning collecting ropes. We toss them over the balcony railings and they land in a heaping mess in the courtyard. Hollis reaches the pile before I do and heaves the whole jumble of ropes over her shoulder nearly wrapping herself from head to toe. Thick ones, thin ones, brown ones, and white ones.

I chuckle at her. "Want me to carry some?"

"That's okay," she says. "I've got it." She prances off happily to the dungeon with no more sign of a limp.

We walk around the empty dragon's cage together. I haven't been down here in months. I notice Hollis must have come down here at some point because the dragon's gate is closed. She sighs as we turn the corner toward the outside. The breeze pushes her hair back from her face tickling her shoulders. It has grown a little since it was hacked short. Kava helped even it out from the jagged way it was slashed off her head. I've never seen a girl with hair cut to the jawline. I think it suits her.

At the edge of the cave opening, we can see the prairie beneath us. It is beautiful. The few trees are all budding light green leaves. In several spots, there are patches of yellow and purple wild flowers.

"I hope there is enough rope," Hollis says as her load hits the ground in a plume of dust. I notice a second pile of ropes near the cliff's edge.

"Where did all of this rope come from?"

"I collected it all over the castle before I invited you," Hollis says out of breath.

"How long have you been awake? The sun is barely up."

She beams proudly at me and I can't help but chuckle. I find it weird that she wakes up chipper. I wake up feeling dull and when anyone talks to me before I'm fully awake it's as if they are eating my soul.

I wrap the pulley's anchor rope several times around one of the few large stalagmites jutting up from the cave floor. I knot it and double knot it making sure it is secure.

Hollis ties all the ropes together end to end. She hands me the first knot and says, "Tighten, please."

I pull at the ends so hard the rope scrapes my palms. She hands me another and another to tighten. As she gets to the last one, she ties it to the rope already threaded through the pulley and tosses the rest of the rope off the side of Ellery and howls into the wind.

"Wooohooo," she yells, her voice echoing behind us through the cave.

The ropes topple and whip out of view below. I can't stretch my neck out far enough to see how close it is to the ground, so I lay on my belly and crawl to the edge. So much for my clean shirt. The rope doesn't reach the ground.

"We need more rope," I state. Relief pours over me. I'm glad to postpone this daring idea, even for a few more minutes.

Hollis says, "I have an idea," and races back toward the dragon's cave. Moments later she returns with another rope and an armload of leather straps. I secretly hope it still doesn't reach. I don't want to die trying to drop to the ground to fetch her stupid flowers.

I already regret agreeing to this as I reel the dangling ropes back up, hand over hand. She ties the extra rope on the end, including one leather strap with a metal loop on the end. I tighten them. An idea strikes me and I wrap the leather straps around my thighs and torso to ensure I don't splat my guts all over the pretty flowers below.

"What are you doing?" she asks.

"I'm making a harness, so I can hook it to the rope."

"You're making the harness for me, right?" She nods with her eyes wide. Pausing, I consider the fact that she wants to do this dangerous stunt, and realize that's the way it has to be. She'd never be able to pull me back up with her little arms.

"I'm making a harness for you, apparently."

"Thank you," she says, dancing and clapping.

Suddenly it's as if I'm doing the wrong thing again, following along with another one of Hollis's ridiculous schemes that isn't going to end well. My ears start to ring. I want to drop everything and back out but listening to Hollis whistle as she tucks in her shirt, changes my mind momentarily.

"Please don't break your other leg," I beg. She is overly thrilled to do this because she bursts into that obnoxious high-pitched laugh.

It startles me. I take a deep breath, giving myself a moment to get my hearing back.

Hollis steps excitedly into the harness. Trying not to touch her, I secure the top around her waist. She asks me to tighten the thigh straps. I am embarrassed as I accidentally graze her butt with my knuckles. She makes me even more uncomfortable when she shoves an empty grain sack down the front of her tunic. She doesn't even notice that I almost saw down her shirt. It's getting hot out here.

Shaking the thoughts from my head, I say, "Please be careful." I latch the hook from the harness to the loop on the end of the rope.

"I think that might be on you, Ledger. Just lower me gently." She sits on the edge.

I snatch up the ropes, worried she'll plummet before I am ready. Uneasy about letting her descend to the ground, especially alone, I imagine the look I will get from Tolliver if this goes badly. My gut gurgles.

I nod as she rolls on her stomach and climbs downward. I keep the rope tight and watch it scrape on the edge of the cliff, sending rock shards over with it. Gently releasing more and more rope through the pulley, I lower Hollis down the side of Ellery toward the ground. I can't look out over the edge to assess how she is doing, but she hasn't cried out yet. So she must be okay. Once all the rope is gone, I gently let the pulley take all of her weight by catching on the huge double knot. I lie down on the edge and see her swiftly walking along the ground with her harness still hooked to the rope. I am thankful she made it.

"Unhook it," I yell. She must not be able to hear me from up here, but she finally gets the harness loose. She lets the straps and ropes hang as she runs off toward a patch of purple flowers. I wish I could hear her. The more flowers she finds, the more she dances and jumps. She gathers them into her arms and races off toward the tree line. Her little legs are a blur.

"No, that's too far," I call, still unable to reach her with my voice.

She is struggling to rip flowering branches from the bushes. I should have sent a knife down with her. She finally yanks off a few branches and tucks them under her arm. I am wildly out of breath as she darts for the next patch of flowers. My head buzzes with a wave of nausea. Bracing myself for something to go horribly wrong, I imagine a wild animal attacking her and I'm stuck up here unable to defend her.

Finally, she comes back to the rope. She places the armful of flowers into the sack and straps it on her back by the drawstring. She reaches for the ropes, having to walk at the same time and tries to hook her harness to the end. Once, twice, three times it takes for her to hook to the drifting island. I run to the pulley and yank on the rope. It is harder to pull her up than let her down. Suddenly the rope snaps loose. I scramble to my belly and peer over the edge. She has fallen on her back on the hard ground. She might be crying or maybe gasping for breath.

"Get up, Hollis," I yell. Her lips move but the wind is battering against my ears and I can't hear her.

Regret clamps down on my chest and I can't help but mutter under my breath, "What were you thinking? You let her risk her life, for what? Flowers?"

Hollis shakes her head and is on her feet running toward the dangling rope. She holds it up at me and shakes her head. Her mouth is moving but I can't hear her. Something must have broken. I pull, pull, pull until the end flops over the side.

I run to the dragon's cave into the storeroom. "Please, please, please," I plead. Flipping over the saddles, I find one strip of leather with hooks at either end underneath the last one.

I sprint back outside, latch it to the bottom, throw the whole thing over the side, and scoot to the edge. She is red-faced walking beneath the island. Inspecting the new piece on the end, she looks up at me confused.

"Put your foot in it," I scream as loud as I can.

She tilts her head, pinching her eyebrows together.

Then I stick my bare foot over the edge and wrap the rope around the bottom of it. I hold for a long moment then look over the edge again. Sure enough, she stuck her foot into the loop and is ready for me to hoist her back up.

I pull with all my strength, ignoring the scratching pains in my hands as the rope rubs against my skin. I groan with every pull, frustration gnawing its way through me. I punish myself with every yank, glad that my hands are bleeding.

"You are supposed to protect her, Ledger. You are such a powerless fool for putting her in danger—again." Tears sting my eyes.

Finally, her choppy blonde hair pops up over the ledge. Tugging one more time, she scrapes her way onto solid ground. Quickly wiping the tears away, I drag her from the overhang. She lay, gasping for breath, looking up at the high ceiling. I inspect her from head to toe to make sure she didn't break anything. There aren't any limbs laying at odd angles. Thankfully.

"You are never doing that again," I groan.

"Yes, that was a stupid idea. Who came up with that?" she asks with a wild grin.

"I don't know, but they should be punched in the neck," I say, and we laugh.

WINDS OF CHANGE 30

Day 194

Hollis shuts herself in the throne room making Kava a few special things out of the flowers she fetched yesterday. Hopefully, no one will find out about them until the ceremony, so they won't be too mad at us. Angus and Tolliver build a bonfire in the center courtyard.

Kava is making a meal of meat stew and mush. Luckily, we have a few pieces of jerky left to make it a little more special.

"Ledger," Hollis whispers. She pokes her head out the throne room door and waves me over. Yanking me through the door, she reveals a path of petals from the door to the middle of the room along the golden rows of tiles. It's actually quite beautiful. "Can you help me with something?" Her blue eyes sparkle in the torchlight. She is still wearing the grass stained tunic and trousers. Without waiting for me to respond, she instructs, "I need these over there."

She is pointing at several tall iron candlesticks on either side of the thrones on the platform. It takes me several minutes to drag all four candlesticks to the center of the room. They screech hideously along the stone floor, sending shivers up my spine.

"There," she says, "Our Hundred Harvest Tree." She smiles and runs a hand through her hair. "Your job is to make sure the wind doesn't wreck the petal path. I have to go get ready and help Kava."

I laugh, and she lowers her eyebrows at me feigning seriousness.

"Okay," I say with hands raised in surrender. She gives me a few more directions and prances out the door.

A little while later, after I've paced the entire room three times, there is a bang on the door. I open it slightly. It is Tolliver and Angus. "Where are the girls?" I push my face through the crack in the door.

"They're coming. Let us in," Angus demands.

"No, Hollis said not to let anyone in until we're all here."

At that moment, Kava and Hollis walk around the corner from the dining hall. Kava is dressed in a floor length white dove-down silk dress with a daisy crown on her head and a bouquet of wild violets in her hands. Tolliver gasps and Angus says, "Whoa."

Kava looks beautiful, but next to Hollis there is no comparison. Hollis found a light pink dress that drapes to her knees. Her short vibrant hair and rosy cheeks, slender body and dainty features make my heart skip.

They stop before the door and I can't take my eyes off her. I don't notice her eyes go from excited to irritated.

"Open the door, Ledger," Kava demands. I jolt to attention and drag the large door open. They enter and Kava gasps at the beautiful petal path that leads into the room. I quickly push the door closed behind them, so it doesn't get blown apart.

"Thank you, Hollis," Kava whispers and hugs her.

We create our own silent processional down the petal path to the center of the room toward the rod iron Hundred Harvest Tree.

Angus leads them in the blessing of the union and their future offspring. Kava and Tolliver gather a handful of petals in their hands, kiss them and toss them above their heads. They fall all around us as if they are falling from the Hundred Harvest Tree. My whole body aches with nostalgia.

Tolliver unfolds a white piece of fabric he brought. He drapes it over her head and touches her face gently. Her cheeks push back into a pleasant smile. Happy tears pool in her eyes.

Angus claps a rhythm. We put our hands together to the beat and dance for several moments. It doesn't matter to Tolliver and Kava that we don't have any drums to pound out the rhythm. We laugh together at the awkwardness as our claps echo around the room.

I hand Tolliver a piece of coal, symbolizing our family trade. Hollis hands Kava a leafy branch. "Pretend it is an herb," Hollis whispers and winks.

Kava chuckles and nods.

We walk together down the petal path, out the door into the courtyard. The flames of the bonfire are small, whipping back and forth. But it serves the purpose.

Tolliver and Kava lift their tokens and say together, "Through life into death, we combine into dust, never to be separated." They toss the branch and coal into the flames.

Before leaving the bonfire, Tolliver pauses and kisses Kava in front of us. The Balfour ceremony never includes kissing, partly because some of the unions are arranged marriages. But Tolliver and Kava's show of affection is quite fitting for their unique ceremony in the sky.

We walk to the dining hall and sit together around a high stone table. Angus fetches the meal. We eat the meat stew and talk about the future.

"When we get back, I'm going to build myself a house," Angus says.

"You can build me one too." Kava smiles and touches Tolliver's hand.

"When we get back, I'm going to go fishing." Tolliver swallows a bite of Kava's delicious meal. "And never eat grain again." We laugh together filling the hall with our voices.

Hollis says, "I'll go swimming. I'll climb an apple tree and eat fifteen apples. And," she pauses dramatically, as a smile spreads across her face. "I'm going to make a cake."

They all laugh at her comment, but I jam another bite of stew into my mouth. I don't say anything because I'm not ready to go home.

***

Day 203

"You did what?" Tolliver asks.

"I wanted it to be special," Hollis says crossing her arms.

"And you were involved with this?" He looks at me with intense brown eyes. I put my hands up, staying out of it. I take a step back and sit on the edge of the courtyard fountain. I distract myself by picking up tiny bits of gravel and tossing them into the fountain.

Hollis crosses her arms and pouts, "I survived, didn't I? It worked, didn't it?"

Tolliver stops for a moment and I see a revelation light in his head. He is concocting something.

"What?" I toss a stone into the pool with a plunk.

"Maybe we can climb down and hunt again." He scratches his head and says, "I miss a decent meal."

Hollis and I exchange glances and she winks at me. Swallowing back a laugh that almost burps out, I toss the rest of the gravel into the fountain.

"Show me how you did it," he says. Hollis uncrosses her arms and swiftly leads the way to the dungeon. We light a few torches at the bottom and make our way around the dragon's cage and out the underside of Ellery. I show Tolliver the pulley and gather the rope, ready to toss it off.

"Wait," he stops me. "What is that?"

We all look to the ground below. There are men wearing glistening silver armor on horseback riding in pace with Ellery. The island is closer to the ground than where Hollis gathered flowers.

The men notice us standing at the mouth of the cave. They could be shouting, but we can't hear them. Their arms wave wildly. Without helmets, I can see their skin is painted a solid color. Some are red, some blue, yellow and a few green except for the man leading the charge. His hair is brilliant white with skin that is pale and nearly as white.

Hollis waves to the men. I lean out and look around the

side of the rock toward the east and see a vibrant path before us. There are long rows of flowers leading to a castle in the distance.

"Look at that," I exclaim.

"What is going on?" Tolliver leans out to see. "Let's go up top for a better view."

Dropping the ropes, I follow Tolliver and Hollis back through the belly of Ellery. He calls for Angus and Kava as we race through the courtyard and around to the east lookout tower. We get to the ledge and gaze out at the expanse of colorful rows of flowers. It looks as though they are planted in a pattern along the path of our floating island. They lead to a city with a massive castle at the center.

Standing in awe at the sight, Hollis chatters on and on about the flowers, big and small, red and purple, how she wished she could climb down now for Kava's wedding flowers.

When Kava and Angus arrive, we don't need to direct them to the view because it is so vibrant and eye-catching.

"Holy goose farts!" Angus exclaims.

"I've never seen anything so beautiful," Kava gasps.

"Look, soldiers," Angus says, pointing to the northeast. I squint, just able to make out rows and rows of men in silver armor.

"There are horsemen riding directly beneath us too," Tolliver says. "We saw them out the dragon's cave." He puts the spyglass to his eye.

"Do they seem angry?" Kava grabs Tolliver's arm. "Are they going to attack?"

"Actually," I interject, "They seem happy to see us."

Scanning the landscape and the gray castle beyond, Tolliver says, "There are mounds of bags near the castle with soldiers guarding them. Maybe bags of food."

"For us?" Hollis asks.

"Not exactly us. For the Ellerians. Remember, it will be another three or four full moons until we reach the location where the Ellerians were lost," Tolliver explains.

"These people don't know the Sky People are gone." Hollis peers into the distance.

"We need that food," Angus says.

"We are never going to get down there to receive it," Kava says with sadness in her voice. "Besides they would notice we don't have wings."

"I don't want to risk getting captured again," Tolliver says.

"That was not fun," Hollis agrees.

"So, what do we do?" I search for an answer.

"Nothing," Tolliver replies. "We wait until we pass, then maybe we can talk about getting down to the ground to hunt again."

Angus looks at him with wide eyes and a bit of excitement as Tolliver explains our stunt to pick flowers. My face warms with embarrassment because of how silly it sounds. Angus, of course, who always loves a challenging adventure, loves the idea. My stomach fills with bile at the thought of trying it again.

31
COLORFUL WORLD

Day 203

The sun sets behind us as the castle of the colorful people comes into view. I inhale the scent of flowers and my heart thrums in my chest. The floral patterns become more intricate and swirl north and south as we near their city.

"Anything new happening?" Hollis walks up behind me, puts her hands on my shoulders, and rests her chin on her hands. I can smell her warm, sweet breath on my face.

"We're getting closer to the castle and there is something happening on the wide road in front of it," I say directing her attention to the ground before us.

She climbs up next to me on the tower's railing. "They are having some sort of ceremonial dance," she marvels.

"Yes, with twirling flags."

"I wonder what this would look like from Tristeh's cave," she says.

"I don't know if you could see all of it because the opening faces too far north."

We debate the path Ellery will take and decide we'd see it best if we walk out on the surface. Leaving the tower, I take a detour to the king's chambers to grab my blankets and a few small pillows to sit on. Hollis races off to find the others. I meet all four of them on the east side of the island. Tolliver and Angus bring an entire mattress to sit on, rendering my blanket idea useless.

Hollis jumps up and down clapping, unable to contain her excitement.

"Calm down, Hollis," Tolliver says.

She scowls at him and bounces on the balls of her feet. I shake my head with a smirk because she is acting the way I feel inside.

Tolliver and Kava settle into a comfortable position in each other's arms. Angus plops next to them and picks at his worn leather boots. I sit on the opposite side and Hollis joins me a little too closely. I give her a small pillow. Our hands graze each other, as she stuffs it in her lap. While she is distracted, I shrink away from her touch.

The parade below becomes more animated as we get closer. There are hundreds of colorful people. Their dark hair flails about as half of them twirl their vibrant flags.

"Oh my goodness," Hollis squawks, "Can you hear that?"

I hold my breath and strain to hear drums pounding a rhythm. Hollis bops to the beat. The thumping becomes more audible as we arrive at the castle of colorful flags and people.

The flag twirlers are wearing white swishy dresses, though the spectators surrounding them are dressed in miscellaneous drab colors of black and brown. Interspersed throughout the crowd are large tan circles. Three men surround a large drum, pounding them with mallets. They all play together, sending up a delightful rhythm.

The flag women toss their colorful flags and switch out flags mid-throw. They spin in circles with only blue flags matching the large one at the center of their castle. Their twirls and stops match the beat of the drums.

Hollis can't sit still next to me. She is on her knees bouncing up and down. Her eyes are bright, and a goofy grin is stuck on her face.

Tolliver and Kava nod to the beat. His arm is wrapped around her resting peacefully on her stomach. I have a flash of worry that she could end up with-child on this island.

Hollis jumps to her feet and yanks Angus off the mattress. I am grateful she makes him dance with her and not me. He stands with heavy feet and lets her dance around him. She twirls and grabs his big hands. As Hollis yanks herself back and forth, Angus laughs and bobs his head.

Tolliver and Kava laugh together. The evening sky fades to navy. We adjust our mat to stay within view of the celebration below. Sitting on the northern most point of the island's edge, the dance ends with a heavy drumbeat. I realize when it is all done I can barely see them under the cover of night.

We hear cheers rising up to the sky and I am filled with awe. All the voices, high and low blend in the air, sounding like a rushing river. A sudden noise explodes behind the castle. Hollis grabs me abruptly, squeezing tightly. I fear something has gone terribly wrong. We all pause, waiting for something bad to happen, when blue flames scream through the air at us, like hundreds of lit arrows.

My gut wrenches and Tolliver yells, “They are shooting at us!”

Hollis yelps and buries her face in my chest, pinching me in several spots with her tiny fingers. Tolliver gathers Kava to himself and we all run back to the safety of Ellery’s walls, when another pop is heard. Seconds later, the explosion lights up the sky again. Hollis screams. I cover her with my arm as we run.

We reach the entrance to the castle and race through the door, all except Angus.

“Where’s Angus?” I shriek.

“Did he get hit?” Kava’s voice wavers with panic.

Hollis cries and I rub her back, comforting her.

“Stay here,” Tolliver commands and steps out into the fray. I disobey, peering around the corner, worried for Angus. He is standing on the stairs gawking at the sky. After each explosion, sparks shoot through the heavens. My heart is pounding wildly in my chest.

I notice each pop is a different color. I can’t help but watch them burst into the air. What a spectacle. The sparks never come close enough to hit the island and gradually, we all emerge from our hiding places. In amazement, we watch the loud display of exploding colors and popping thunder. The sparks remind me of hammering a red-hot piece of metal on the anvil.

Hollis has long since released me, but I feel the need to be near her. Stepping behind her, I wrap my arms around her shoulders, and rest my chin on her head.

She sighs beneath my touch.

The powerful display in the sky ends with several quick

blasts igniting at the same time and showering us with several colors at once.

Hollis breaks the silence, "That was the most amazing thing I have ever seen."

Nodding in agreement, I look to the east. A glassy surface shimmers in the distance. More water. We follow Tolliver back to our mattress and blankets. The people below are dispersing. Torches are glowing all along the road leading to their castle and across the front to the surrounding white buildings with wood crosspieces. We gather our stuff off the rocky ground and head back inside.

I walk through my room to the balcony and sit on my favorite perch. Looking eastward, I think about the beautiful dance, playing it over and over in my mind. All of it was for the Sky People—for Alouette. I am surprised having seen how they are treated with such reverence.

I wonder why Balfour stays in such a remote location. They could be here, with these exciting, colorful people. Their lives are more advanced, with their lit streets and buildings of wood. With their enormous castle of thousands of people and best of all, their performance of dance, music, and sky flames. I think of Alouette and all the amazing things she's seen every year. I think of how small Balfour must be to her. She must think nothing of me. I am just another insect beneath her lofty world-traveling life.

Looking at the starry sky, I get the feeling I'm on a foolish mission in the scope of all of this. The Sky People probably found a lively city in which to settle and enjoy the lavish things of these more advanced settlements. Alouette is probably better off without me.

***

Day 211

Missing home, I hang my feet out over the edge of the dragon's cave and watch the surging waters. I think of Father's blacksmith workshop and how often I would tire of all the work he needed me to do, endlessly pumping the bellows to keep the furnace hot enough for an entire job. Sometimes I would have to stop a project right in the middle to assist my mother in woman's work. I daydream about my mother. I can feel her disappointment in me over the distance between us. She needed me, and I left her.

Sitting in the cave at the base of Ellery watching the sea pass below, it pulls at me. I want to drift away and not be here anymore. Suddenly, leaning too far, the wind catches my back just right and my body slips from the ledge. I instinctively scramble to hold onto something. Hollis's rope is a good arm's length away and I flail reaching for it. Grabbing hold at the last second, the rope burns and scrapes my hand as I fall a few feet off the side. I hold on for dear life and cry out, "I want to go home!"

My body is shaking, and my eyes are teary. I can't even muster the strength to hold on, let alone climb back up. My mother's face flashes through my mind, then Killian, Mila, Hazel and the new baby born only weeks before I left, and Father. I remember Hollis in the river splashing water on my good tunic. I laugh aloud in wild desperation and it echoes off the rocks in mock of my stupidity. I look below at the drifting surf and decide to climb. Hand over hand, I climb my way up the rope. The most difficult part is pulling myself over the ledge. The rope helps a little but the small sharp rocks dig into my chest and hands as I drag myself aboard.

I roll away from the edge and cry.

I cry and wail, not caring who hears me.

I want to go home.

***

Day 225

It's getting difficult to care about anything anymore, passing over another large body of water with no land in sight for days. I fear it will take as long as the previous ocean. I lay in my bed and stare up at the tan stone ceiling. It arcs up from the four corners of the room and peaks in the middle. In the center, a rod iron candelabra dangles from a rope hooked to the ceiling. The rope reminds me of Hollis, but I dismiss her blue eyes as fast as they come.

I imagine the king's servants, or helpers, or whatever he calls them, entering his chambers in the evening, unreeling the rope, lighting the candles, and hauling them back up. I wonder if it lights the room fully.

"Ledger," a small voice whispers my name. I don't answer, too tired to talk. Hollis enters and walks gently to my bedside. "When are you going to get out of that bed?"

I blink and look away, refusing to talk.

"I was thinking we could make a swing and hang it in the courtyard," she says.

I hear her, but my whole body feels like it is somewhere else. Some place dark and heavy.

"I brought the rope from Tristeh's cave and tied it six

levels up. It's pretty sturdy, I think." She leans over me, her words flowing, my body still in protest. "I may have tried it once without you. The knot on the end makes for a great seat. All you have to do is jump off the second floor railing."

Leaning close to my face, she reveals small pearlescent teeth. I breathe out and hope my rank breath wards her off. Her eyes wince slightly and she starts talking again. "Anyway, it is exhilarating. It's almost as thrilling as the time you dropped me off the bottom of Ellery. Almost," she says, poking me.

I don't want to think about her lying flat on her back wheezing in pain. That's my fault. A tear comes to my eye and I blink it quickly away.

"Oh, Ledger, come on. Come back," her voice sounds distant. I stare up at the ceiling. Sadness weighs on me, pressing me into the bed. My throat aches to swallow, and I can't even do that.

"You will find her." Hollis sits beside me on the bed. She places her small hand on my bare arm. I am so powerless as the tears threaten to surface again. I don't want Hollis to talk about Alouette. "She is probably out there waiting for you to find her," she continues. "And you will. I know you, Ledger. You're so stubborn. When you want something, you get it. You grit your teeth and dig your feet into the ground. You are unmovable when you're determined."

When she looks out the balcony door, I sneak a peek at her face. All I see is sadness hidden by a thin layer of pleasantness.

"But there's no sense in sitting around getting all sad and smelly." She catches my eye before I can go back into my dark hole. “You do stink, Ledger. Badly. I mean, like three-month man sweat and skunk kisses.”

My body involuntarily snorts in an attempt to stifle a laugh. I scrunch my forehead down and appear mad.

Hollis giggles and continues, “So, what do you say I draw you a bath and you stop offending my nose?” She pokes me in the side and I make a weird squawk. A tear comes out with it.

She leaps to her feet and talks about water temperature and soap. I don’t really care. My eyes betray me as tears spill down the side of my face. I don’t think we will find her. Alouette is probably far away from the path of Ellery. Or worse, killed by savage people who hold no honor for them. Maybe we should just ride this island home and I can go back to normal life. My familiar and safe life in Balfour. I should stop having big dreams that risk other people’s lives and get people into trouble.

PLUCKING 32

Day 232

Thankfully, the next few days are hazy. The yearlong wait is crushing. I refuse to leave my bed, so I don't have to see the endless water.

I think about what happened this morning. Hollis may have stripped me to my undergarments and pushed me in a bathtub, which she failed to heat sufficiently. I may have sat there in my own filth until my fingers were wrinkly. I got out when my teeth chattered, and my body convulsed from the cold.

After throwing on a new set of clothes, I set out in search of a bed that doesn't smell like skunky man sweat. Upstairs, I find a home no one has used. I walk to the back bedroom in a trance. Pulling back the neat blankets, I crawl inside.

Then I hear her. "Ledger?" Hollis's voice echoes up the tower. "I'm going to find you."

I grab a pillow and put it over my head in hopes to hide from her. I must have fallen asleep because in what seemed like moments later, Hollis squeals, "There you are."

She scuffs her way into my space and whips back the

blankets.

"We cannot do another day of this. It's just," she thinks for a moment and says, "not healthy."

Wrapping two little cold hands around my ankle, she drags me from the bed. The only thing that crosses my mind is the impossibility that her tiny frame can pull me off the bed and slam me to the floor. I must be losing weight after days of not eating much.

"Hollis, I need to be alone," I whimper, hating the way my voice sounds.

"No, I'm bored and need to do something fun or I will die."

What she needs will kill me. I curl into a ball on the floor and wait for her to leave. Then her bony fists start hitting.

"I need assistance on my exciting new swing."

I groan. As soon as the word 'Fine' escapes my lips, she stops punching and helps me up. I drag my body from the ground and follow her out. Grabbing the rope, she shows me how to sit on the knot and jump. I hear her voice, see her mouth move, but my mind is foggy. I don't care what she is saying, probably more chatter and wordy excitement. She jumps and goes sailing halfway across the courtyard. Her squeal echoes up the tower as her hair flies in streaks of yellow, eyes wide and full of the thrill. I sigh as she comes to a stop, climbs over the railing in front of me and offers me the rope.

I shake my head and she spends several minutes trying to convince me to do it. I can't. I just can't. She tries to put the rope into my hand. My arms hang limp at my sides.

"I want to see you do it again," my monotone voice

requests.

"Really?" She gladly takes another ride. I pretend to laugh when she attempts to land on top of the fountain in the middle, but kicks the statue in the face instead.

She laughs and laughs so hard she can barely get herself back over the railing. I have to help her up. I force a big fake smile trying to participate in her joy, but I am hollow and tired.

"Hey, come check this out," Tolliver shouts from below.

Hollis bounds down the stairs and I follow slowly after. When I reach them on the east lookout tower, my eyes sting from the bright sun bouncing off the beige stone. We are approaching land. The edge of the sea meets a steep cliff with a series of roads and white washed houses made of some sort of smooth white clay. Mountains jut out to the northeast.

Peoplc come and go from their homes: a woman hanging up wet clothes, a man walking a mule with a load on its back up a path. There are little blackened windows in each home and some have pots of small red flowers adorning their stoop. As we float by, we are probably the width of Ellery away. There is no chance of jumping across that gap.

"How beautiful," Hollis marvels. I blink emotionless and wonder why I have to care anymore. Hollis waves and yells, "Hello."

"They can't hear you," Tolliver says.

"I know that." She waves again. "What's that?" She points at an enormous boat with white fabric draped across the top.

"It's like Thelonious's raft," Tolliver explains. "Except bigger."

"Let me see," Angus says grabbing the spyglass. I am having trouble staying focused on everything I'm seeing. I can't care anymore. I walk away and wonder if I can make it back to my new clean bed before my brain shuts down.

***

Day 237

"We are passing through hill country," Hollis explains even though I don't care. "They're covered in trees. It's quite beautiful. Oh, and Tolliver said tonight is the last new moon before summer solstice. Can you believe it? Summer is almost here." I nod, trying not to hurt her feelings, even though her words are invading my space. "I came to get you because Angus and Tolliver went hunting yesterday. Kava is making roast duck." She smiles and continues to chatter on about food and vegetables and stuff that doesn't matter, while playing with a handful of feathers.

"Why?" I ask suddenly. I'm not prepared to say it aloud, but out it comes.

Hollis stops, a little shocked that I said something. "Why what?" She lays her hand on my arm.

"Why do you keep finding me and talking to me?"

She opens her mouth to say something and I interrupt her answer. "You could easily ignore me and go on with your day."

"I love you, Ledger," Hollis's lower lip quivers and her eyes sadden. "I know you're not doing well and I want to cheer you up."

I suddenly don't know what to say. Of course she would

say that. What was I expecting? I am so foggy I don't even have any sort of reply in a conversation I initiated. I grind my teeth and try to think of something to say. But, it doesn't matter. She fills the silence.

"You did it for me when I broke my leg," she says. "Remember all those stupid stories you made up?" She half laughs, half shrugs. "I needed you then, and you need me now."

And that is all there is to it.

My eyes sting with tears at her sad truth.

"So, that means I have to sing a song for you." She grabs a couple sticks from the pile of kindling near the fireplace and taps them on the mantle, while singing a weird made-up song about hunting ducks, plucking ducks, and eating ducks for dinner.

I really want to laugh for her, and even though my insides are stuck in a permanent frown I manage to smile at the sweet girl with the sticks.

***

Day 303

"Ledger, wake up," Tolliver commands, jolting me from a dream. "We are being boarded and we have to hide."

I sit up slowly, my head swimming with sleep. I cannot grasp whether Tolliver is really here until he shouts, "Get up!"

"Okay, I'm up," I groan.

"Put this on." He hits me in the face with the clean white tunic. My body complies before my brain realizes what I am doing.

"We've already got everything we need," he says. "This time we are going up the tower as far as we can get before they get here."

As soon as the shirt drapes down over my chest he grabs a handful of it and hauls me out of bed. "If you don't walk, I will throw you over my shoulder."

Bleary eyed, I rub my face and follow him out the door to the stairwell. He bounds up the steps two at a time. Taking a deep breath, I scurry after him, stumbling a few times. Round and round we go, up and up. Gradually, I lose feeling in my legs and they move on their own. When we reach the second floor from the top of the tower I have to stop to catch my breath. The air is thin and my lungs are aching to draw a substantial breath.

"Come see what they are doing," Angus calls from one of the homes. "They shot some sort of hook into the side of the island and are climbing up."

Tolliver swears. We follow Angus to the back window. We lean out one at a time, because the upper windows are smaller than the ones on the lower levels.

Breathing is still difficult as I lean out and see men climbing onto Ellery. They are all dressed in black from head to toe with only their eyes showing. They sneak across the surface toward the grand entrance.

I barely feel the weight of this intrusion. The thought of encountering strangers makes me want to get back in bed and sleep until we get home.

"Let's barricade the door," Angus suggests.

Tolliver agrees, and they set off together to move

furniture in front of it.

Kava announces near the window, "They're inside."

"Now we wait," Tolliver declares, sitting on the bed. Hollis clutches her chest and looks around anxiously. Kava busies herself down the hall near the hearth, organizing the food they brought all the way up.

I walk around to the other side of the bed that is really a pile of mattresses and curl up.

When I awake again, unsure of how long I slept, I hear Tolliver and the others in the kitchen.

"There are so many of them. They are searching the castle. Eventually, they will find us, so we should probably make a plan now, just in case we are captured."

They discuss a few things that sound stupid to me.

I hear Hollis say, "Why did we come here? This is such a waste. We're all going to die." I hear something slam. "And for what?" she demands.

Someone hushes her. I'm not sure if it's to keep me from hearing her words or to keep the intruders from locating us.

"Don't shush me, Tolliver!" Hollis squawks. "Ledger brought us all here to die!"

"It's not only Ledger's fault," Tolliver whispers. He continues so quietly I have to hold my breath to hear him. "I'm as much to blame."

"What the blazes are you talking about?" Hollis asks.

"Shhh, I found out something last harvest," Tolliver's voice wavers.

Last harvest, what happened last harvest? I wonder.

"Just say it, Toll," Kava says.

"I found out I am Ellerian," he says. The confession

strangles me. I attempt to swallow. My heart thrums in my chest.

"I caught Ledger with an Ellerian girl. I told my mother who he was with and she explained where I came from. I am a wingless Ellerian. They kill the wingless ones. She said they pitch them off the island." I hear the anger in his voice. "I was smuggled off Ellery and into Balfour when I was only a few weeks old."

"My stars, Tolliver," Angus says. "Why didn't you tell me?"

"What was I going to say?" he asks. "Hey, Angus, I'm not really your cousin, I'm your enemy?"

Angus chokes out a single laugh, but it isn't funny. He stops himself short. They continue talking about an escape plan and my mind is shutting down. This can't be real. This can't be true. The more I deny it, the more my heart slows. I let the darkness consume me again and dream of Alouette. Her people find us and rescue us from black dragons with masks that reveal only their eyes.

SKY PRISON 33

I awake to a scuffle. There is shouting in a language I don't understand. My head is heavy and when I open my eyes, black hands pluck me from the bed and drag me to the kitchen. I am pushed face first to the ground. My cheek burns from scraping the stone. A foot presses down in the middle of my back.

More words I don't understand.

Then Tolliver begs, "Please, please don't."

I hear Kava cry out and twist my head to see what is happening. One of the masked men has a hold of Kava with a knife to her throat. Angus is crushed beneath all the furniture that is shoved away from the door. His eyes are closed, and he isn't moving. Panic claws at my dull mind.

"We don't know where the people of Ellery are," Tolliver garbles. Another man has him pushed against a wall with a forearm pressed against his neck. I squirm looking for Hollis. She is gone.

"Hollis," I squawk. "Where is Hollis?" My temples hurt from the pressure inside my head and on my back.

The man holding Kava says something and drags her out the door.

Tolliver yells after them and his captor does a quick move, yanking him off the wall and whirling him around so that his arm is twisted behind his back. He pushes Tolliver out the door.

Strong hands grab me by the collar and haul me to the balcony. I don't fight the man in black escorting me down the stairs, so he doesn't throw me down the way Tolliver's captor does.

Tolliver tumbles down three steps and hits the landing hard. With two hands, the man rips him from the floor and pushes him toward the balcony railing and yells something in his face, probably warning him not to struggle or he will throw him over.

I take a deep breath, keeping my pounding heart under control. Tolliver makes eye contact with me and his confession comes flooding into my mind. He is Ellerian. I can't even think about it right now. I shake my head adamantly at him, warning him not to fight back. Tolliver relaxes his muscles and complies.

It takes a long time to descend all the way to the ground floor, but we don't stop there. The masked men escort us down the stairs leading to the dungeon. We walk swiftly through the hall of prison cells lit with torches.

Hollis wails at the end of the hall and my insides twist as Tolliver and I are thrown into separate cells.

"Hollis, are you okay?" I yell to her. My shoulder hits the hard ground and pain jars me. Her screaming cuts through me, forcing me off the floor as the man in black locks the door and leaves. "Hollis, are you hurt?" I yank at the cell door. It doesn't budge. She doesn't respond. I must find a way to get to her. Pacing around the dark cell, I inspect all the shadowy corners for some way to escape, dig or pry. There is no window. There is no other exit.

"Hollis," Tolliver calls. "Hollis, please stop."

She continues to cry uncontrollably. Her voice echoes so loud it garbles in my ears.

"Hollis," Kava says several times unable to calm her down.

Eventually, her weeping slows.

I push my face between the bars hoping to see the cell she is in. The one across from me is empty. "Hollis," I say with a scratchy throat. "You're okay."

"No, I'm not, Ledger!" Hollis screams at me sounding like a wildcat. She weeps for a moment and says, "We're not okay. We're locked in a prison. You saw what happened to that person that got locked in here with no water."

"I just meant—"

"I know what you meant, and I don't care," she growls. "We're all going to die down here." She sobs. I imagine her rocking back and forth, holding herself.

Not saying anything for a long time, our predicament churns around us like rising floodwaters. Hollis is losing it. Angus is missing. Tolliver is Ellerian. And we're locked in a dungeon. Sadness ebbs at the edge of my vision and I refuse to give it a chance to flow through me again. Gritting my teeth, I think, I've got to find a way out of here. I can't shut down. I won't.

***

Day 305

Two days the men in black masks have left us down here without food or water. My head aches with thirst. Shortly after they locked us up, they dragged Angus down and tossed him into the cell across from me in a rumpled heap of brown clothes and red hair. He woke up on the second day with a huge lump on his forehead.

Footsteps echo from the stairs and scuff down the prison hall toward us. I scoot away from the door to avoid being seen. Something metal hits the floor outside my cell and scrapes against the stone. It's a bowl of boiled grain. I scramble to the bowl and eat it without taking a breath. The moisture of the gray mush soothes my dry throat. I finish it quickly and my body aches for more. I sigh, thinking about the fact that I desire this nasty slop that I've been sick of eating since the second week on this island.

"Thank you," a female voice says from the end of the hall. Probably Kava.

"You are welcome," the guard responds with an unfamiliar accent.

"Wait," Tolliver calls. "You speak our language?"

"A little," he says.

"Why are you holding us?" Tolliver asks.

"I am not. My master is."

"Will you let us go?"

"I cannot," the guard says.

"We are starving and my friend, he is hurt."

The man pauses and says, "I am sorry. Master wants

payment."

"Payment for what?"

"We supply Ellery with," the guard stops for a moment then continues, "Items they need. Difficult to find. We find. Ellery pays much."

"But they are gone," Tolliver says.

"Yes, and he want someone to pay," the man says.

"Why don't you tell him we don't want the items?"

The guard walks up the hall, stopping near my door and replies, "I cannot." He is covered from head to heel in black, with black boots and a black mask. His eyes are far apart and when he looks at me, I shrink back from the torchlight.

"He can have Ellery. We will get off the island, and he can have it. The whole thing. That can be his payment," Tolliver says.

The man snickers. "He already took it from you." He continues to the stairs.

"Wait, please," Tolliver calls.

The sound of his footsteps fades into the darkness.

34
OH LITTLE MUSH

Day 306

The next day, more mush and a pouch of water are sitting outside my cell when I awake. It is Hollis's water pouch—the small tan, bean shaped pouch. I draw it to me and practically hug it. I want to scarf down the food, but decide to eat and drink sparingly. I may not eat again until tomorrow.

"Why are you doing that?" I peer over into Angus's cell and his dish is empty. He is shirtless, pushing his body up and down off the floor, exercising his arms. His face is almost as red as his hair and his eyes are focused. I can hear his loud raspy breaths. He stands up and lunges forward with one leg, then the next.

"Just in case I get the chance to kick that man in the mindyberries," Angus replies, flashing me a smile.

I chuckle halfheartedly and stand to mimic Angus's actions. Lunge right, lunge left, back and forth. On the floor, push up, let down, push up, let down. My arms and chest burn. It makes me angry, but I keep going. I think about Hollis and how afraid she must be. I wish she were across the hall from me, so I can see her. So I can read her face and understand why she hasn't said anything since yesterday.

"This is the season, Ledger," Tolliver's voice carries down the hall. Anger rises from deep in my gut. I don't want to hear his voice. I can't deal with him right now.

"The season for what?" Angus stifles a cough and continues with his push-ups.

With clenched teeth, I finish my last set of pushups. Sweat drips from my face.

"When the Ellerians went missing," Tolliver says. My mind snaps to attention as I sit back on my knees.

"We have to get out of here, so we can scout for them," I say.

"Even if you found them, what makes you think they'd want to get back on this floating rock?" The bitterness in Tolliver's voice is unmistakable.

"I don't know." I think for a moment about what might happen if I say her name in front of Hollis and take a deep breath. "Alouette would have told me they were leaving the island. So something must have happened. They are in trouble. I just know it."

"Maybe," he says with a deep sigh. "If we ever get out of here and back home, promise me one thing."

"What?" I try not to sound hateful.

"No more traveling."

I don't answer because frustrating questions bubble to the surface about Tolliver. I don't get it. I can't sort out whether he is telling the truth and why he hasn't told me about being Ellerian yet. Should I bring it up? The thought of arguing with him makes bile churn in my stomach. I dismiss the thoughts as I hear a quiet scuff up the hall and wonder if someone is coming. Several minutes pass and no one emerges from the prison entrance. Maybe they have a guard posted down there.

"Hollis," I call.

There is no answer.

"Can anyone see into her cell?" My voice echoes down the hall.

"No," Tolliver replies. "She is across from Kava."

"Kava?"

"She's fine, Ledger," Kava says with snide disdain. I imagine Hollis and Kava glaring at each other from across the hall in agreement about my unacceptability.

"I wanted to make sure she is still breathing," I say. It is the wrong thing to say. I wish I could have said something sweet or witty. But nothing comes to mind. So I go back to sweating. I leap to my feet and jump up, legs outstretched, hands up, jump again with legs together and arms down, up, down, up, down. Anger boils to the surface and disappointment leaks out of my skin in sweat droplets.

The next day when the mush is plopped in front of my door I sing, "Oh little mush, slimy on the outside, squishy in the middle. Oh little mush." My voice echoes down the hall. I know Hollis can hear me, so I keep singing. "Oh little pouch, warm and tangy water, smelly like old man feet. Oh little pouch."

I hear Tolliver laugh, but not Hollis. I keep going, "Oh little mush."

"Oh my stars, stop it!" Kava yells.

"Little gray bird droppings, slides on down like mucus. Oh little mush."

I hear a little girlish giggle that might have been Hollis. Kava yells, "Gross! Please stop singing. You're going to make me vomit."

Satisfied getting one little laugh from Hollis, I acquiesce.

We will survive this. I remember what Hollis said about me being stubborn. She is right. I can dig my heels in and wait for the perfect moment to escape.

***

Day 309

By the sixth day in the prison, I have Hollis singing with me about the mush and its gooey chewiness when the man in black brings our food. The hole in my chest fills with every giggle that comes from the golden-haired girl in the cell across the hall and two doors down.

I continue to work my muscles with Angus. It hardly pains me anymore to push my body off the ground, lunge forward, or squat and jump. Angus teaches me how to fist fight and high kick. I jab the rock wall, bruising my knuckles, but I don't care. I am stronger each day even though I'm cooped up like an animal.

"We need to get out of here," I say to Angus.

"You have any ideas? I'm up for a challenge." Breathing heavily, Angus swings his foot in the air at the invisible attacker.

"If we could just get out of these stupid cells, we could climb down the ropes Hollis and I used to gather flowers." I grunt and step forward kicking my left leg in the air. I practice over and over, swinging higher each time.

"Can't," Angus says mid-kick.

"Why?"

"I used those ropes," he says.

I want to scream at him. I take a deep breath reaching down in the pit of my stomach and pull out some patience. "What did you use them for?"

"To make a rope ladder."

His response surprises me. When did he have time to do that? I wonder, and he answers my thoughts.

"When you were crazy as a whistling pig, I made a rope ladder for Tolliver and me to go hunting. Remember the roasted boar we had?"

The word roasted causes my stomach to growl. "We have a rope ladder?" I say with a smile, leaning on the bars of the door to catch my breath. That's perfect. "So maybe it's time we get a hold of the guard and break his fingers until he unlocks these cells," I say.

Angus bursts out laughing. I want to laugh with him. But I'm pretty sure he is laughing at me. His face flushes and he bends over holding his knees. It ends with a short coughing fit. "I've never heard you say a violent word in your life." He chuckles and clears his throat. "That's not a bad idea. But you couldn't break someone's fingers. I'll do it."

I smile at my cousin and let him have it. "I didn't mean I would do it. I was just making suggestions."

"Sure, Ledge, sure you were." Sweat glistens on his forehead as he winks his dark blue eyes at me.

***

Day 310

"What was that?" Hollis asks from down the hall. Several of the torches have burned out and the darkness is encroaching. But I don't care. We have an escape plan. It just takes the right moment.

I am laying on the floor with my feet propped on the wall. "I didn't hear anything."

Then I hear a distant screech.

"There it is again," she whispers excitedly. "Sounds like Tristeh."

"Who is Tristeh?" Tolliver is confused.

"My dragon," Hollis says.

We all listen as the shriek gets closer followed by a loud thud. Bits of stone fall from the ceiling into my eyes. Sitting up, I rub them.

"Something's happening," Hollis's voice wavers.

A roar peals through the halls and my heart leaps into my throat. "It's in the grand hall," I say, finally free of the dust in my eyes.

"Oh, that's not Tristeh," Hollis says disappointed.

"How can you tell?" Angus asks.

"That one is much lower," she explains. "And more intense. It might be an older dragon or a male."

"Oh, my lucky pig, I've never been more glad to be locked in a cell," Angus exclaims.

Footsteps scramble down the stairs into our hall. "It is time for you to go," the man in black says. With jingling keys, he unlocks the cell at the far end first. Hollis's door swings open with a squeal and a clunk. Then Kava's and

Tolliver's. His dark eyes focus on unlocking my cell door.

I assess Tolliver through the bars as they approach my cell. His pale hair is long and hangs in his face. His jaw is scruffy with auburn stubble. I bottle the questions and anger as if corking an agitated bottle of ale. I can't deal with him right now, I decide.

Another screech rips through the air. A loud thud shakes the ground below and rocks above, dropping dust and pebbles on our heads as my door swings open. Hollis grabs my arm. Her tunic and black trousers are coated with fine gray dust.

"Wait, what is happening?" Kava's face and brown dress are dirty and disheveled.

"Obviously, the castle is under attack by a dragon," I snap.

"You don't know that," she says. "It could be something else."

"Three dragons," the man says. "Need to go."

Angus grabs the guard in a chokehold when his door is unlocked. "Where are you taking us?"

The man gasps for air and replies, "I help you get off Ellery."

"Angus, let him go," Tolliver says, putting a hand on Angus's bulging muscles clamped around the guard's neck. Angus drops his arms. Instead of reacting defensively, the guard leads us through the hall. He starts to ascend the stairs. Tolliver stops him. "Where are you going?"

"Out. My men leaving, climbing down."

"This way." Tolliver redirects us toward Tristeh's cave.

We run down the stairs in the pitch black, all the way

around Tristeh’s cage to the mouth of the tunnel leading outside, headlong into a dark and angry sky. Intense winds hit us in the face.

UNDER THEIR WINGS 35

A storm rages all around us. Lightning flashes and thunder booms hitting Ellery, making the entire island shake. On the far side of the cave opening lies a huge pile of ropes and wooden rungs. I can't conceive how long it took Angus to put together such a lengthy rope ladder. Tolliver and Angus grab the end and toss section after section over the side. Thunder growls through the air, as the ladder unravels on its own off the side of Ellery.

"Kava will go first, then Hollis, Ledger and Angus," Tolliver explains. The thunder obscures his voice momentarily. Hollis's body jolts at the sound and I put a hand on her back. Tolliver waits for it to stop, then points northeast to a grouping of birch trees and says, "Hide in that tree line over there and wait for me."

"Are you sure this is safe?" Kava worries with her hands on her cheeks, watching the last section of the ladder topple over the side.

"Of course it's safe. I built it," Angus says, offended. "We've already used it to hunt on the ground once, remember?"

"Just be careful," Tolliver says and kisses her forehead.

A deafening bolt snaps through the air startling Kava. "I'm more concerned about getting struck by lightning."

"Maybe I should go first," Angus offers. "Then I can help them off the ladder." Kava is relieved to not have to go first, relaxing her tense hands.

"Fine," Tolliver says. "Watch how Angus gets over the edge. That's the hard part. Climbing down is the easy part."

Angus adjusts the ladder, so it lays flat against the ground. He sits on the gravel surface and rolls onto his belly, sliding his knees over the edge. With a hand on each rope, he shimmies down until his feet land on a rung of the rope ladder.

I catch a glimpse of a bright streak cutting through the forest striking a tree north of the spot where we're supposed to meet. Hollis is startled by the sudden crack. Then another sound makes her arms prickle and my heart rate accelerate. A dragon's high shriek peals through the sky above. Before Angus climbs down, he looks at us with terrified eyes and nostrils flaring.

"Just go, man," Tolliver shouts. Angus's throat bobs as he swallows hard and descends out of view.

The sky grumbles all around us as Kava gets into position. Her skirts lie in a heap at her feet and she looks pleadingly at Hollis. Pulling away from me, Hollis helps tie her skirts together between her legs, like big ballooning pants. Tolliver kneels on the other side of her and says to Hollis, "You hold that arm, and I'll hold this one as she gets her feet on the ladder." She nods.

Breathing heavily, Kava looks at Tolliver with tears in her eyes and says, "I can do this." She lowers herself over the edge. He smiles at her and lets go as she climbs down into the tempest.

Hollis doesn't waste any time sitting, rolling over, and sliding out over the drop off before I have time to assist her. I get on my knees beside the rope ladder and watch as she disappears below.

"Get them into the woods where it's safe," Tolliver says. Another violent crash of lightning strikes the island and anger rolls through me at his command. I can't stop shaking even after the thunder stops rumbling. The sheet of rain is almost upon us. I bottle up all the thoughts that are stirring in me—about Tolliver, about climbing down a rickety ladder in a dangerous storm and force myself across the gravel. It takes a second for my foot to find a rung. Once I do, I scrape my chest along the edge and lower rung-by-rung into the blustering wind. The muscles in my arms twitch with each release and grab. The rope ladder jerks underneath me and I worry that someone has fallen off. I can't see directly below me, but I look up to see Tolliver gripping the ladder and climbing down toward me.

A bolt of lightning streaks across the sky and an unmistakable roar rips through the air. A giant mass of flesh and scales topples from the surface of Ellery. I halt, watching a black scorched dragon roll and plummet to the ground. It lands in a grouping of trees and sounds like another clap of thunder as branches crack and break beneath its enormous weight.

My heart beats wildly as I hurry my descent. Tolliver

is only a few rungs above me and I'm only halfway down. Once I pass the end of the jagged rocks on the underside of Ellery the wind thrashes relentlessly. It pushes and twists the ladder. I could fall at any moment. The rain rushes in and I wait for it to soak me. Instead, Ellery blots it out and aside from intermittent mist on the wind, the rain misses me altogether.

The lightning strikes come quickly now, hitting all around. A crash to the east, a boom to the north, I can hardly hear the torrential rain until I reach the end of the thrashing ladder.

Angus is on the ground below, unable to reach the last rung with his hands fully extended above his head. I search the ground for Hollis and Kava. They are nowhere to be found.

They must have had to jump. If they can jump, I can jump. I hear Angus's voice through the splatter of rain. He is telling me to climb down and jump. I follow his directions, until I am hanging from the last rung. I gulp, count to three and let go as a clap of lightning rattles my teeth together. I hit the ground, biting my tongue and pain shoots up my left leg. Angus hauls me upright by the arm and yells, "They're over there!"

The solid ground fills me with resilience. I dash into the gushing rain to the small grouping of birch trees where I find Hollis and Kava shivering under the shielding leaves. I run to Hollis and hug her. I lift her and squeeze a giggle out of her. I'm glad we are alive.

Tolliver leaps from the ladder and runs through the torrent toward us.

"Come on," Tolliver says, not slowing down. "Let's go."

"I'm ready," I say when another lightning bolt claps around us. A masked man surprises all of us barreling through the brush. Hollis screams and Tolliver shields Kava. Angus puts his fists up, ready to defend. My insides jolt and I step in front of Hollis.

"You have a better way down," the man in the black says, bowing slightly.

"Oh, it's you," Angus says, recognizing the guard's voice. He relaxes his fists.

"My name is Jin," he says and removes his wet mask. Out topples a long black braid. His face is wide and his chin is smattered with facial hair circling his mouth.

The canopy shields us from the pounding rain. Beneath the branches only a few droplets make it through. As the sky continues to rumble, we tell him our names.

Hollis gasps. Standing out from under the trees looking up at Ellery, she points and says, "There are three of them. They are enormous."

We all take in the view of Ellery swarming with dragons. One is perched on Ellery's surface, another circles the air above it and the third is crawling out the grand entrance with a man in black clutched in its powerful jaws. Relief floods my body as I realize what we just avoided.

Lightning surges through the clouds and strikes the surface of Ellery. I leap back at the violent crack that sends shards of stone into the air.

"We need to find somewhere safe to hide," Tolliver says and Jin agrees. They lead us up the side of the hill into thicker brush and trees until we can no longer see Ellery. The rain gushes down on us until we can barely see very far in front of us. Hollis is soaked and her hair clings to her face and neck. As we crest the top of the hill we stop short of a small clearing.

Through the sheets of gray rain, I gape at what we find hanging dead. Lightning lights up the opening in the trees, making it difficult to miss the two Ellerian men hanging upside down from tall posts. A shocked silence washes over us. Expansive wings stretch double their height. The display of their disfigured and decaying bodies hits me like a mace to the chest. Swallowing back bile, I am unable to move. Terror pours over me like hot oil burning my resolve as my friends make their way across the clearing.

"Come on, Ledge," Angus encourages. He wraps a strong arm around me and we walk under their wings.

No one says a word as we follow a well-beaten path away from Ellery and away from the ghastly sight. I don't need to push back the tears; they just blend in with the rain and pour down my cheeks. Hollis takes my hand, pressing her tiny fingers between mine.

"It's probably not a good idea to follow this road right into the dragon's home," Tolliver says.

"Dragons didn't do that," Hollis says.

Jin agrees, "Not dragons." He directs us up the side of a wooded hill. We walk a short distance into the wilderness within view of the path below. The wind carries the storm east. Each rumble of thunder sounds farther and farther away. The rain tapers off to a steady drizzle and I wipe my face, regaining my composure. At the top of the next hill, Jin halts and signals that he will take a look first. He crawls to the top and watches for a moment. Waving us up, we sneak up the hill.

In the next valley, a castle is being built. On all sides, winged men and women work on the structure with shackles on their ankles. They lift heavy stones, building another wall. But the chains keep them on the ground. Their wings are dirt-spattered and their movements are sad and slow in the sprinkling rain.

On the eastern side is a row of men with their ankles chained together digging a slimy muddy ditch. They swing and scoop the muck together. Water rushes into it swirling the brown silt.

Nausea fills me when I remember who I am here to find. Alouette is in this place. Dizzy with fear, I wonder, what have they done to her? Is she even alive?

I look for a girl with dark hair, but they all have dark hair. I look for her little green dress and white wings. They are all in brown rags and dirty tunics. Their wings are wet and matted from the rain and mud.

Tolliver pulls us back. "Whose castle is this?"

"They call him Roi du Ciel," Jin says. "He started building many moons ago. I did not know he made slaves of Ellery." He shakes his head.

"We have to save her," I blurt.

At that moment, three dragons call to each other in the sky as they fly over our heads low enough to the trees I can see straps and a harness on their underside. Men ride them.

"Look, Hollis, dragon riders," I say.

We watch them land on the east side of the castle. Men in tan robes dismount from the dragons, hook lead ropes to their saddle harnesses and walk them into a cave on the far side of the valley.

"What if Tristeh is in there?" Hollis is full of hope.

"No," Tolliver replies, "We are not rescuing a dragon too."

ENSNARED BIRD 36

"I must go to my men. I need to see if alive," Jin says.

"What? No," Hollis pleads. "We need you."

I elbow her and scowl. She backs away in a pout.

"I must." He bows slightly and places a hand on Tolliver's shoulder. Their eyes meet and Tolliver nods.

Jin wraps his braid around his head, pulls his mask down over his face and scurries off into the wilderness. I watch him go, barely hearing his footsteps. His stealth and agility conceal his movements.

We follow the ridge around the east side of the mountains toward the dragon cave. We walk quietly out of sight of the castle and the winged slaves.

I need to find Alouette and her family and make sure she is okay. Not knowing where to start, I consider sneaking down among the Ellerian prisoners and asking them, but I'm not sure who is holding them captive or their capabilities.

"This is a bad idea," Tolliver says, following behind Hollis and me.

"I have to see if she is here," Hollis says. "You don't

have to come."

"Hollis and I can go in together," I state. "You guys can stay outside and stand guard."

"No way," Angus answers. "We don't have any weapons. Maybe we can find some in there."

"We stay together," Tolliver says.

The cave isn't being guarded. Inside are enormous cages built into the walls. Metal bars block off branches of caverns. We peer into several along the main corridor finding dragons in each. One hisses at us as we pass, another looks with mild curiosity. Shrieking and clawing echoes from farther down the tunnel.

"I don't think we should go down there," Kava says. "This is far enough."

"Please, please let me see if she is in here," Hollis pleads with determination in her eyes. She rumples her hair and shakes water droplets all around like a wet dog.

Tolliver nods and says, "We'll stay hidden here. You sneak around that corner and take a look." Tolliver guides Kava and Angus into a small, dark crevice in the wall.

"I'm going with," I whisper and follow her.

We slide along the wall and crouch low to look around the bend in the cave. Beyond a wall of bars, there are seven men surrounding a large green dragon in the center of a huge round cavern.

Several men hold torches and one at the head holds a rope tied to its muzzle. The jaws are clamped shut. Letting out a muffled shriek, it rears up on its hind legs.

"It's not her," Hollis whispers, shoulders drooping. "Maybe she couldn't fly this far."

"Come on, Hollis," I say. "Let's go."

She hangs her head and follows me back to the crevice. When we return, the others are gone. "Where are they?"

I wrap an arm around her. As we inch forward, I tiptoe making sure my footfalls are as silent as Jin's. Hollis scuffs a couple of times and I point at her feet then put a finger to my mouth shushing her.

We creep back through the cave until we hear voices. My ears perk up at our language echoing down the halls. "What do you want me to do with them?"

"Take them to Ciel," a man says.

"I'm not taking them. You take them," a nervous voice says. "He will not be pleased to hear we allowed trespassers in the stables."

"Then don't tell him. Say you found them in the woods."

I look at Hollis. She is nervously chewing on a piece of her hair. Looping my finger around it, I gently pull it out.

I am startled by a loud crack from behind us as a sharp pain shoots through my lower back. A man with a whip swings it in the air preparing to lash out again. I gasp and whirl around facing him, blocking his access to Hollis. He snaps the whip with a flick of his wrist and wraps it around us both. Hollis screams as it bites into her skin. It's like a hundred bee stings all in a row.

The man is a head shorter than I am, but his wings unfurl aggressively behind him making him appear taller. He gestures toward the mouth of the cave, forcing us to join our friends, where he untangles the black leather whip from around us.

The man with the whip asks, "Who are these children in

my stables?"

"We are taking them to Roi du Ciel," the taller one says with a blade in his hand.

"Then do it," he barks. They tie our hands behind our backs with strips of rope. I inspect their large gray wings, powerful and moving as if they were an arm or leg. Hollis is wide eyed gaping at them. She winces when one of them walks by and grazes her arm with his feathery tip. I can't help but wonder if they are Ellerian, unless there is another winged race in this enormous world.

It is a long walk through the muck to the castle. I slip several times and nearly fall on my face because my hands are tied behind my back. As we walk across a makeshift bridge over the ditch the winged slaves are digging, some of them stop and stare.

The mud cakes on the bottom of my feet and I tiptoe carefully to avoid slipping again. Inside the archway of the east gate we follow the taller stableman into a wide hallway. On one side are tall window openings overlooking a messy courtyard still in the process of being built. There, several women with leather straps on their wings kneel with their hands in the dirt. My heart aches at the thought of Alouette's wings being tied down like some ensnared bird and being forced to work.

Midway down the hall the men lead us through an enormous doorway into a throne room twice the size of the one on Ellery. The walls are a gray stone and the floor is some sort of smooth black rock I've never seen before. I am surprised by how shiny it is and peer down at our reflections. I am dirty and disheveled.

There are several groupings of winged men and women, dressed in fancy clothing and jewels all around the room. They pause mid-conversation and gawk at us being escorted to the king.

On the throne is a wingless man with piercing eyes. His short silvery hair spikes up around a thin gold crown. His eyebrows are dark and tipped angrily at us. My insides clench.

The stableman leads us to the foot of the platform on which the single throne sits. He takes a knee before Roi du Ciel. The man behind us does the same. The entire room is quiet. All eyes are on us. The silence jars me like a thousand stones being thrown at the same time. I don't understand why no one is saying anything. The nervous man grabs the front of Tolliver's shirt and yanks downward. Tolliver falls to his knee and one by one we all lower ourselves before the king. My face burns and my heart thrums wildly. I hold my breath, bringing it under control.

The king speaks in a deep powerful voice, "What is this?"

"Your majesty," the nervous man says with head still bowed. "We found them wandering around the... in the woods." His voice cracks on the last word as he lies and gulps down a breath.

"Perfect," the king bellows. "Our first grounder prisoners. Throw them in the dungeon for trespassing."

Looking around from my kneeling position, I notice several people seated on the right side of the room. Three women sit on a padded bench with a serving of tea before them on a round table. Their white wings are folded neatly, and their dainty hands are poised in the air with teacups. One of them, a woman with dark hair and brown eyes, jolts. Her face goes white and she drops her cup. Alouette.

The teacup crashes to the floor at her feet, breaking the gaping silence. Unable to take my eyes off her, I breathe heavily. The sound of the cup hitting the stone catches the king's attention. My throat constricts as she rises from her seat. She curtsies in a wispy gold dress that is gathered at her narrow waist by a wide burgundy sash. Her thick brown hair hangs over her chest past her elbow. Her face is solemn but as beautiful as I remember, with wide cheekbones and dainty pink lips.

The king nods at her.

"I apologize," she speaks. Her voice is like music filling my ears, singing a song that my soul has ached to hear for a long time. "I know these people." She is being strangely proper and closed off, unlike the free spirit I remember.

The king's eyebrows relax. "Who are they? And what do they want?"

"I believe they came," she looks at me with intense eyes, "To visit me." Her wings swish and spread to either side as she curtsies low again. "May I take leave and walk with them through the courtyard?"

Surprisingly, the king is actually considering her request.

"You may," he says, moving one finger in her direction, his tone easing. She has favor with this tyrant. I loosen my jaw and take a deep breath.

Alouette gathers her long golden skirts in her hands and hurries to me. She tells the stablemen to untie us and waves them off as she leads us to the door. I reach for her hand, but she pulls away. An ache shoots through my chest.

"Lonan, escort Alouette and her guests," the king commands as we head for the door.

She has favor, I think to myself, but not full trust.

Tracing our steps across the path of smooth black marble, I follow Tolliver, Angus, and Kava. Hollis walks beside me rubbing her wrists. Her eyes reveal confusion beneath her furrowed brow. Alouette walks quietly behind and my mind floods with questions.

As soon as we turn left out of the throne room, I spin around, mouth open, ready to speak. Alouette shakes her head vigorously, scowling at me. I swallow back the torrent of questions that swell behind a crumbling dam of patience.

At the end of the hall, she grabs my dirty sleeve and directs us through an archway into the unfinished courtyard. Alouette tells the guard to keep his distance so he pauses with his hands behind his back, wings blocking almost the entire doorway. We proceed down the only paved path and stop in the middle of the courtyard.

The sky is still gray and threatening but the rain has stopped. The wind tosses Alouette's dark hair and ripples through her white wings.

"Leave us," Alouette commands the wing-bound women working in the courtyard. They obey and scurry out of the area. Tolliver eyes her and looks at me, adding more questions to mine. The pressure of their weight bears down on me.

At the center of the rectangular garden, Alouette stops abruptly. "What are you doing here?" Her eyes finally reveal her surprise and delight that I am here.

"What am I doing here? What are you doing here?" I demand. "When you didn't come back, I thought…"

Alouette looks around and whispers, "I'm sorry. I had no way of getting news to you."

I sense Tolliver getting antsy, but I don't care. I need to know what is happening. "What is all this?"

"Our new home," she blushes and shrugs at the mess around us. "I'm so glad you are here. How? You travelled all the way here, didn't you?" She touches my face as if she can't believe I'm real. I can't look away from her deep brown eyes. They are like my mother's eyes. Except on this exotic beauty, they are outlined with thick lashes and hold many secrets.

"Yes, I built a—" I interrupt myself and get right to the point, "It doesn't matter how. I've come to rescue you."

"Rescue me?" she scrunches her nose and her fearful eyes lie. "I don't need rescuing."

"Are those your people chained to the ground, forced to work?" The look on her face confirms what I already knew. "Your people are enslaved to that—that man in there!" I shout.

"That man?"

"Where is King Halcyon?" I ask.

"He is dead." Alouette looks away, brows scrunching. She smooths her golden dress. "There was a shift in power and my father—"

"He is dead?" I ask. "Did that man kill him? Did he drag all of you here to force your people to build him a castle?"

"Ledger, silly boy." She reaches for me.

Feeling patronized, I yank my hand away. "I'm not a boy

anymore."

"I know. I'm sorry," Alouette puts a hand to her forehead. I'm making this harder on her, but I'm frustrated because I don't understand what is happening.

"I'm getting you out of here." To Tolliver and Angus, I say, "Let's go."

I offer her my hand and she reaches for it slowly. Her hand is a warm earthy color compared to my pale skin. When I pull her, she doesn't move. Her eyes are sad, unwavering. "This is where I belong, Ledger. Stay with me."

"What are you talking about?" I am in shock.

Her cheeks push back with an almost-smile as she says, "Stay here with me. I don't have to marry Dayson. You and I can marry, with my father's approval, of course. And this can be our home."

This is not what I was expecting at all. I look at Hollis. Her blue eyes overload me with questions. The dam breaks. I'm confused by Alouette's request. I can't stay here. This is not my home. I don't understand what is happening or what Alouette is thinking.

At that moment rumbling fills the air. I cannot figure out where it is coming from. Then rocks crumble from the castle walls. Looking up at the ominous storm clouds, men in black masks crest the top of the walls, set hooks into the stone and rappel down into the courtyard around us.

37

INTO DARKNESS

Chaos breaks out around us. Lonan, the guardian sent to escort Alouette, unsheathes his sword. He swings at the first intruder that hits the ground. The stealthy man pulls a sword and unhooks the rope from his harness in one smooth movement. Three, four, and five men overtake Lonan.

"We have to get out of here," Tolliver says and we take off running.

Several men in black masks open the front gate from the inside and more of them pour into the castle like swarming black flies. Winged guardians rush to defend their castle and we are caught in the middle. The sound of clinking fills the open space as we dash through the archway.

Tolliver puts his arm around Kava, shielding her from the violence as guardians fight masked men. Swords clink, wings flap. A man in black pulls out a horizontal bow and pulls a lever releasing a small arrow hitting a hovering guardian in the chest. He topples in a feathery pile.

Hollis screams. I hold her hand as we scramble down the hallway.

At that moment, a man in black charges us, sword drawn, eyes intense. Instead of attacking, he directs, “Go that way. It is clear.” I recognize Jin’s voice as he continues to run.

“Come on,” Tolliver calls. We follow him through the hall twisting back towards the dragon’s cave.

Once outside, we find men in black freeing the chained Ellerian slaves. I don’t understand why they aren’t killing them. Each one flits into the sky as soon as they are free. Angus pushes us forward over the small rickety bridge toward the woods.

Alouette’s pace slows and her dress scrapes along the ground, gathering mud and leaves. “Please,” she pants, “Please stop.”

“We are not safe,” I state and keep running. “Not yet.”

We make it into the trees and up the hill. After we crest the ridge, we gape at the raid below. Most of the slaves have been freed and have flown to the east, toward Ellery. The last of the masked men are making their way into the castle. An alarm blares in the distance and we hear the grating cry of a dragon.

From the entrance of the stables, flies the large black dragon that had attacked the island. Its talons are sharp, the spikes on its forehead are jagged, and when it shrieks again flames burst from its mouth.

“Fire,” Hollis whispers in awe. “They breathe fire?”

I suddenly feel foolish for handling Tristeh. She could have killed us that entire time.

Another screech and a gray dragon emerges from the hold, followed by the large green one. His muzzle keeps the flames at bay. We watch the three beasts circle the castle and dive into the middle with riders on their backs. I consider the fact that we had been standing in that courtyard and a lump forms in the pit of my stomach.

The sound of another dragon tears through the valley and Hollis gasps.

She looks to the sky, to the north and to the south, every which way.

"What is it?" I ask.

"Tristeh," Hollis says.

Alouette looks at her with eyes wide. "How do you know that name?"

"She is my dragon," Hollis declares.

"Yours?"

"Your people left her to die in that dungeon," Hollis says, still searching the clouds.

Alouette puts her hands on her hips. "We left in a hurry."

Another shriek and the red dragon soars over the castle. She doesn't aim for the castle or the people; she aims for the green dragon. She dives at him from above, lands on his rider, and wrenches to the side.

"Well, she's mine now," Hollis yells.

The tangle of dragons separates, and a rider falls from the sky. The two dragons soar into the atmosphere, wing tip to wing tip. They dive together for another pass. This time, Tristeh rattles the valley with a roar ending in a high-pitched shriek. Flames thrust from her mouth the length of a tall tree.

"Tristeh," Hollis screams into the sky.

The red dragon twists out of formation and dives at the trees over our heads.

Kava screams and we all hide, except for Hollis. Tolliver

and Kava duck behind a fallen log. Angus, Alouette, and I clamber behind several trees and shrubs.

"Tristeh," Hollis yells out again.

Tristeh circles overhead, descends between the trees and lands before us. Her scales are a vibrant, shimmery red in the daylight. The curve of her jaw and brow are fierce with spikes jutting out. Remembering why I feared her, my whole body shakes while I grip the tree, the only thing between me and the beast.

"What are you doing, Hollis," Tolliver shouts. "It will kill us all."

"No, she won't," Hollis argues.

"Yes, she will," Alouette agrees. "She doesn't have her muzzle."

Hollis boldly steps toward the dragon. Tristeh's nostrils flare, tasting the air. Hollis places her hand on the dragon's mouth. She coos and the dragon ducks her head into Hollis's embrace.

She says, "This isn't our fight. It's time we get back on the island and go home."

"But it is my fight," Alouette emerges from behind a tree. "Those are my people being slaughtered down there."

"We have no way to help them. No weapons. Nothing," Tolliver says. "We only have an escape."

"I'm going to wait it out and see what happens." Alouette frowns, her eyebrows low.

"Why don't we find your family and get out of here?" I grab her hands in mine. "Free anyone else we can so they can go back home to the island."

"What are you talking about?" She frowns. "Ciel is my

father and my mother is dead."

I drop her hands and step away. "But he is wingless," I state.

"King Halcyon clipped his wings when he started a revolution to relocate to the ground," Alouette explains. "For centuries, it's been illegal to leave the island of Ellery. When the king died, my father took the throne instead of his bratty children. He is rebuilding Ellery on the ground, so we don't have to rely on all the people around the world to supply our every need."

Mouth hanging open and mind reeling, I am shocked.

"Your father is enslaving his own people?" Tolliver asks. A great question I would have thought of if I had time to process what she just said.

Alouette looks down, fidgeting with a piece of her dress. "Sometimes examples have to be made," she recites. They aren't her words. They sound like something that has been said to her over and over. I look at the evening sky where streaks of red scratch across the horizon. The setting sun is like an evil eye gazing at me from beneath the furrowed brow of storm clouds. I am lost in the gravity of her words. They knock me down into darkness and heaviness again.

"I can't stand here and argue," Alouette states, head held high. "I must find my father."

As the word 'please' comes out of my mouth, her powerful wings propel her into the air over the treetops back to the castle. Alouette is gone.

"We have to go back to the island," Kava says. "We can make it if we run."

My insides jolt. "We can't leave yet," I say, turning

toward the castle. Alouette will die and this whole thing will be for nothing. I bottle every feeling brewing inside me.

"Ledger, stop," Tolliver commands. "Kava's right, we should go back." Each word he says sends a spike through the thin glass that has been holding me together. "We have to make it home."

With that, something shatters.

"No!" I scream. "You stop! Stop telling me what to do. You're not my father. And apparently, you're not even my brother!"

The words erupt out of me.

"Ledger." Tolliver's shoulders slump.

"Why did you keep that from me?" I yell, leaning toward him pointing in his face.

"I wanted to protect you."

I scoff, "Protect me from what?"

"I needed to find some answers before—"

"Before you stopped lying to me?" I am drawn toward the castle. I can't do this right now. I have to find Alouette and get her out of here. I have to make sure she is safe. I give in to the draw and take off running. Without thinking about it, I just run.

"Ledger!" Tolliver's voice chases me over the ridge and down the side of the hill. "Ledger!"

Slipping my way across the bridge and sliding through the side door of the castle, my head throbs from the painful confrontation. I bite my tongue to push away the tears. The castle halls are vacant. Slowing to a walk, I catch my breath and tiptoe into the throne room. It too is empty.

The faint echo of voices draws me farther down the

hallway. I follow them out the other side of the castle into a small village of wood and thatch homes. There are masked men standing along the only road through the village. A single flame ignites the twilight.

I spot Alouette kneeling on the ground before a masked man with a torch: the master. She is weeping over a body beneath her arms. Her wings droop behind her. I fear she is wounded. Inching closer, I stay concealed behind the first cottage.

"Father," Alouette moans. Her tears fall onto the face of Roi du Ciel. He is laid out on the ground, contorted unnaturally, blood seeping from his side. "Why?" Alouette shouts. "Why did you kill him? I could have helped him—"

"Sometimes an example has to be made," the master says in a familiar accent.

Alouette's head drops to her father's lifeless frame with uncontrollable cries. As her weeping trails off, I hear the hum of many voices. I peer around the corner and notice a cottage with a log propped against the door. I nearly fall when a branch comes loose from the dried mud wall beside me. The rest of the Sky People must be trapped inside that house with the shutters tied shut from the outside.

"Now you have a choice to make," the master says. "Resist us or leave with your life."

"I'm not leaving without my people," she says firmly, "All of them." With such an easy choice, I don't understand why Alouette doesn't just shoot into the sky and go home. Instead, she reaches for her father's sword. The masked men around the circle let out a laugh.

I should do something. The men in black come at her all

at once, several behind, from the sides, and at the front. A man knocks the sword from her hand with a swift kick. They apprehend her easily and drag her toward the barricaded cottage. I grow frustrated that I didn't intervene. I'm not brave, but I do care about her and her people.

Her scream echoes off the walls and rips through my soul. Three men muscle the log away from the door and another shoves her inside. I stand upright and take a deep breath. Darting from my hiding place, I charge at the master right as he throws a torch on the roof of the cottage. I get in a few good punches before his men peel me off. One of the men in black wrenches my arms behind my back, restraining me.

The master chuckles as smoke billows over his head. I scream, "They don't deserve to die!" The man behind me pulls my arms tighter and my shoulder rips.

"Ledger," the master laughs. I jerk in response to my name. He pulls the black mask from his face and a braid topples out. "You came to do the same," Jin says. "But they refuse to leave. They are on our land and my emperor wants them gone."

I hear screams rising from beneath the flames as the entire roof ignites.

"Please, I can convince them," I plead. "They will go. I promise."

"You are too late." He nods to the cottage where the roof and the side wall are engulfed in flames. He commands my captor to release me and I land in the dirt. Jin calls his men and they follow him westward away from the castle.

Now is my chance! I bolt for the flaming cottage and yank at the log barricade. It doesn't budge. I go for the walls, kicking and yanking off branches stuck in mud. My arms are a blur of fists and handfuls of dust.

On the other side of the wall, I hear their screams. I hear her scream. Scrambling over to Ciel's body, I snatch the sword. Charging back to the house, I hack at the ropes tied between the handles of the shutters. As soon as the last fiber is sliced, the wooden panels burst open and smoke wafts in my face. "Alouette!" I yell her name, reaching in, grasping at anything. A small hand clutches mine.

38

FLAME KISSED

My eyes sting, refusing to open as arms and legs climb over me through the small window. The smoke chokes me as we all topple out together. A sharp pain shoots through my neck as the blazing cottage falls down around us. Prying my smoke-filled eyes open, I pull on the small hand in my grip while strong arms around me drag us both out of the rubble.

The heat from the burning thatch singes my face. As we drag Alouette's lifeless body from the flames, I realize Tolliver and Angus are helping me.

Suddenly, the roof tumbles inward and screams cut through the sky as several Ellerian dart out of the toppling building. One plummets to the ground unconscious. Another lands and rolls in the dust, quenching the flames on his wings.

"Help them," I say to Angus and he races over.

Alouette breathes and coughs. She is alive. I check her arms, wings, and torso for burns. Her dress is singed, but she is surprisingly unscathed. She struggles to sit up.

"You're okay, Alouette," I say.

She looks at me with big sad brown eyes then at the fire

that is spreading to the next cottage. “It will never be okay,” she says. A tear spills down her dirty cheek. Getting clumsily to her feet, I hold her elbow as she gains her balance.

Her soiled wings pump once, lifting her into the air above me for a moment. I open my mouth to ask her to wait, and she shakes her head. She looks at the burning house and flits overtop, inspecting, searching.

Night has fallen, but the spreading fire lights up the small village.

“Seven of them made it out,” Tolliver says. I am unsure of what to say and shocked he didn’t leave me behind. My throat constricts as tears fall.

“I’m sorry,” he says. “I should have told you first.”

I nod.

“I was being selfish,” he admits, blinking back tears. “I didn’t want you to look at me differently.”

In that moment, I remember what Grandmother said about him, Trust him and remember who he’s always been to you.

“I should have trusted you,” I say. He grabs me and hugs me tightly. A sharp pain shoots through my shoulder with a familiar sensation. I am burned.

“I’m just glad you’re alive,” he says, pulling away. It takes a moment for me to catch my breath from the pain in my burned skin.

Alouette lands nearby and tiptoes toward her father. She sits beside him and tears stream down her face.

Angus helps the singed Ellerian man assist his unconscious friend. They stand him up and the winged man tries to lift his lifeless body from the ground. He fails several times, lacking the strength to lift the deadweight and his own.

"Alouette," the man calls. She looks up from her father's dead body. "Alouette, help me."

"Dayson, can you help me with my father first?"

I recognize the name. He is the man she is supposed to marry. He lays his friend on the ground and joins Alouette beside Ciel. She gently lifts his head and removes his crown and a necklace from around his neck. It is a silver bird with a branch in its mouth. I recognize it and pull the trinket from my grandmother out of my tunic. Mine is a tiny version of it. They lift him together and I join their efforts, carrying him to the raging fire. Heat licks my fingers as we lay him down. Alouette stares into the orange flames as they dance across his chest and consume his body. Tears fall silently down her cheeks and Dayson wraps an arm around her. The funeral pyre lights his dark hair and dark eyes.

When Dayson says, "We need to go," she meets my gaze with a question in her eyes. Before she asks how I will get back to Ellery, we hear that familiar high-pitched shriek through the sky. The moon casts a shadow for a sliver of a second then the ground shakes around us. Tristeh lands only a stone's throw away and Hollis is strapped into a saddle on her back. It's not the dreaded white saddle, but a dingy brown one.

"Your ride is here," Hollis sings.

Alouette puts the unconscious man's limp arm over her shoulder. I nod to her and she says, "Meet you on Ellery." She blinks with a realization. "I never thought I'd ever say that to you."

I smile in agreement.

Dayson and Alouette lift the man together and I watch them disappear into the night sky. It feels like goodbye watching her leave with him, but it's only see you later.

I sigh and gaze at the girl with the dragon.

"I could only make three harnesses with the straps left in that dragon cave back there." Her voice is full of energy and confidence. "Someone will have to wait here, and I'll come back to get you."

I exhale deeply, and my heart does a strange thing watching her climb down the red scales. I imagine myself charging straight to her, grabbing her face, and pressing my lips to hers. My heart jolts into action, but my body is frozen in place. It is neither appropriate, according to our custom, nor am I able to build up the nerve. Frustration chokes me, and I swallow it back.

"Ledger can ride with you and we'll use the harnesses," Tolliver says yanking me from my daydream.

"Great idea," Hollis bounces over. She leaps at me as Tolliver says, "Careful, he's burned."

Her arms land around my neck and shoulders. The pain cripples me and there are spots at the edge of my vision.

Hollis pulls herself off me. "Oh, Ledger. My apologies."

Her politeness makes a chuckle shoot from my gut. Tears pool in my eyes in a very unmanly fashion. I hunch over gasping for air, recovering from the searing pain.

Hollis touches my face, "You breathe through that, while I get everyone ready." She dances off.

The harnesses consist of four straps: one looping each leg, one around the waist, and one hooking them all together ready to fasten to the dragon. By the light from the burning cottages, Hollis helps Kava into her harness with her skirts puffing awkwardly. Tolliver fastens his and shows Angus how to latch the loops and hooks. I catch my breath and try to act normal watching Hollis tend to Angus. Just being near her makes everything feel like it will be okay.

"Well, I hope you're not afraid of heights," Hollis teases. Angus just eyes her. "I have these two long straps to hang over the saddle, so they don't cut into Tristeh's skin."

"Scales," I correct and flash a smile.

She raises a single eyebrow at me and continues, "We'll drape them over then I'll get Tristeh in the air, so you can hook yourself to the straps underneath. Simple."

A nervous laugh trickles from Kava's lips and she shifts uneasily from one foot to the other. Tolliver puts a hand on her shoulder.

"Are you sure she can carry all of us?" Angus steps into the harness.

Hollis laughs. "I saw her rip a tree out of the ground today. I'm pretty sure she'll be fine."

Angus's mouth hangs open and Kava's eyes are so huge I can see the reflection of the moon in them.

"What about me?" I ask.

Hollis tosses me a single strap that could be confused for a belt. I hold it up and look at her with no idea what to do with it.

"Come on," she calls, racing toward the dragon. My gut wrenches, because we don't even run up to our horses in Balfour. They would startle and possibly rear up. But the beast stands still as the girl with the golden hair climbs like a mountain goat up Tristeh's wing. She lays the two long straps across the saddle and they dangle to the ground on either side.

"Ledger, can you hook all the ends together?" Hollis calls from atop the dragon.

"Maybe." I eye the beast warily.

I force my body to approach the dragon with no bars and no muzzle to protect me. Tristeh sends out a low growl as I near her shoulder.

"Tristeh, stop it," Hollis commands and she obeys.

The burn on my shoulder aches as I warily reach for the straps. Hands shaking from the thrum of adrenaline pumping through my veins, I am only able to grab three.

"Come on, Ledger, she's not going to cook you," Hollis giggles.

"That does not help," I whisper. Taking a deep breath and slowly reaching for the fourth strap, I hook them all together on a large metal loop used for cinching the rigging of a saddle.

I back away and air fills my lungs again. Tristeh blows in my face. I squawk like a startled chicken and race back to Tolliver and Kava.

Hollis's laugh echoes off the hills around us and she calls me to mount the beast. I decide it's better if I pretend Tristeh is a horse. Otherwise, my body may not obey.

Tristeh is a gentle pony, I tell myself as I crawl up her leathery wing. *A pony with giant bat wings.* I have to touch the scales with my bare hands to crawl to the saddle on her back. They are like seashells laid in a perfect pattern all over her body.

Gentle pony, I recite in my mind.

I sit just behind Hollis on the saddle, half on and half off. I watch her grab the two pieces of leather that we didn't know what to do with when she rode Tristeh the first time and hook them around her waist, latching herself in securely.

"Oh, that's what those are for," I say, not realizing I am saying it aloud.

"Would have been helpful that first time." She smiles at me. "Now wrap yours around you and hook it to mine."

I follow her instruction and it pulls me tight against her. My head is dizzy and my heart pounds as I sit on this gentle fire-breathing pony. I am glad to be this close to Hollis. Grabbing my hands, she wraps them around her narrow waist. My body buzzes with excitement as I embrace her. It feels like home.

39
TO THE SKY

Hollis clucks, “Fly, Tristeh.”

The dragon leaps into the air, pressing down with enormous wings. We swoop through the night sky and make a circle. Hollis encourages her to hover over our family on the ground stirring the flames of the burning village.

Tolliver hooks Kava, Angus, and then himself. They are strapped face to face. Kava wraps an arm around each one and they do the same in a little circle of arms.

“Ready?” Hollis calls. “To the sky!” She jerks her body to the southeast and Tristeh responds in sync. The giant wings gently lift us above the trees toward the midnight blue sky. The moon lights our way as we soar over brambles and streams.

I am surprised how far Ellery has drifted and how long it takes us to reach it. When it comes into view, relief trickles through me. Moonlight reflects off the top of the castle. The cool night air flows in and out of my lungs. I am at peace in the air. Exhilaration rises in my chest and I want to howl into the wind like a wild man. I keep it in, worried what Hollis would think, until she crows unabashedly into the night sky, "Waaaacaw!"

Shaking my head, I laugh at myself. What am I thinking? I can be myself with her. So I join her weird screams of delight. Letting all the joy and frustrations blend together and relieve me from hiding one for the sake of the other.

Hollis shouts something to me but it flies by with the wind and never reaches my ears. I ask her to say it again, but she doesn't, guiding the dragon toward the surface of Ellery. Tristeh comes in for a slow landing, flapping her giant wings and hovering just shy of Ellery's grand front entrance where the Sky People await our return. Tolliver, Kava, and Angus land safely and unhook their harnesses. Tolliver waves and Hollis nudges the dragon away from the island.

Tristeh's wings flap powerfully and she shoots us toward the moon, like a sky flame. I think of Alouette and realize the worry in my gut is gone. She is safe. It is strange and new to see her among her people. Alouette belongs with her people. They have a lot of healing to do together.

Hollis and I lean with the dragon as she circles around the tiny castle below. My lungs plead for a breath as Tristeh dives back to Ellery. We lean to the other side and soar around the structure jutting from the floating island. Then round and round the jagged rock hanging below the surface.

Coming around the north side of Ellery, the dragon slows our approach and ducks through the opening to the cave. Her talons scrape on the gravel. There are torches all along the cavern lighting our landing.

Unhooking her belt, Hollis's laugh echoes off the cave walls. My belly fills with her joy like a glutton at a feast.

I detach my strap and crawl off the back of Tristeh. Hollis follows, balancing on her feet all the way. I slide down the wing and land feet first in the dust.

"Catch me, Ledger," Hollis calls.

I turn just in time to raise my arms and catch her little body against me. I wince protecting the burn on my shoulder as my breath is stolen. Less because of my shoulder and more because of her. I can't look away from her blue eyes and vibrant smile. I gaze at her lips and forget everything else. Leaning in, I press mine to hers. Warmth grows in my belly as I inhale the smell of her: strawberries and summer wind.

She leans away and looks into my eyes. "Ledger," she says out of breath with a pleased shock.

"I love you, Hollis," I say. She begins to speak, and I stop her. "I have always loved you, even when I was pushing you away. When you are gone, I am lost. You are my home."

She tightens her hold and hugs me.

"It's about time," she giggles. "Everyone else knows it."

I groan and let her feet touch the ground.

The sting of my burn returns as she pulls her arms from my neck. I draw a sharp breath and she says, "Oh, I'm sorry. Your burn. I guess jumping on you was not a good idea."

"Yeah," I agree. "I wonder who thought of that."

We laugh together and Tristeh breathes a growl that echoes through the cavern. Hollis gasps, startled. I turn around finding five guardians with swords poised for a fight.

THANK YOU

Thank you for reading *Wingbound* by Heather Trim. Independent Authors rely heavily upon reviews and word-of-mouth to reach new readers. If you have a moment to spare, please leave a review on your preferred site. Honest reviews, short or long are greatly appreciated.

Leave a review on Amazon:

Leave a review on Goodreads:

ACKNOWLEDGMENTS

Thank you, Kevin, for letting me get lost on Ellery. You've made this dream a possibility and a reality. Daisy, thank you for your constant input and sharp skills at brainstorming and decision-making when I got stuck. Daphne, thank you for your peaceful support and creative drawing skills that helped me form Tristeh. Gabe, thanks for being who you are because you make Ledger more interesting. Amaryllis, thank you for falling in love with my fantastical world, even though I'm boring. Violet, thank you for demanding I keep reading at the end of each chapter and being mad at the characters for all the right reasons.

Mom. Dad. Thank you for letting me be a daydreamer and encouraging my fiction-writing fixation. Thank you to my siblings (and BFFs) who let me just be me: Erin, Jason, Lucas, Pam, Amber and Justin.

Thank you to my crazy awesome, mismatched team of Beta Readers, who each saw a hole and helped me fix it: Pam Mather, Lisa Coetzee, Becki Czerwonka, David Dudley, Becca Hickman, Suzette Lambert, Shannon Johnson, Scottie Snipes, Leah Rollins, and Lauren Shields. Thank you, Shayla Eaton and my trusty Book Launch Team, for supporting me.

Thank you, my Lord, for the beautiful sky that distracts me while I'm driving or riding or sitting outside. I couldn't keep my head (or my imagination) out of those clouds. One of them looked like a floating island with a castle on top and it made me wonder what it would be like if there were people who lived on it. Surely, they would need wings, something I was born without. I wonder if my spirit has wings? My wedding dress sure did.

ABOUT THE AUTHOR

Heather Trim, an award-winning author, the executive director of Bear Creek Ranch, and a professional daydreamer, inspires with her unique perspective of spirituality and the world. She lives in Georgia with her husband, Kevin, and five lively children. Heather enjoys bullet journaling, graphic designing, and reading too many young adult novels. She can be found on Facebook, Instagram, and her website: www.heatheraine.com.

Sign up for Heather's Newsletter:
http://eepurl.com/cLd0D1

Connect with Heather:
Facebook: facebook.com/heatherainetrim
Instagram: instagram.com/heatheraine5
Goodreads: goodreads.com/heatheraine
Amazon: amazon.com/author/heathertrim

WINGLESS

WINGBOUND SERIES: BOOK TWO

In the second installment of the Wingbound Series, four wingless friends are imprisoned on the floating island. Ledger must get home before an assassin strikes at the heart of Balfour. Facing the dangers of land and sky, he must help them escape and lead them home.

But his adopted brother, Tolliver, won't leave just yet. He is determined to find his winged family, the ones who threw him away at birth. Will they accept him or execute him? Either way, Tolliver intends to try.

Turn the page for a sneak peek at WINGLESS.

PROLOGUE

TOLLIVER

"Father sent me for you, and Mother said you were out here." I pause at the sound of rustling in the bushes. Ledger grabs my arm. He's hiding something. "Wait. There's something in the—"

"It's nothing." Ledger tries to lead me away, but a muffled sneeze comes from the leafy mass.

I knew it! He is *doing something sneaky.* Knocking my little brother to the side, I crouch, peering beneath the branches. "Hello," I say.

"Hello," answers a female voice.

Ledger is sneaking off with a girl? I frown at her. "Who are you?"

She attempts to stand, but the branches are tangled around her. "I am Alouette."

Ledger introduces me. "This is my brother, Tolliver."

"Who is this?" I ask, confused by the foreign name. "I've never seen *her* before." I know every face in Balfour. She has beautiful brown eyes, smooth olive skin, and a white smile.

"She is a…visitor." Ledger's vague answer piques my curiosity. We never have visitors.

"From where?" I politely offer her my hand as she struggles to get out of the bushes. She accepts it, and I pull her free. Enormous white wings snap out of the shrubs and into the air behind her, vibrant and alarming. A gasp escapes my mouth and I yank my hand away from the enemy. My fists ball in an instant.

"Tolliver, I can explain." Ledger's voice squeaks with panic.

"She is Ellerian!" Anger spreads through my body like a brushfire. She is an intruder, a spy.

"It's okay, she's not a threat."

"Not a threat? She is one of them!"

The trespasser leaps into the air above us and off our land.

"Wait, don't go," Ledger calls with one hand reaching out to her. "I know she is one of them, but…" He stretches the other hand out to me.

He has betrayed us all. Frustration flares into my tone. "Does Father know?"

Ledger shakes his head with the look he always has when he is in trouble: wide eyes and bottom teeth bared. It irritates me to the core how he is silent, stubborn, and refusing to face facts. I back away, disgusted with him.

"Please, don't go!" he begs.

What does he think he is doing with the enemy? I square my shoulders and lower my brows at him. "This is unacceptable."

He looks skyward. "Please stay."

"Goodbye, Ledger." The girl darts to the cloud layer. A blanket of navy and gray conceals her.

My muscles tense. Someone needs to knock some sense into him. I wouldn't mind doing it myself.

"Please calm down," Ledger says.

"How can you do this? Betraying your own people!" I almost call him a cruel name to get his attention and bring him into reality.

"It's not betrayal. She's my friend." His hands shake as he shoves them in his pockets and hunches his shoulders.

"Making friends with the enemy is exactly what betrayal is." I rub my head in irritation. He isn't making any sense.

"She was only a little girl when we met. She was curious about us," Ledger explains. "Mother knows, but no one else can."

Shocked Mother would tolerate this, my fists clench over and over. I bite my tongue to protect Ledger from the furious words threatening to fly out. He's lucky I sift through it all. He deserves a reprimand, but not ranting, so I groan and walk away.

"Please, Tolliver. No one can know." Ledger's voice echoes down the mountains side.

My feet grind pine needles against the rocky path as I stomp over the mountain pass to the Hundred Harvest Tree. By the time I reach the clearing, my jaw aches and my teeth are pulsating from the tension.

Blazing through the village, I burst through the door of our cottage, where Mother is darning a black sock. Ledger says Mother already knows, so her face will tell.

"Ledger is a traitor," I announce.

Without looking up from her chore, she takes a deep breath and lays the sock aside. There is no surprise in her eyes, no defiance of the truth, only sad eyes and downturned lips.

Panting from the trek, I want to yell again, but the way she silently walks to the back bedroom quenches the red-hot anger in my belly. I follow her. The window over the bed lights her movements to the dresser. She pulls open the bottom drawer all the way out and lays it on the floor. She reaches into the dark space and pulls out a leather book with a strap wrapped around it.

Facing me, she says, "Close the door."

Dread washes over every last ember of anger, throwing me into darkness. I don't like not knowing what she's going to say. It's as if I've fallen into a cavern and have to find my way out blind. I push the door shut and sit beside her on the large bed.

"There is something I've wanted to tell you for quite some time. I've thought of a hundred ways to say it, but nothing seemed good enough. I know you, son. You jump to conclusions and argue when you're wrong or unsure about something. So all I ask for the next few moments, Tolliver, is for you to remain silent until I can tell you everything."

She turns her brown eyes toward me, pleading and full of worry. They are wrinkled at the corners, and her brows pinch together with a question. *Will I remain silent?*

"Yes, Mother."

Her expression softens, and she purses her lips. I have no idea what she is going to say.

"You are Ellerian."

The words ignite me. My mouth drops open to argue. I want to reject it.

"Tolliver," she whispers, reminding me of my promise.

She knows me, my nature. Ashamed that I've dishonored her, I wait for her to continue. *I'm better than that.*

"Each year Ellery returns, and on the second day of battle, I journey to the lake. I meet an Ellerian guardian carrying a package. The midwives of Ellery must, by law, dispose of any child born without wings. The king commands them to throw them off the island wherever they are, but many mothers cannot bear the thought of their children being lost to the wind like criminals. So the midwives devised a plan to bring them to Balfour. On rare occasions, the delivered package is crying. Most often they are not. When they are not, I walk over the next ridge beyond the lake and bury them beside their kin."

She stops, wipes a tear, and continues. "But when they are crying, I feed them, swaddle them, and carry them back to Balfour. That is how you came to be in our family."

A torrent of emotions makes my head ache. I press two fingers to my temples. *How can this be?*

She glances at me again. "You were the tiniest child I ever held in my arms. You must have only been hours old or weeks too early. I loved you from the moment I saw you. I was able to hide you in that drawer." She points to the askew drawer on the floor. "After the Harvest Festival, your father went on a two-month hunt in the North Mountains. I tucked a small pillow in my skirts as if I were pregnant, then bigger and bigger pillows. When enough time passed, Balfour met you for the first time as the blacksmith's son."

A deep breath fills my lungs, drawing in everything she is saying. Doubting thoughts reel through my mind. My mouth clenches shut to keep from denying it aloud. *No. I am Tolliver, son of Fergus. I am Balfourian. I will be an elder one day and lead our army against—*

"I know you have questions, so you may ask them now." She wipes both of her eyes and lays her hands over the small book in her lap.

I ask the first thing that comes to my mind. "Does Father know?"

She abruptly looks at her hands. More tears flow as she says, "No, he does not."

I am taken aback. I want to yell at her for the lies, but I don't understand. "How can he not know? He is your husband. Wouldn't he have seen? Or heard?"

"I would have told him, had he seen. But he was not accustomed to living with a woman when we were first married. He didn't know how it all worked. Then the hunt was planned, and I had the perfect opportunity. I told him I was due the week after he was to return. He promised to be back in time. So I made sure to bring you forth before his return. When I presented you to him, he was so proud and full of love for you. It didn't matter to me that you came from another woman, another father, another land." Her voice trails off.

Another woman. This small woman at my side is not my real mother. Someone else is. Someone with wings.

"She is a midwife."

"Who?"

"Your mother." Grief shows on her face as the confession

spills out. "She was one of the ones who would send the wingless children as the women birthed. I wasn't always the one who would receive them on the ground. There was another before me, who handed me the responsibility when she was unable to make the trip anymore. This was done years and years before me. We even buried winged children because families sometimes exceed the allotted number of children permitted by Ellery."

The more she shares, the more horror must be evident on my face. "It's okay, Tolliver. I give them a proper burial and honor them, when the Ellerian king thinks it's right to throw them out like spoiled vegetables."

"What am I supposed to say to all this? It seems too crazy, too unbelievable. I cannot possibly be Ellerian." My head won't stop shaking back and forth. It can't be true.

Mother opens the leather book in her lap. She turns to the middle. It appears that each page is dedicated to one child. A small sketch with a baby's face, rounded cheeks, closed eyes, and a tuft of hair fills half the page. A name is at the top: Lilstar. A date, probably birth date. A list of attributes: girl, wingless, pale skinned, blonde, blue eyes. Another date: deceased. My chest constricts at the thought of the dead child. She was only a month old when she died.

She turns the page slowly, and my name appears on the next sheet: Tolliver. With a completely different name below it.

Tylanu?

The weight of it all presses down on me until my neck aches, so I rub and stretch the tight muscle.

"You were so small." She strokes the sketch. Eyes open,

hairless, wingless, and alive.

She gives me the book with shaking hands. "I need you to know, you can tell your father if you choose. I will not stop you from being who you truly are."

"And who is that?" I don't mean to sound angry, but the pain shoots out of my mouth like a poison dart from my soul.

"Whoever you choose."

My pointer finger touches the birth date. "This isn't right."

"It is the real one."

I shake my head, realizing how long she had to wait to bring me out of the drawer. Four months. *Can this be true?* My head throbs against the only reality I've ever known, raging against this new truth. My throat constricts as fear and anger choke the air from me.

A tear drips onto the page.

I am a wingless Ellerian.

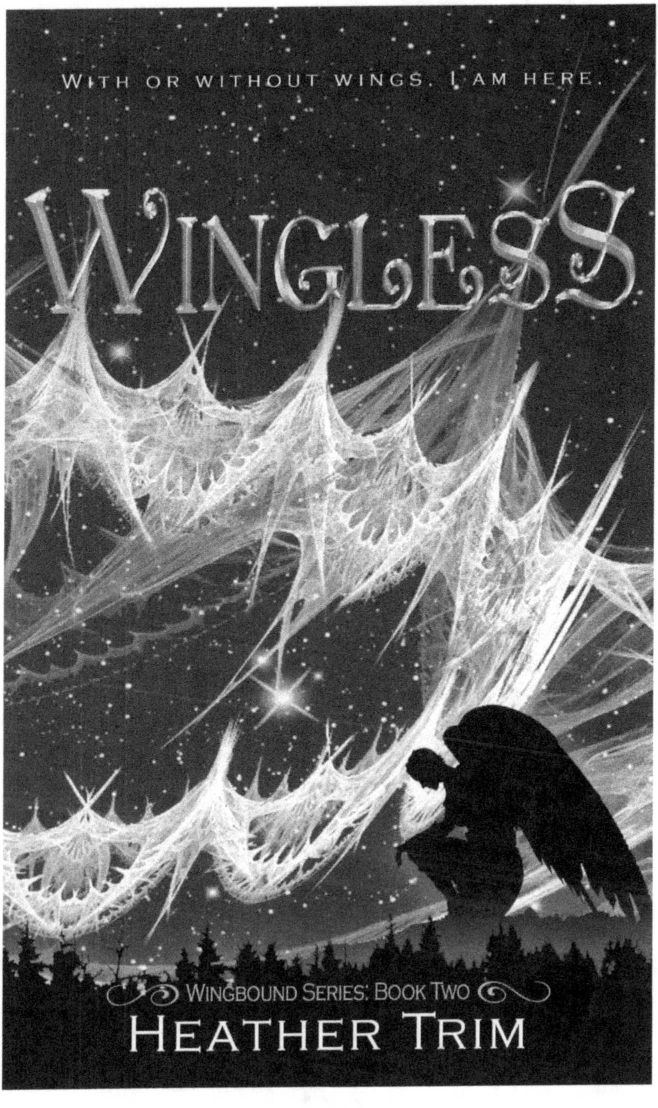
With or without wings, I am here.
Wingless
Wingbound Series: Book Two
Heather Trim

Buy now...

www.ingramcontent.com/pod-product-compliance
Lightning Source LLC
Chambersburg PA
CBHW060537310726
48982CB00009B/1287/J